G000167074

Dr CASSW

by

SARAH FISHER

CHIMERA

Dr Casswell's Plaything first published in 2001 by
Chimera Publishing Ltd
PO Box 152
Waterlooville
Hants
PO8 9FS

Printed and bound in Great Britain by
Omnia Books Ltd, Glasgow.

This book is sold subject to the condition that it shall not, by way of trade or otherwise, be lent, resold, hired out or otherwise circulated without the publisher's prior written consent in any form of binding or cover other than that in which it is published, and without a similar condition being imposed on the subsequent purchaser.

The characters and situations in this book are entirely imaginary and bear no relation to any real person or actual happening.

Copyright © Sarah Fisher
The right of Sarah Fisher to be identified as author of this book has been asserted in accordance with section 77 and 78 of the Copyrights Designs and Patents Act 1988

Dr CASSWELL'S PLAYTHING

Sarah Fisher

This novel is fiction – in real life practice safe sex

'You have to understand who is in control here, Miss Morgan,' he growled in her ear, his breath laden with garlic. 'And trust me, I will teach you. I really will.'

He moved away, his intrusive hand leaving her, and Sarah strained to pick up some clue as to what would happen next, although she had a pretty good idea, and then she tensed as she heard an unmistakable sound, and strained to catch a glimpse from the corner of her eye of the waiter pulling his leather belt from his trouser loops and handing it to Mustafa. Her fat tormentor folded it double in his fist, and then moved out of her sight.

There was a terrible silence, a few seconds deep and dark and full of a cruel promise. Sarah swallowed hard, every sense and nerve braced for the fierce kiss of supple leather.

Sarah Morgan closed the door of her car and looked up at Dr Casswell's country house. Moonlight picked its way between skeletal trees, reflecting in the windows of the mansion, giving them the appearance of cold, unseeing eyes. On the lake below the terrace, a chill autumn wind stirred the oily black water into life. She shivered and pulled her coat up around her shoulders, wondering if coming here had been a mistake...

Accepting Dr Rigel Casswell's offer to help him translate the erotic diaries of a medieval servant girl, Beatrice de Fleur, leads Sarah Morgan into an intriguing secret world. After being broken in by the doctor and his manservant, Chang, Sarah rapidly discovers the delights of pleasure, pain and submission.

As academic interest in the diaries mounts, Dr Casswell takes Sarah to the house of his godfather and mentor, Oliver Turner, where the old man is hosting a conference of interested parties. But this is no dry academic get together, rather a meeting of masters, sexual connoisseurs and their compliant slaves.

Dr Casswell's Plaything follows Sarah's continuing adventures in search of the secrets and passions of Beatrice's life, while also undergoing her own erotic education.

Chapter One

In the garden room of his mansion, Oliver Turner refilled his and Rigel Casswell's champagne glasses. Both men glanced around the shadowy interior. Oliver had wanted to make sure everything was ready for the arrival of his guests. He had settled on a medieval theme to echo the history of the diary before they heard the delegates' findings that perhaps the book was a mere brilliant forgery.

The room was divided by a row of ornate columns that supported the glass roof and had been hung with great garlands of ivy and lanterns. Set with a row of trestle tables and benches, the whole room resembled a medieval banqueting hall. Rigel Casswell took a long sip of the champagne. Already a couple of the other delegates were at the bar. The atmosphere all afternoon had been a little subdued and Egon had not arrived yet from Florence with his 'very important news' – damned man.

Oliver lifted a hand of greeting to his guests. Crouched beside the delegates were their two body slaves, naked, chained and masked. One was a tall thin boy with a shock of white-golden hair, sporting a flurry of strange ritual tattoos over his arms and legs that gave him an almost serpentine quality. The second was a girl of mixed race whose skin had been oiled so that it looked as if she was carved from some glorious exotic golden wood. As Rigel looked at her she glanced and smiled, revealing neat white teeth. Her eyes were dark and leonine, as black and untamed as the forest night. As she stretched and eased the heavy chain that joined her to her master, Rigel could see that her body was scarified, her face, arms and breasts covered in complex swirling spirals of white scars that were at once both fascinating and deeply disturbing.

Close by the band began to play.

'Lonely?' whispered a familiar voice from behind them. Both men turned to look into the masked eyes of a slim blonde creature dressed in an exquisite peacock-blue silk corset. Amelia, Oliver's spirited slave girl, smiled at them. Her corset was laced tight, emphasising her slim waist and full hips, delicate wisps of lace barely covering her nipples, while below she wore black silk stockings tied with lace garters, and high-heeled lace-up ankle boots.

A matching peacock-coloured mask was framed by intricate ringlets twisted into her tumble of blonde hair, and despite all the odds, there was something about the way she looked that evoked the middle ages. Oliver Turner smiled, and leaning forward pressed a kiss to Amelia's cheek while at the same time sliding his fingers up over her thighs.

Amelia smiled and then wriggled closer, long slim legs opening a little to give the old man greater access.

'Missed you too,' she purred, licking her lips like some sleek, well-fed feline. She began to rub against him, her body rippling in waves in time to the music. Amused by her delicious performance, Rigel shook his head and looked away.

Chang told him that he would prepare Sarah Morgan for the party, and all he had to do was wait and watch the comings and goings of his fellow guests – and there was much to observe. Around them the garden room was rapidly filling up. Although the air amongst the guests was still subdued, the arrival of the delegates' slaves was gradually altering the atmosphere. Each was part of their master's fantasy, and reflected a stunning array of tastes;

they were exotic, outrageous, bizarre – and utterly compelling.

The music drew a handful of dancers out onto the floor. Some naked, some dressed, and every shade in between. By the bar stood Dr Ford, who had brought twins back from the Far East on his last trip – the two delicate oriental sisters, naked except for their masks, collars and silver patent high-heeled shoes, waited like puppies at the end of their leash for their master to command them. Across the room, Leonra Stevenson, one of the few female guests, was dancing to the strains of the band, accompanied by her boy, who was dressed as a medieval minstrel, complete with bulging codpiece.

Rigel glanced down at his watch and when he looked up again, saw Sarah Morgan framed in the open doorway. Led by Chang, who was dressed in a simple black silk Mao jacket, the girl looked stunning. On the end of a fine silver chain, Sarah was wearing a sleek, close-fitting bodysuit that appeared to be covered in black feathers, and combined with the mask it made her look like some wonderful exotic bird. The bodice had long sleeves and she was wearing black stockings, but the fabric thinned over her exquisite breasts so that her nipples peaked through the finer, silken fabric. It was a heady invitation to linger and explore further. Rigel smiled; the pale creamy swell of her hairless sex was framed in a tumble of black silk and curling feathers that reflected inky shades of green and blue in amongst the coal-black fronds.

From behind her mask Sarah stared around the room. It was if she had been led to the darkest shores of passion. Rigel Casswell extended a hand and took her lead from Chang. 'Good evening, my dear. You're looking very beautiful, I must say.'

She nodded, almost afraid to speak. Her silent

acknowledgement appeared to please him. Oliver Turner looked at her too; she could sense that he also was delighted with what he saw.

In those few seconds, Sarah glanced around the party. The other slaves were all stunning and exuded an intimidating sexuality, dressed in fantasy costumes, all beautifully made up – they reminded her for all the world of a selection of tasty morsels as enticing and inviting as the sumptuous buffet that lined one wall.

Other delegates looked up upon her arrival – they must know she was new and although their glances were covert, they did not disguise the fact that many appraised her body with the eyes of potential purchasers.

Outside, beyond the huge glass windows, the night sky was a cloudless band of stars, while inside there was a sense of electric desire bubbling to the surface – not overtly seductive as yet but with an intense erotic promise of things to come. Sarah shivered, trying hard to get a grip of the wild fluttering in her stomach.

Amelia uncurled from Oliver and ran a finger over Sarah's arm. 'You and I have a little assignation,' she purred. 'Come with me.'

Sarah stiffened and glanced up at Dr Casswell for some kind of confirmation. He inclined his head towards her, eyes bright and hawkish.

'Do as Amelia says.'

Sarah's senses were reeling and without a word she followed Amelia across the now crowded room. She noticed that Chang, a figure that hovered in the shadows, had slipped away. She wondered what his departure signified, but before reaching a conclusion, Amelia grabbed her hand and guided her towards a slightly raised platform.

Sarah gasped. 'What are you going to do?'

Amelia laughed. 'Trust me; you and I are the cabaret

tonight, precious. Just relax and play along – you will love it.'

The conversation in the room faded to a low hum and Rigel settled against one of the pillars that overlooked the stage. A spotlight picked out Amelia, clad in her leather corset. The wisps of lace circled her shapely breasts, framing their heavy contours. And the costume framed her sex, emphasising her ripe pallor.

The music rose again and Amelia thrust her pelvis forward dramatically, while with one finger she teased at the open lips of her naked pussy. With the other hand she picked up a whip from the stage, and as her finger found the tight bud of her clitoris she cracked it, threw back her head and howled like a wolf.

Casswell allowed himself a wry smile; Amelia was a natural exhibitionist. Sarah was watching her performance, completely stunned, open-mouthed as the woman prowled around the small stage. Under the spotlight's glare, unseen hands had arranged a wooden café chair, over which were draped a pair of handcuffs.

As Casswell watched, Amelia suddenly leapt off the stage and grabbed Sarah. Instinctively the girl protested and writhed, fighting the lithe blonde woman, who relentlessly dragged her onto the stage. As they struggled their way into the spotlight, Amelia seized the top of Sarah's feather-trimmed body and with a single violent movement ripped it down, revealing the milky-white curves of her breasts.

There was a wild cry of approval from the audience as her tormentor cupped one firm breast in her gloved hand and squeezed it speculatively, tweaking the ripe pink nipple. Sarah sobbed and squirmed miserably but Amelia had no intention of stopping. She guided the girl towards the chair, all the time her fingers working at the girl's body, ripping away the remainder of her exquisite costume. Sarah mewled unhappily, naked now except for her stockings, the feathery mask and a pair of high heels.

Casswell sipped his champagne, impressed by their performance; he could sense the growing excitement, not just of Amelia but Sarah too. The slim blonde threw her new slave onto the floor and then thrust her hips forward, a single finger teasing at her quim, holding the lips open.

Sarah cried out, whimpering a protest while Casswell stared on with pleasure, feeling the heat and excitement rising deep inside him. 'No, no, please,' she sobbed, her voice echoing around the enrapt audience in the garden room, but Amelia was without mercy. She caught hold of Sarah's hair and pressed her face into her groin.

The girl let out a stifled sob of fear, trying to push away, and then surrendered, her tongue working up and down the flushed lips of Amelia's sex.

From his vantage point, Rigel Casswell could hear the wet sounds of Sarah working at the blonde girl's quim, and see the way Amelia's breasts flushed and swelled, nipples hardening as the hapless Sarah circled and nibbled at her clitoris. He could see that Sarah was overwhelmed.

It was almost as if he could feel the tendrils of pleasure creeping up through Amelia, who was moving under the magic of Sarah's increasingly competent caresses. The blonde threw back her head and began to move in earnest, rhythmically, thrusting her hips forward in time with the girl's tongue.

Casswell could sense Amelia's orgasm approaching, like the tense heady promise of a summer storm. At the very final second, just as Casswell felt certain that Amelia was falling helplessly into the void, she tore herself away from Sarah and dragged her to her feet. With a single smooth movement she turned the dark-haired girl around, and without a whimper Sarah straddled the chair. An instant later Amelia snapped her into the handcuffs, securing her tight to the bentwood frame.

To Casswell's delight, Sarah could no longer sustain the pretence of real fear; her eyes glittered with anticipation, her flesh glowed with an inner fire. Behind her, the corset-clad Amelia flexed the whip speculatively and let the tip cut through the air.

Sarah shivered, eyes widening, pupils dilated. The second swing was closer, a crueller stroke slicing through the air with an icy hiss. Casswell could feel the goose bumps lifting on his skin. He glanced around; every pair of eyes in the room was fixed on the stage.

He could see Sarah tense for a split second before the next stroke hit her squarely across the shoulders. Then she screamed – a cry that came from the pit of her soul, a wild desperate mewl of pain. Her whole body seemed to leap forward, her breasts thrusting forward, nipples darkening.

Casswell could see, framed by the wooden arc of the chair's curved back, the open lips of Sarah's naked sex. Its interior the flushed inviting colour and texture of ripe pomegranates, it glistened like treasure under the spotlight's single eye.

The hue of Sarah's flesh was changing, a strange unnerving flush that seemed to seep through her, as behind her Amelia twisted to apply the next stroke.

The blow was lower this time, making Sarah's legs and pelvis surge forward, pressing fiercely against the chair. Her face was contorted into an ecstatic grimace, while her hips thrust forward again, offering her sex to the audience like a ripe fruit. Mesmerised by the spectacle, Casswell's mouth was watering from the sheer erotic charge the two females created.

Sarah was breathing hard, trying to retain some control, and then the whip fell again and her head jerked back. Amelia smiled from under the mask – her teeth pearly-white and feline – and then she planted a kiss on her victim's gasping mouth.

Around him Casswell could feel the erotic temperatures rising, the guests and their slaves willing their way towards release as a single body.

Four, five – the whip cracked again and again. By now Sarah had surrendered entirely to the compulsive beat of the erotic pain. Casswell shivered as he imagined the raw kiss of the leather cutting into his back.

Six and seven – Sarah was pressing herself forward, straining and desperate, trying to rub her glowing, wet sex against the smooth wooden frame of the chair.

Eight and then nine – Casswell wondered how much longer Sarah's beating could continue. The atmosphere in the garden room was strung as tight as a piano wire.

Ten – and a final decisive blow cracked around the crowded room and reverberated through Sarah's flushed, perspiring flesh. As if she knew it was the last stroke, she fell forward, sobbing hard, struggling to catch a breath.

Behind her Amelia threw the whip onto the stage and undid her victim's handcuffs, then dropping onto her hands and knees she crawled across the stage. The submissive pose was completely at odds with the erotic scenario that preceded it.

Casswell wondered if the entertainment was over and looked away just as a man in a long dressing gown stepped onto the stage beside Sarah and Amelia. He looked back, and realised with a shock that the man was Oliver Turner. Amelia slithered across the floor and rubbed against her master's legs, a feline dripping with sexual promise.

Amongst the crowd was a low murmur of recognition

and approval. Their host smiled with all the warmth of a basking shark and stroked Amelia's pale blonde locks. She purred with delight, and still nosing and rubbing against his thighs, undid his red brocade robe. It fell open to reveal that Oliver was naked beneath, his great cock arched and angry. Under the spotlight he looked better endowed than Casswell remembered.

Amelia cradled his phallus in her fingers and began to suckle at the end where a single teardrop of excitement glistened. She sucked greedily, hungry to pleasure him, with one hand lifting to cradle and caress his heavy scrotum.

The old man's expression was impassive as the lithe blonde stroked herself into a frenzy, long fingers dipping into the wet ripe confines of her sex, then using her juices to smear over Oliver's cock and balls. Moans of intense pleasure hummed out from the junction of her lips where they closed around his throbbing phallus.

Sarah Morgan sat in the shadows, and only her eyes betrayed her passion, as bright as a flare in the intense darkness. Until she met him, she could have had no idea that things like this ever went on.

Amelia started to pull away from Oliver, breathless now, but before she could her master grabbed tight hold of her hair and pulled her closer. She snorted and wriggled as if fighting to be free of him, saliva trickling down her chin as he forced her to bring him to release. Between her legs, her fingers still worked their own particular magic, meaning that she too was on the great spiral of orgasm.

Casswell could sense their growing pleasure despite Oliver's apparently unfeeling expression. Suddenly the man let out a throaty sigh and jerked his cock from between Amelia's lips; a great arc of semen flooding out over her body, splashing across her face and breasts.

At almost the same instant Amelia began to twitch and shudder, drowning in a great well of orgasm as her fingers worked in the sopping pit between her legs. Beyond the heady images of the couple on stage, the room was draped with a strange stillness and quiet.

Amelia collapsed at Oliver's feet, his cock, wet from her kisses, still jutted above her like a sword. To Casswell's delight, Sarah climbed off the chair and crawled across the stage towards the couple – her action as erotic and glorious as it was unexpected. Dropping onto all fours beside the prone body of the exquisite blonde she began to lick the glistening semen off her breasts. Crouched over Amelia, open and excited, her richly fragrant sex was an invitation Casswell was tempted to take up. But as the thought formed in his head, one of Turner's other guests climbed up onto the stage. The man was in evening dress, but it took him no more than a few seconds to undress, kneel and place his erect penis into Sarah's sex. Casswell looked away; he knew it would not be long before the party disintegrated into an orgy, and his tastes were more discriminating and he had no great desire to participate.

Then almost as if some benign but debauched god had heard his prayer, Chang appeared at his shoulder.

'Egon has just arrived from the airport, sir,' he whispered. 'He is waiting for Mr Turner and yourself in the drawing room.'

Casswell smiled; on stage his protégée, Sarah Morgan, was on the very brink of orgasm, while above her, still naked except for his dressing gown, Oliver Turner was looking on with the greatest of delight. Casswell indicated the elderly gentleman with a discreet nod of his head. 'Give our host a few minutes to compose himself and then tell him where we are, Chang. I'll go and entertain

Mr Egon.'

Minutes later, Sarah, her body flushed with the aftermath of orgasm, gasped for breath and rolled over onto her back, her male companion already back amongst the crowd. She could hardly believe the way she had behaved, but also knew that there were no excuses – watching Oliver Turner and Amelia provoked some dark side of her soul that wanted nothing more than to be part of their passion, part of their desire.

Now, as her breathing slowed, Amelia looked across at her, her face arranged in a sly smile. 'See, I said you'd like it, didn't I?'

Sarah laughed and then glanced around the darkened function room, out over the sea of faces. Most of the couples and threesomes were already engaged in passions of their own – but to her consternation, Rigel Casswell was nowhere in sight. She picked up a thick white towel that had been left on the edge of the stage and wiped her face; sweat had appeared like raindrops as she fought her way out to the very edges of desire.

A few feet away, Chang clambered onto the stage and whispered something to Oliver Turner, who nodded, pulled his robe shut and tied the belt tight. Indicating that Chang should lead, Oliver fell into step behind him while Amelia followed her master, leaving Sarah alone on the stage. Part of her wanted to stay, but instead she picked up the towel, wrapped it around her shoulders and headed after Chang and the others.

At the door to the drawing room the little oriental turned, opened the door for Oliver Turner and Amelia, and then waved Sarah away. 'They're talking business,' he said gently. 'Go upstairs and wait. I'll tell him where you are.'

Sarah looked at Chang and swallowed down the anger, but amongst the many other things she felt about him, she trusted him to take care of Casswell. 'It's about the diary?'

Chang nodded and the sense of elation she felt on stage with Oliver and Amelia trickled away like iced water. Without another word she hurried upstairs. What would happen next? Would this mean she would have to leave Casswell Hall, leave her master and the diaries? The thought horrified her. Staring at the familiar outline of the transcript on the table in her room, she closed her eyes, willing the outcome to be a good one.

Sarah perched on the end of her bed for what seemed like an eternity, until finally she contemplated going back downstairs. Perhaps amongst other people the time would pass more quickly. But to her relief, almost as the thought formed in her mind, Casswell opened the door and strode into the room.

Part of her wanted nothing more than to run into his arms, prostrate herself at his feet, whatever it took for things to be right. In an odd way she felt as if they had both lived through Beatrice's worst fears. For an instant she held back, wondering if she dare speak to him, but she could not contain herself.

'The diary,' she began, aware that she had his undivided attention. 'I finished reading it this afternoon. Chang has told me about the things Gilim said…' Her voice faded as she struggled to find the right words. Would Casswell be angry with her for speaking out of turn, for knowing so much? 'Was that the expert you were expecting? Is the diary genuine? I have to know…'

Dr Casswell allowed himself a narrow smile. He looked her up and down, eyes as dark as crystal.

'So you have to know, do you, Miss Morgan?' he said, taking a glass from the tray on the side table and settling in the chair Sarah had so recently vacated. 'How very interesting. One day, my dear, you will learn to be silent. Now take off that towel and let me look at you.' His voice was barely above a whisper.

Sarah did as she was told, letting it drift to the floor. Already her pulse had quickened. She dropped her gaze in an act of submission.

'Good,' Casswell said, beckoning her closer, and without thinking Sarah dropped onto all fours and crept to him, delighted and relieved and lifted by his presence, although unable to explain why. He stroked her hair, pushing it back off her face. Her breasts, still naked, trimmed by the torn remnants of the feathered costume, brushed against his thighs.

'You are a precious creature,' he said, cupping her breasts, toying with the erect nipples as he spoke. 'The bad news is that the diary you and I have been working on is a forgery.'

Sarah felt her heart contract sharply. As she struggled to find something to say, Casswell continued in a low voice. 'The expert who flew in this afternoon has seen the authentic article in a museum in Turkey. Our volume and at least one of the other diaries that follow it are stored there.

'The manuscript we have been working on is a clever and apparently very accurate copy, by a master forger at the beginning of this century when an inventory was taken of the books at Father Orme's old abbey.' Casswell paused and looked down into Sarah's eyes. 'I have to admit; I'd already suspected it wasn't the original, but it is important you understand, Sarah, that the diary is not a fake. All the stories about Beatrice are true; those are her words, her thoughts, her passions and pains, just transcribed by another at a later date – much as you and I are doing.'

He lifted her chin and wiped away the single tear that meandered onto her cheek.

'Oliver Turner has already asked me if I would like to go to Turkey to examine the original book, and its companion volumes if I can track them down. He's agreed to finance the whole expedition.' Casswell paused for a few more seconds to let the words sink in. 'I've told him to arrange for Chang and my personal assistant to travel with me.' Sarah stared at him, sorting through what he had said. 'I'll need someone I can trust to type up the transcripts. I plan to leave at the end of the month, and will make arrangements for you to come with me.'

Sarah, tearful with relief and gratitude, dropped her head into his lap and nuzzled there like a faithful dog. She could feel his cock hardening as he pulled her closer, so slowly she unfastened his fly and began to lick and suck his thickening shaft; a slave to her master. She moaned softly as she tasted the nectar of his excitement, and like Beatrice, she savoured a sense of coming home.

Chapter Two

'My dear Casswell, it seems so long since we have seen you, my friend.' As he spoke, Uri Weissman poured iced tea for Sarah and Dr Casswell from an elegant glass pitcher. 'I am delighted that at last you and your companion are here in Turkey, in my home. Delighted too that I can finally repay your hospitality after all these years. I trust your journey went well?'

The first floor room into which they had been shown, was furnished with an eclectic and exotic mix of European and Middle Eastern artefacts. Along the cream washed walls, long sofas and low tables were set amongst ferns and ornaments and complex panels made from brass and carved hardwoods. The late morning air was heavy with the scent of incense, sandalwood and ylang-ylang burning in a thurible, its perfumed smoke rising effortlessly in an idle twisting plume to the ceiling.

In an ornate cage hanging from a beam sat a handsome red and yellow macaw, watching the proceedings with a tired, world-weary expression.

Although the room was relatively cool compared to the streets below, Sarah felt beads of sweat on her face and in the valley between her breasts.

Their host, an eminent Austrian businessman, had a home in one of the coastal towns on the Aegean, a short drive from Marmaris and just a few minutes by car from a small museum where Casswell had been told at least one of Beatrice's original diaries were now housed.

Sarah thought Uri Weissman looked like a concert pianist.

A tall man, he had great wings of golden hair shot through with grey, which swept back off his high forehead, framing sharp aristocratic features. From time to time his icy-blue eyes would move effortlessly from the conversation to appraise Casswell's latest companion.

'Indeed, we're delighted to be here,' said Rigel Casswell, his tone suggesting he was bored with the social pleasantries. 'When can we see the manuscript?'

Uri Weissman laughed, revealing perfect white teeth. 'You never change, do you, Casswell? You're always the same – always so very eager when it comes to your precious antiquities. Have no fear; we shall begin our quest tomorrow. I have arranged for the curator of the museum to give us a guided tour, and then for an extra little consideration to have uninterrupted access to the manuscripts. The trustees are remarkably proud of their archives, so despite my best efforts, I am afraid you will have to translate in situ, at least for the present.'

While the two men spoke, Sarah sat quietly on one of the huge cane sofas that gave a view into the narrow streets below. Above her an ancient ceiling fan cut through the hot air like a sword blade, but worked to only disturb the heat rather than cool the room.

Despite Casswell's convivial comments it had been a long day of travelling – the early journey from Casswell Hall, the flight from London, the drive out along the coast road from the airport. Tired and heavy-eyed, Sarah's attention wandered away from the two men, her eyes drawn again and again into the alleyway below which gave a glimpse of the main street beyond. It was like a carnival, noise and dust and unfamiliar smells and colours, merchants and tourists mixing with women out to do their marketing, here a donkey, there a man carrying a pile of baskets on his head; the Moorish and Ottoman influence obvious on the buildings and on the faces of the local population.

Weissman's grand white Moorish house was tucked away in a back street and seemed a million miles from the bleak beauty of Casswell's isolated country estate.

'And I assume this is your latest acquisition, eh?'

Aware that both men were now looking at her, Sarah's attention snapped back to the discussion in the room.

Casswell nodded. 'Indeed, this is my companion, Miss Morgan.'

Sarah glanced briefly towards her host, eyes lowered, expression demure and guarded.

Uri Weissman nodded with appreciation; there was no doubting her role. 'You always did have excellent taste. I shall look forward to acquainting myself with your latest pupil when time permits.'

Casswell smiled. 'I'll send her up to you this afternoon during siesta, if you wish.'

Weissman smiled. 'How kind, I'd be delighted to accept.'

Sarah reddened, part of her still unsettled by the casual trading and use of slaves. It seemed that her body was little more than a delicacy to be tried and tasted, a token to be traded or exchanged with whomever Casswell decided deserving.

Uri Weissman eyed her again with interest and as he did, Casswell indicated that she should stand so he could inspect her more closely. Sarah knew better than to refuse, and turned slowly.

For her trip to Turkey, Casswell's manservant, Chang, had dressed her in a white cotton blouse with breast pockets, a slim-fitting cream linen skirt, broad brown leather belt and high-heeled sandals. Despite looking like an English Rose abroad, beneath the clothes Sarah Morgan was totally naked, her quim shaved and oiled, her body always available to Casswell or whomever he might choose to pass her to.

Weissman beckoned her closer and indicated the blouse. Without a word Sarah undid the buttons, eyes lowered, colour rising, as she slipped it back off her narrow shoulders to reveal pert breasts with large dark nipples. She still found it hard to overcome her natural modesty and blushed as the blouse dropped to the floor. She could smell her own body, crystals of perspiration rising in the pit of her throat and along her collarbones. The slight breeze from the fan contracted her nipples into stiff peaks and filled the room with the delicate perfume of perspiration mingled with the heady scent Casswell liked her to wear.

She felt like a prize filly, sweated up and on show. Despite her natural reticence, there was something about being at the beck and call of the two men that excited and frightened her at the same time.

Glancing down into the street below Sarah wondered how many passers-by might look up and see her, framed by the doors of the balcony. She knew too that if Casswell asked her she would beckon any peeping Tom to join them, whoever he might be. She would take him into the room, suck his cock, and let him fuck or whip her, and the prospect induced a ripple of pleasure in her belly. She was his to command and however disturbing it might be, it excited her beyond all reason and measure.

Weissman grunted his approval at her unquestioning obedience, and then indicated that she should come and kneel closer so he could handle her.

'Personally I would have her pierced,' he said conversationally, weighing first one breast and then the other in his large hands. He nipped thoughtfully at the puckered nipples, rubbing them between thumb and forefinger. 'I know an excellent man locally who would do it for you while you're here. He does a good job. He would do her sex, too. It looks good and marks her as your own.'

Casswell laughed. 'If you look at her you'll see I've already marked her as my own.'

As he spoke, Weissman lifted her skirt and turning her a little, saw the brand mark on Sarah's buttock, and nodded his approval. 'Very good, but I would still consider a piercing. I find it helps with training and improves the appearance greatly.' The Austrian slipped his hand up between Sarah's legs. He was far from gentle. It felt to Sarah as if he really was handling horseflesh, firmly and without compassion, so she understood this was business, not tenderness or affection or even genuine interest. A single finger roughly breached the outer lips of her quim and without prelude drove deep inside her. She winced as her body resisted his invasion.

'A little dry,' he said, and withdrawing, spat into his palm and having rubbed it unceremoniously into the folds of her quim, tried again. This time he had no trouble, pressing deep into her, his thumb sliding back to brush her clitoris. Sarah gasped as she felt a little ripple of pleasure and instinctively flexed her buttocks, her body drawing his finger deeper still.

Uri Weissman laughed and nodded approvingly. 'Tight, good breasts, and keen too – I'm very impressed, Casswell. You always did know how to pick them. Not bad at all. I shall look forward to this afternoon—'

There was a knock at the door. Sarah froze, uncertain whether to cover herself or stay as she was.

'Come in,' barked Uri Weissman, making no effort to move.

Sarah felt her colour deepen and looked down at the

floor.

'Rigel darling, how wonderful to see you again,' gushed a female voice that, like Weissman's, had a heavy Teutonic accent. 'How are you? I see you have brought another one of your pets along with you, and of course my brother would need to try it out. He is so boring, so predictable.'

Reluctantly, Weissman drew his hand from between Sarah's legs and turned to greet the new arrival. 'Casswell, you must remember my sister, Anna?' He turned his attention to the striking young woman. 'If I had my way I would hand you over to Casswell so he could train you, you little vixen, and then perhaps you would have some manners and understand what it is that women are truly designed for.'

Sarah glanced up into ice-blue eyes of a statuesque blonde who bore an uncanny resemblance to their host.

'Oh, I know exactly what they're for, Uri. And I like them for all the same reasons you do, darling. Here, I brought you this, Rigel; a little something to whet your appetite.' She handed Casswell a neatly folded sheet of white paper.

He opened it, and after a few seconds smiled. 'My God, is this it? This is what I'm here to translate. It's wonderful. How did you get hold of this?'

Anna laughed. 'Oh please, how do you think? I've been working on the Head of Antiquities, Mustafa Aziz, for weeks. He is a perverse little bastard, but he adores women too, particularly women who adore other women. I have therefore promised him something very special to get us access into the vaults of his precious museum.'

Seeing Casswell's expression, Anna laughed. 'Did Uri not tell you? The items you want to see are considered to be highly sensitive. Certainly not available to the general public.'

Anna glanced back at Sarah, those diamond-hard eyes crawling slowly over her.

Casswell followed her gaze and smiled wryly. 'Whatever it takes.'

Anna poured herself a glass of iced tea. 'Funnily enough, Rigel, I guessed you would say that. Now tell us, what does it say? I'm very curious.' She indicated the sheet of paper Casswell cradled in his fingers. On it was a facsimile of two tiny pages covered in close script. Even from the fleeting glance Sarah had she recognised it as similar to the pages of the diary that she and Casswell had already translated and transcribed back in England.

After a few seconds Dr Casswell began to read. For Sarah, stripped to the waist, waiting in front of Uri Weissman, her sex wet from his invasion, it was like hearing the voice of an old friend – an old friend whose life and circumstances uncannily echoed her own.

...Bound hand and foot I was carried from my master's bedchamber to the feet of my master's most honoured houseguest, strung on a pole like a prize doe, fresh from the hunt, naked save for the studded collar my master had given me. To be gifted to a stranger thus both terrified me and yet at the same time lit a dark light low in my belly. His highness the king, who has graced the castle with his presence, is an old man, and his sumptuous robe does little to disguise his fragility. Flanked by his entourage he drank in the details of my nakedness, my long slim legs, ripe breasts, full hips, oiled and perfumed and all tied and ready for his pleasure. As I caught a glimpse of him my first thought was that surely such an old man was too feeble to have much use for me. I could feel the eyes of the great hall on me and began to tremble, wondering what would become of me if the guest of honour indeed had no use for me. Would my master's gift be seen as an insult?

Slowly the old man stood up and gestured to those servants who carried me to bring me closer. My feet were cut free and the pole lifted so my arms were above my head. Now it seemed I was his to explore and use as he wished. He beckoned them to carry me closer still so he could inspect me. In his hand I caught a glimpse of a riding crop and guessed at once where his tastes lay.

Behind him stood two young men – noble men or thanes by their rich dress and arrogant bearing, I knew not which – watched the king, their eyes alight with desire as the old man ran a thin and wrinkled hand over my trembling flesh. I knew better than to meet his gaze and looked down demurely at the rush-covered floor. His hands lingered on my breasts, cupping them thoughtfully in his pitifully gnarled fingers.

'It seems my host has sent this creature as a gift to tempt me from the path of righteousness,' the old man hissed angrily. 'What say you, my sweet boys?'

Behind him the two young men nodded and murmured agreement.

'I am a refined and noble man pledged to mother church, pledged to one woman for a lifetime.'

Was this a game or was he truly upset? I felt a rush of fear in my belly. He let the head of the whip trail across my breasts and belly, and last of all over the rise of my maidenhood before sliding it between my legs. I moaned in anticipation of what I imagined was to follow. It was impossible not to.

The old man snatched the whip away and shook his head in disgust. ''Tis true that this wench is a harlot indeed. Ripe for correction, ripe for redemption.' He held the whip out. 'Who will undertake this deed for me?'

As he spoke, the servants who bore me set the pole to which I was tied into a frame, erected, I realised now, for that very purpose.

One of the king's young companions stepped forward, breathing heavily, lips slack and moist with greed and lust, eyes bright. My fear quickened. The old man would barely raise a weal, but this young buck could easily whip me without so much as raising a sweat. I felt my pulse begin to race and began to struggle against my ties.

'Let me, father,' said the man. I could see now that he was dressed in the raiment of a priest, although it was so fine a robe it was hard to tell if he was a man of the cloth.

'See,' he said, as I pulled again at my ties, 'she is spirited and full of fight; she needs the devil beating out of her for certain.'

From the dais the other said, 'Aye, and then I, brother.'

The old man nodded his approval. 'You shall share in the creature's correction; ten strokes each to begin with. Let us see if such a girl begs for mercy – after all, are we not merciful?'

I knew I would beg, but not yet; that was not the bargain I had struck when I became my master's plaything. I knew he was somewhere in the room watching me, he and his good friend Lord Usher, who shared my favours many a night. I would not disgrace him. I closed my eyes and held my breath as the first of the young men drew back his arm.

I heard the whip cut through the smoky air, holding my breath as I imagined what would follow. The blow hit me square across my bottom and I screamed as the shock roared through me. This man, with his strong right arm, truly thought to beat the devil out of me. Although from the look on his brother's eager face I suspected that when the beating was done they had other plans – more base plans on how best to redeem me…

'That is all there is,' Casswell said, as he stopped reading and with regret folded the paper into his jacket pocket. 'You say you got this from the local museum?'

Anna Weissman nodded in confirmation. 'From their private archive. Apparently it was bequeathed to the museum, along with several other pieces that were stored in a relic chest, back in the nineteen-fifties.' She handed him a photograph, which Casswell glanced at. 'It seems strange that something so important should end its days in a tiny museum here in Turkey.'

Despite the businesslike words, Sarah could see from the woman's expression that hearing the extract had excited Anna Weissman. Beatrice de Fleur's voice was still as fresh and as sexually charged now as it had been so many centuries ago, when she first scribed her compelling and intimate diaries.

Casswell looked particularly pleased with the find, although unlike Anna it always seemed his excitement was more academic than physical. 'The tone, the appearance of the script looks promising, and it is written almost exactly as the others were, or at least the fragments and extracts that I have seen.' He pointed to the photocopied page. 'Beatrice's style is unique, written in an obscure central European dialect; there is always an element of cipher and encoding in the entries. Although, I have not seen or heard this particular incident documented before. It is just possible that you've come across a new volume in the museum.'

Anna looked intrigued. 'So this entry is not the one you translated before?'

Casswell shook his head. 'No, which makes this find all the more exciting.'

There was a discreet tap at the door and Weissman glanced down at his watch. 'Perhaps we can discuss the matter over lunch? We eat lightly in the middle of the day and dine more sumptuously in the evening. If you would care to join us?' He got to his feet and indicated the others should follow him.

Casswell nodded, Sarah retrieved her blouse, and as she buttoned it up, it struck her that once this meal was done she was promised to their host to share his siesta.

Rigel Casswell lit a cigar and lay back on the bed watching the plume of smoke drift and swirl up into the oppressive afternoon air. It felt good to be on the trail of Beatrice de Fleur once again, and how fitting it was that Sarah Morgan should be there with him. He put an arm behind his head and closed his eyes. After they had eaten Chang whisked her way to shower and ready her for their host, Uri Weissman. Casswell smiled at the idea as he considered taking up Weissman's offer to watch their encounter. Despite the rigours of the trip and the heat of the day, he was very tempted.

In the adjoining chamber Sarah did not resist as Chang dressed her in a fine red and gold embroidered caftan and matching sandals. He drew her hair back, and outlined her eyes with a fine kohl line. A veil was the final touch. Sarah glanced at herself in the mirror; she looked like a slave from the harem.

The room she had been given was long, with a high ceiling, and doors at one end with a balcony overlooking another narrow street. A fan burred overhead. The room was painted white and gold, the bed up on a raised platform draped with creamy muslin mosquito nets.

As Chang admired his handiwork, Sarah longed to ask

the imperious oriental about their host, but knew from bitter experience that the rule of speaking only when spoken to extended to him as well as Casswell. During their flight from London, Casswell's valet had sat silently in economy class while she joined the doctor in first, but here in the quiet of the bedroom it was Chang, not Sarah, who had the upper hand.

'There,' he said, fastening the veil over her hair. Sarah suspected he was talking to himself, but nevertheless nodded and looked again at her reflection in the mirror.

The caftan was made of delicate cotton voile, so fine that her body was visible through the folds. Chang had rouged her nipples, set a faux jewel in her navel and added a delicate gold G-string so fine that it just covered the lips of her sex and sat snugly between the shapely orbs of her bottom. As a final touch he had put a narrow black leather collar around her throat and added a fine gold chain to it.

It was odd how quickly she relinquished her modesty to this apparently impassive little man; this man who used her as and when he pleased, her compliance a perk of his servitude to Dr Casswell; this man who regularly shaved away her pubic hair, and who attended to her body in the most intimate and private of ways.

Without another word Chang caught hold of the chain and led Sarah back down the stairs to an ornate set of double doors. Beyond them Uri Weissman was already waiting for her.

Gone now was the European tropical suit of cream linen jacket and tailored trousers of their earlier encounter, and instead Uri Weissman was dressed in a long fine white cotton robe. He looked Sarah up and down and had her turn around before his critical gaze. Then as Chang went to leave, Weissman stopped him.

'Secure her and stay,' he ordered.

Set up in front of a large mirror on a heavily patterned carpet was a frame not unlike a tall piano stool, with a long padded seat with cuffs and chains attached to all four legs. Sarah shivered, knowing full well that the device was meant for her.

As Chang bent her forward and fastened the restraints tight around her wrists and ankles, she experienced a moment of total fear as she surrendered to whatever would follow – after all, she did not know this man. She only knew she trusted Casswell's judgement. Catching sight of her reflection for an instant, she saw the image she presented to Uri Weissman.

The stool was built so that her buttocks were high, her knees slightly bent, legs apart, her breasts pressed hard down against the upholstery, her lithe body draped with the soft red fabric. As she watched, Chang lifted the skirt of her robe to reveal the creamy white orbs of her bottom, the gesture like some terrible parody of a bride being unveiled for the groom.

It was disconcerting and compelling at the same time to watch Weissman's progress across the room towards her. Chang moved to one side and stood with his hands folded behind his back – the model of a perfect servant.

Weissman prowled, hungrily absorbing the delectable view of the bound girl. In his hand he carried an old carpet beater, made from bent willow. Sarah shivered and let out a little sob of fear, trying to imagine what its broad face would feel like as it cracked across her delicate and vulnerable flesh.

Weissman flexed it thoughtfully between his large hands before taking up a stance behind her. As the seconds passed, all Sarah could hear was her rapidly rising pulse beating in her ears and then, in the mirror she watched Weissman's arm go back, heard the air rush and then screamed out in shock as an instant later the face of the beater exploded against her skin. A red-hot sensation rolled through her, making her writhe.

The stool was bolted to the floor, because the frame moved not an inch as her body contorted from the strike. The gold G-string tightened as she flexed, pressing tight against her clitoris, its grazing touch a bizarre and unexpected counterpoint to the great flash of pain. Weissman struck again and this time her body arched, its progress cruelly stopped by her restraints, her cries rending the still afternoon air.

Tears of discomfort and rivulets of perspiration ran down Sarah's face as the beater found its mark yet again.

'Please,' Sarah sobbed, 'please,' as always not quite knowing whether she was begging her tormentor to stop, or whether she was crying out for him to continue.

As she bucked and twisted, Sarah felt the terrible firefly glow light deep in the heart of her sex, a spark that ignited that same tantalising need, that same madness that kept her so close to Casswell and all he offered her.

As Weissman found a rhythm her cries broke up into throaty sobs and incoherent pleas, the heat suffusing her body like a tidal wave, her breasts rubbing hard against the damask, her clitoris pressed and restrained by the tight G-string. It was a heady and terrifying combination.

Above her, Weissman grunted and lay the beater on again and again until Sarah lost count of the strokes that exploded across her tied frame. The sensation washed away all reason until at last the Austrian threw the beater down and crouched over her glowing buttocks, ripped the G-string to one side, and gripping her hips pulled her back towards him and drove his cock deep into her wet sex.

Sarah cried out as he plunged home, his flesh against

hers a stunning contrast to the angry heat of the beater, although the sounds were strangled and fearful in her dry throat. With one hand on her hips, the other tangled in her hair, Weissman dragged her up in a bow towards him.

'Untie her,' he growled at Chang, who complied instantly.

Allowing Weissman to guide her, the Austrian pulled Sarah down onto the floor in front of the mirror and rolled her onto her back. His expression was triumphant. He hunched over her and tore the G-string off, with one hand still working in the folds of her sopping sex, his thick cock slid back into her, while with his other hand he lifted her breasts up to his lips, first one and then the other, sucking and biting at her aching nipples.

Sarah whimpered in delight and began to writhe beneath him, her excitement building towards a terrifying crescendo. Weissman, his eyes glazed over with a mixture of pleasure and need, suddenly pulled back and roughly lifted her legs over his shoulders, allowing him to plunge deeper still. The sensation of his weight and the glow of her bottom rubbing against the floor were almost more than Sarah could bear, and without thinking she slid her hand down to touch her engorged clit.

Weissman snorted and leered down at her. 'You truly are a find, Miss Morgan. Come on; fuck me and let me feel you come. Suck me dry with that tight little pussy of yours.'

The words sounded so incongruous, grunted in his thickly accented, educated tones, but even so Sarah did as she was told, rocking furiously against him until moments later she sensed his impending climax and with it her own. As the lights exploded inside her head she closed her eyes, and the last thing she saw as the waves of pleasure stole her away was Chang watching the two of them, his expression quite unreadable.

In the small viewing room that overlooked Weissman's bedroom, Casswell watched his pupil with interest and delight. It was hot and dark, and beside him on a small sofa Anna Weissman was straining forward, any pretence of sophisticated indifference long since forgotten. Her eyes were alight with pure excitement.

Casswell knew from what had been said earlier that it was Sarah's exquisite body and her unquestioning obedience, not some incestuous desire for her brother, which shortened Anna's breath and induced the expression of intense interest on her handsome face.

Not that Anna was averse to male flesh. Her tastes, as he remembered, moved in many directions.

As if she was completely oblivious to Casswell being there, Anna slid her hand down between the sleek, well-toned flesh of her thighs. As she found the right spot she gasped and then threw her head back, eyes closed, and began to work her fingers back and forth, eagerly stroking the little bud that nestled there, while dipping her fingers into herself.

Casswell smiled; the show in the hidden room was nearly as interesting as the one in Weissman's bedroom.

Suddenly Anna's eyes opened, pupils dilated with desire, and she stared at Casswell as if seeing him for the first time. It was obvious what she wanted, but to make sure Casswell understood, Anna took his hand, put it over her own in its fragrant hiding place, and then parted her fingers. Her sex was wet and warm, covered by just a wisp of soft damp silk.

She was more than ready for him, but Casswell smiled down at her and shook his head; whatever Anna Weissman thought, there was no way she was going to call the shots.

As her face registered consternation, Casswell dragged his hand out from between her legs and pulled her roughly off the sofa onto the floor. The only way she was going to have Caswell was on his terms. As she started to resist, he ripped open her blouse and bra, dragging them off her suntanned shoulders, while his lips sought out her heavy breasts.

She squealed in pain and protest but Casswell sensed her resistance – although genuine – was little more than an excited reflex, a token to appease any last shred of decency. This was exactly what Anna Weissman wanted. She was desperate for him to take her, to dominate her, to make her his and give her the pleasure she longed for.

As she began to relax and move with him, moaning as he sucked hard at her engorged nipples, his hands crept under her pencil skirt, this time ripping away the silk panties. All the time his lips were pressed to her breasts, nipping and sucking, but now he moved lower, licking her ribs and belly while his hands further pulled up her skirt.

If for an instant Anna Weissman thought she was in for tender pleasures, she was mistaken. With two fingers deep in her wet quim, Casswell could sense how close the vixen was to an orgasm, and just before she reached the point of no return he pulled away, as if done with her.

'Please,' Anna sobbed, 'don't stop now, please.' She begged while her fingers sought the spot his lips had abandoned, but before she could bring herself to a climax Casswell grabbed tight hold of her wrists.

'Get up on all fours,' he snapped, and without hesitation she did exactly as she was told. Casswell smiled wolfishly. Weissman was right about his sister; despite all her bravado she was ripe for training.

Waiting for him now, crouched there in the shadows,

Anna was a picture of submission. Her blouse ripped, her elegant skirt rucked up around her narrow waist and between those long legs her quim was wet and ripe, hungry for his attentions.

Casswell let her wait for him, and just as he sensed she was beginning to relax he unzipped his fly, and releasing his turgid shaft he thrust deep into her, making her cry out with surprise, discomfort and pleasure. This time his fingers found her clit and pressed on its delicate hood, all the while driving in and out of her, their movement an echo of the one they had just witnessed in the room beyond the two-way mirror.

Anna Weissman sobbed as he thrust into her, her body matching him stroke for stroke until he felt her sex start to contract rhythmically around him, and Casswell knew then that he was lost to everything except the pleasure of the moment.

Beneath him Anna pressed back and rode on, drinking in the last few ripples of delight, her tight quim milking him, and they both sprawled on the floor, gasping for breath, sweat coating their faces and bodies.

Chapter Three

Sarah lay in bed listening to the unfamiliar sounds of the Turkish night. Outside the sky was black and sensual. A slight breeze, swirling up from the sea, rippled the curtains on the balcony, and now the day was done she could hear the lapping waves of the Aegean against the harbour wall from somewhere close by.

Sleep eluded her even though she was exhausted, her body heavy from the thrashing administered by Weissman. Part of her was uneasy about her role on the trip to secure and translate the diary, although her role had seemed clear when she was back in England with Casswell.

In stark contrast to the events of siesta, over dinner Uri Weissman had played the perfect host while his sister Anna spent the entire evening unashamedly flirting with Casswell. Sarah shivered as she imagined Anna's full lips, pouting and eager, her body so slim and yet so ripe in a silver lamé sheath dress, moving close to him, smiling and touching his arm. It was as if Anna was offering herself to him on a plate.

Sarah made sure she did not catch the Austrian woman's eye, although she was shaken by Casswell's apparent delight at so obvious a creature. She wondered if her position in Casswell's life was tenuous; in theory she was his personal assistant but realistically good secretaries were ten-a-penny, although she hoped her role in his life as an obedient slave was less uncertain.

Alone in her bed, Sarah bit her lip to hold back the tears. She loved Casswell more than she could possibly say.

The realisation took her by surprise. Watching him laugh and joke with Anna Weissman made her jealous and unhappy beyond anything she had ever felt. But beneath the jealousy was something else – instinctively Sarah did not trust the elegant woman, although she could not work out why.

After coffee and liquors were served, exhausted by the long day, Sarah was pleased when Casswell suggested that she might like to retire early and wondered if he would call for her to share his bed.

Chang had already informed her that their suites adjoined, but so far no such summons had come. It was a long time after Sarah had gone to bed that she finally heard Casswell entering his room, and she suspected he was not alone, so feeling tired and bereft she curled up and went to sleep.

'So you want to get your hands on my precious diary?' said the keeper of antiquities, first thing the following morning. The ornate vaulted museum foyer was cool and dark after the heat and clamour of the streets. Around them a steady stream of tourists were already making their way into the cool shadowy depths of what one of the tour guides was currently describing as a former palace of a minor prince. Unlike its curator, the building was indeed magnificent.

Sarah tried hard to keep her feelings about the man who had greeted them to herself, and it was a struggle.

The keeper of antiquities and curator, Mustafa Aziz, was grossly overweight with bad skin, foul breath and a badly trimmed moustache. He had an unwholesome, unwashed appearance and an even more unwashed odour. His suit seemed to be made for a much smaller man and the buttons of his shirt strained unpleasantly over his bloated stomach. In one hand he clutched a stained Panama hat.

Conspiratorially he caught hold of Casswell's arm. 'Has Miss Weissman explained the terms under which you can have access to these precious national treasures?'

As he spoke Sarah noted the way the fat curator's eyes worked hungrily, first over Anna Weissman's body and then more slowly over her own. It was impossible to ignore his undisguised interest. As their eyes met, Sarah reddened furiously and Aziz licked his lips as if he had been savouring some particularly favourite delicacy, before quickly mopping his face with a grubby handkerchief.

Casswell peeled the man's fingers from his arm. 'That you have first opportunity to read the draft translations and that none of the original material leaves the building,' he said impassively.

The curator nodded. 'And?' He smiled salaciously. 'And the rest of the bargain... surely you know about the rest of the bargain?

It was Anna's turn to speak. 'Come on, Mustafa, do you really want to discuss your sexual peccadilloes out here in front of the tourists?' She spoke just loudly enough, for one of the parties being guided in turned to look at them.

The fat man reddened furiously and made a show of mopping his brow. His expression implied that Anna would regret her remark.

'Casswell knows the score,' Anna continued. 'Now are you going to show us down into your precious dungeon or not?'

He nodded, his eyes all the while working backwards and forward over the two women. It was evident that the blonde's offhand and aggressive manner infuriated and offended him.

Taking a heavily carved key from his pocket he beckoned them to follow, their prize it seemed was down a flight of steep stairs carved from the most exquisite marble and which lead them into a vaulted cellar, built under the main hall of the museum. Although it was cool in the catacomb, the air was heavy with the smells of dust and decay.

Amongst row after row of battered shelves, display cases and filing cabinets, the curator set up a trestle, lights and two swivel chairs. On a tray in the centre of the desk stood a glass cabinet, two pairs of white cotton gloves and a magnifying plate.

Casswell smiled as he approached the little cabinet. Inside, laying on a special acid free fabric that absorbed moisture, was a tiny red book, four inches by three at the most, the edge of the pages brown with age. Glancing around the makeshift office, he said, 'Anna told me that you promised to provide a computer and printer for my secretary.' He nodded towards Sarah. One of the museum's stipulations was that they did not bring in their own machines, so the state-of-the-art laptop that Casswell brought from England was languishing on Sarah's dressing table.

Mustafa grinned. 'Indeed I did, my friend. You shall have them tomorrow, but today you surely have nothing for her to work on?' Before he could reply, Mustafa puffed out his chest. 'And last but not least it gives me great pleasure to present you with a gift made by local craftsmen to remind you of your time in our humble town.'

He clapped his hands and two lackeys appeared from the shadows carrying a wooden crate. Mustafa waved them to set it down and open it. Inside, amongst a great tangle of wood and wool, was a section of pillar, perhaps two foot high. 'It is a replica of a roman pillar,' Mustafa said enthusiastically. 'Handmade at the local quarry. It will look very fine in your garden, yes?'

It was a very peculiar gift, and polite as ever, Casswell gave his thanks and turned to look at the contents of the glass case, but the Turk had not finished. 'And so today I will have Miss Morgan all to myself while you begin work. That was the deal made by Miss Weissman.'

Casswell looked up momentarily and glanced at Anna.

Sarah stiffened.

Mustafa held up a hand to silence any protest. 'It was the promise I was made. I have honoured you by opening vaults, by giving you a gift, by allowing you access to my most treasured possession. In return, today I have your woman all for myself and then later the two of them together. Miss Weissman, she has promised me.' He glared angrily at Anna, who merely smiled at each of them.

'You know you really owe me for this one, Casswell,' she said.

Sarah cringed at the prospect of what was developing; it was the most appalling thought, but Casswell's expression was unreadable as he turned to the glass cabinet that housed the diary.

Mustafa beckoned to Sarah. 'You, you come with me.'

Sarah looked from one face to another, but there was no right of appeal. It appeared that Casswell's mind was elsewhere. He was busy putting on a pair of cotton gloves, his attention fixed on the contents of the display cabinet, Anna Weissman close beside him.

Mustafa's expression hardened. 'Now,' he snapped, and Sarah, feeling utterly abandoned, reluctantly followed him.

Without another word, the fat Turk led her back through the maze of shelves, opened a doorway and took her into another part of the cellars, out through a tangle of ill-lit corridors to a darker, more isolated area. Finally, after what seemed an age, he opened a door in the stonework and beckoned her inside. What choice did she have? Sarah stepped past him and Mustafa immediately shut and locked the door behind them.

She looked around with a growing sense of fear. They were in windowless room with a beaten earth floor, lit by a single bulb, and empty except for a camp bed, a low table, a chest of drawers on which stood a bottle of water and two glasses, and a battered armchair.

'So, let me see what it is that I have traded my treasures for,' he drooled, excitement thickening his accent as he settled against the chest of drawers and lit a cheroot. 'Strip for me. I want you naked. Now.'

Nervously, Sarah began to undo the elegant linen dress she was wearing. Mustafa watched her with dark eyes, mopping his slack lips with the filthy handkerchief.

'Come on,' he snarled impatiently, ' don't play around. Let me see.'

Sarah stood tall to face him, attempting on the surface at least to appear defiant and collected, while inside she was shaking like a leaf. She slid the dress slowly off her shoulders.

Mustafa nodded appreciatively as she stood before him, naked except for high-heeled sandals. Sarah's flesh seemed to glow like a candle flame in the shadowy room.

'Good, that's much better. Now turn around slowly. Let me look at you.' Sarah did as she was told, her discomfort rising with every passing second until finally the sleazy man snapped, 'Come here!' He indicated the armchair. 'I want you to sit down, like this.' Stumbling over the words he showed her with his hands. 'One leg over each arm so I can see you. I want you to touch yourself, play with your tits, finger your wet little slit, your whole body. I want you to stroke and touch and twist those pretty little nipples. I want you to pleasure yourself for me – make yourself come for me.'

Sarah hesitated, and the curator's expression hardened. 'Do you dare to disobey my wishes, Miss Morgan? I'm warning you, it is not in your best interests to disobey me.'

Sarah started to shake her head, but moving with a speed that belied his bulk, Mustafa caught hold of her hair and jerked her close to him. She winced and let out a cry.

'You do exactly as I say,' he growled. 'Without you and me down here now, there is no manuscript for your precious master to work on. No translation, no computer, no nothing. 'You do exactly as I say or he is out of here.'

Sarah gasped as his fingers tightened, but her tormentor had not finished with her yet.

'And then tomorrow you will come down her and fuck that ice queen, Weissman, down here in the dust and filth, on that bed, straddle her, sit on her face and I will watch her lick you like a dog. And when she is done, you are going to stick your pretty little tongue deep inside her, make her writhe and cry out for mercy and then trust me, Miss Morgan, I will fuck you both.'

He caught hold of her hand and pressed it hard against his engorged cock, and bending her hand inside his he held it tight to him. 'You understand me?'

Sarah gasped and tried to nod again, but this time he pulled her to him, kissing her hungrily, his tongue plunging deep into her mouth, coarse hands grabbing at her body, mauling her. He tasted of cheap tobacco and coffee. It was pointless to resist him. He was like a hungry animal and groaned and snorted as he cupped the rise of her sex, his thick fingers seeking entry. The smell of his body and breath made her feel nauseous, yet she had no choice but to co-operate.

After a few minutes he pushed her away. He was panting

and slick with sweat. 'There is time enough for me to touch you later. For now you touch yourself, for my pleasure.' He smiled with salacious triumph as she hesitantly sat on the chair and very slowly draped her legs, one over each of the arms.

He nodded. 'Good, good,' and waving her up a little, slipped a cushion under her bottom so he could see exactly what was on offer.

Sarah closed her eyes, humiliated and ashamed, but intimidated by the filthy man's attention, she reluctantly began to toy with her breasts, fingers circling and teasing the soft peaks into stiffness while her free hand slowly traced a path down over her belly to the contours of her sex.

But it seemed that this was not good enough for him. 'No, no!' he snapped furiously. 'You think I am a fool, eh? Let me see your face. I want to see your eyes, look at me. Look at me! Do it as if you mean it or I will call one of my men in here to do it for you. That great ape who brought in your master's present – he would sell his soul for the chance to fuck a white girl like you. You want me to call him?'

Sarah felt her eyes fill with tears as she stared up at his bloated features.

Mustafa sneered. 'You are so defiant. Think yourself better than me, do you?'

Sarah shook her head. 'No, no,' she murmured. 'I'm just nervous.' It was true; she was nervous and repelled by him.

Mustafa did not look convinced. 'Get up,' he snarled. 'I will show you who is the master here,' and catching hold of her arm he dragged her off the chair. Before she could gather her senses he sat down and pulled Sarah down with him, folding her over his knees.

'I see you already know what happens to those who disobey,' he said huskily, fingering the bruises and weals that still lingered across her bottom. 'You should take more notice.'

For a few seconds his hand worked across her buttocks, stroking the soft orbs. Settling himself, he then drew back his hand and slapped her hard. Sarah shrieked as the raw sting of the blow flushed through her, and she jerked on his stout thighs.

Mustafa grunted; it seemed this was exactly what he wanted; her over his lap, naked and completely at his mercy. Sarah sobbed as he struck the next blow, the pain and heat of his hand intensifying as it cracked across her buttocks again and again. After a dozen or so strokes he stopped, wheezing heavily.

'Enough now,' he panted, sweating even more than before. 'You understand what I want. You do exactly as I tell you.'

Sarah understood only too well, her bottom glowing with the imprint of his hand.

'Get up and give me what I asked for or I will beat you with a stick,' he growled, tipping her without ceremony to the filthy floor.

Sarah clambered back into the chair and this time – seeing no other option – opened her legs wide apart so the fat man could explore with his eyes and fingers the most delicate and secret parts of her body.

He smiled, his wet lips slack, as she began to move against her own caresses, looking her over as if she was little more than meat.

'That's better,' he said. 'And don't mess with me, I will know if you are faking. Harder now. Harder, I want to see you writhing with pleasure.' He caught hold of Sarah's wrist and pressed her fingers down into her sex.

As he moved closer she could feel him drinking in the details of her body. She felt the humiliation surge through her veins. Mustafa moved closer and crouched down low, sniffing at her sex before running a grubby finger up over the moistened folds.

'Good,' he murmured, sliding the same finger in and out of her wetness, trailing it out onto her creamy flesh. 'I have a little something for you – something I want to use on you now and later on that Weissman woman.' From the depths of a pocket he produced a package wrapped in a square of silk.

Inside was a large ivory-coloured dildo, a series of thick rings set with beads around the base. Sarah stiffened as the man slipped the head of the thing between the inner lips of her quim, easing it in and out on the very edge of her sex. It felt cool and pliable against her and her rogue body opened to let it deeper. With a hand on hers, the curator guided her to take over and she began to move against it, realising the rings and the beads were meant to touch her clit. Sarah shivered and pushed the dildo deeper still, working it back and forth, beginning to lose herself in the sensations of the moment, her finger flicking back and forth over her swollen clitoris.

Mustafa refused to be excluded. 'Look at me,' he grunted, catching hold of her chin.

Sarah had no choice, and as she spiralled out towards the point of no return his eyes were locked on hers. At the very last minute he dragged the dildo out of her.

Sarah gasped – she was close, so very close. It felt as if she was falling over the edge of the world. He jerked her down in the chair and ripping open his trousers, thrust his engorged cock into her pulsating quim.

His manhood was so broad she cried out in fear as he drove it in. Her body was teetering on the edge of an orgasm and the very first stroke from his enormous shaft was enough to drive her to oblivion. It was over in seconds, Sarah's body closing tight around his great cock. Mustafa Aziz gasped as he felt her body holding him, squeezing him dry, and he thrust once, twice, and was spent.

Seconds later he pushed her off him.

'Good,' he snorted, wiping his flaccid cock on his handkerchief. 'That is better, tomorrow you will come back here with that blonde bitch and I will fuck the pair of you.'

In the cellar at the other end of the museum Anna Weissman soon got bored watching Casswell read from the diary and scribble notes in a pad, and disappeared into the shadows. The doctor rubbed the bridge of his nose and looked back over the new work. The journal in the cabinet was one he had not seen or heard of before and the more he read the more certain he was that they had stumbled across a previously unknown volume. The implications were heady. Certainly his good friend and benefactor, Oliver Turner, would be delighted. The material not only commanded a good price in the hands of those connoisseurs who appreciated such things, but would improve his already worthy reputation as a patron of historical research within their select and well connected membership.

Having transcribed the page that Anna had teased him with, Casswell continued to translate from the end of the section the blonde had photocopied. It was slow work even with good magnification; the handwriting was tiny and tucked and twisted around itself. Even so, he was pleased with what he had achieved. Pushing himself back from the desk Casswell began to re-read the notes

…It was no game. This man, with his strong right arm, truly thought to beat the devil out of me. Although from the look on his brother's eager face I suspected that when the beating was done they had other plans on how best to redeem me.

I thought I should lose my mind from the pain. The second brother, a tall blond boy with cruel eyes and even crueller touch, laid on his ten strokes with such terrible vengeance that it seemed the two of them were in some contest to see who might strike the hardest. Ten strokes each sounds so little when spoken, yet between them they took me to the shores of madness.

Oh, doubt me not, I begged and sobbed and pleaded to be set free, beseeching mercy they so cruelly promised, fighting against my restraints, but despite their talk of salvation they seemed deaf to my cries as I twisted, bucked and strained under the kiss of the leather.

Finally, when it seemed I could take no more, they cut me down and as I tumbled to the floor, the two of them set about me like hungry wolves. Those two young men, their eyes bright with lust, lapped and sucked at my poor body; exploring my sex, pawing at my breasts, sucking and biting and forcing their way into me with fingers and tongues and cocks; into my mouth, into my quim, and into that secret place where no man should venture, fucking and touching and impaling me again until I thought I would go insane from their attentions. If this is the Christian virtue and mercy of their king then I fear we are all truly undone.

It struck me that we were not alone in our debauchery – all around us in the great hall my nakedness and beating and the actions of the king's lusty sons had aroused such desires as could not be contained.

Around and over the tables, knights and their ladies,

squires and dames, serving maids and lads, all coupled and entwined and fornicated without thought for the consequences of their actions, in twos and threes and fours their bodies pale and sweating in the rush lights, rolling around in the dust. Where one brushed against the other they joined and mixed and changed partners until the night air was thick with the cries of passion and scented with the perfume of bodies. Lord Usher was no doubt enjoying the sport along with the rest, but did my lord look out for me amongst the throes of wild passion?

Lying on the floor of the great hall, my sex was coated with the silky cream seed of the kings' sons, my back raw, my breasts, face and belly splashed with the remnants of their passion. From his throne the king looked down upon my nakedness, taking in the details of my disgrace and the heavy mass of bodies around the hall.

'Is the devil that haunted this brazen creature gone?' he whispered to them, his voice low and tight. 'Seems we have beaten it out of her and unleashed her wicked ways on the rest of the assembled crowd.'

Half naked and sweating, the two of them agreed that whatever temptation or dangers I previously offered had now been beaten from me. The old man nodded and held out his hand. One of the young men bowed and held the whip in his gnarled fist before he beckoned them to bring me closer.

I could barely walk and could not guess what was to follow. To my consternation the two boys picked me up and bore me to the old man's throne. While one unfastened his robe the other held me, and then between them they manhandled me onto his lap and guided his cock into my poor exhausted body.

I felt him slide inside me, my body closing around him. The old man had no need to move now, for the two young men guided me up and down on his shaft in time with his thrusts.

The old king grunted and pressed home time and again, his old hands raking my bruised and throbbing flesh. With renewed vigour he thrust into me again and I heard his breath quicken and knew that such regal seed as was left in that dry old husk was about to be spent. He thrust up into me, moaning and grunting, holding tight to the instant of release, and it was over.

Once the old man had stopped twitching and gasping, the young men pulled me away from his exhausted cock, and they set me down on the dais while they attended to their master, wiping him and covering his nakedness.

I was forgotten, and all around the coupling and pleasure went on. I closed my eyes and curled like a cur at the feet of the king, his sons and his courtiers. In the half light the revels and feasting continued until who knows when. I must have slept, for when I was aware again it was darker and quieter and the old man and his entourage had gone.

Someone had dropped a cloak or robe over me to cover my nakedness but even so, lying there amongst the reeds I was cold. As I roused myself, I saw my master looking down at my abused body and wondered if it had been his voice or his touch that had woken me.

With unexpected tenderness he gently lifted me up and carried me to his chamber. In the months since my mistress had been banished from the castle I have shared his bed night after night, curled in his arms ever faithful, waiting for his command.

Tonight he was as tender to me as any nurse, bathing my aching body and rubbing balm into the welts and bruises inflicted upon me by his king's cruel sons.

I sensed his anger at their treatment of my body, but not a word did he speak to betray his king. Rather when he was done, my master picked me up and set me in his bed. All night long I lay in his arms, feeling safe, his strength and touch brushing away my pain. When the candle burnt low and the sun brightened the eastern sky, he slipped his hand between my thighs, seeking the tender lips of my quim, and I opened to him like the budding lily…

Casswell paused for a moment to collect his thoughts, and rubbed the bridge of his nose. He was about to hand over the finished sheets to Sarah when he realised she was not there. Instantly he remembered, as if waking from a dream; his delight on finding the new manuscript had made him forget that Mustafa Aziz still had her in his clutches. Sliding the book safely back into its cabinet, Casswell rang the bell the curator had left for him to summon one of the museum staff.

Chapter Four

For once Sarah was glad of Casswell's rule of silence. Not catching his gaze, she watched the rich tapestry of the Turkish port unfold on the drive back to Uri Weissman's house. Beside her, Casswell seemed almost as preoccupied, although when his hand settled gently on her thigh she was grateful of his touch.

It was not far from the museum to the Austrian's home, but the streets were packed with people, locals pushed and jostled for position, their women heading back home to escape the heat of the day. But even though the street life was fascinating it was not enough to wipe out the events of the morning spent with Mustafa in the cellar beneath the museum.

Sarah shivered in the cool blast of the air conditioning. She had assumed that once the fat little Turk had spanked her and forced her to put on the performance in the armchair her part of the bargain had been be paid. However, Mustafa had other ideas and insisted she join him on an impromptu tour of the museum. Knowing that Sarah was naked under her dress excited him and periodically, as they joined other groups of tourists to listen to the commentary from the museum guides, he would move closer and touch her, sliding a hand up under her skirt, clammy fingers groping her. The idea that the other visitors might see him appeared to be an added bonus. In some ways the tour of the dusty sun bleached relics was even more humiliating that the things that had happened in the cellar.

Sarah was relieved when at last one of the museum staff had appeared to say that Dr Casswell was ready to leave and they were to go back to the Weissman's for lunch. As he helped her into the waiting car, Mustafa reminded her that the next day she had another appointment with him – as if there was any possible way she could forget.

Back at the Weissman's house while Casswell went to find Uri, Sarah hurried upstairs to shower and rid herself of the oily smell of Mustafa Aziz. When she was finished, Chang was waiting for her outside the shower cubicle with a towelling robe. She had seen very little of him since their arrival in Turkey the day before.

'So you paid the price set by Anna Weissman?' he said, looking her up and down.

Sarah nodded, not asking how it was he knew about Anna's deal.

Chang made a noise of approval and ran his hand over her naked and bruised flank. 'I will give you a massage, use fragrant oil, get rid of the stench of him.'

Sarah reddened, wondering if she still smelt, and then realised that Chang had taken her clothes away. They must reek of Mustafa's cheap cologne and stale sweat. Chang's fingers moved on up over her hips, breasts and shoulders. His touch was enquiring and firm, making her moan with the delicious pain his fingertips created. In many ways the little oriental was a paradox, cruel and kind; tough one moment, tender the next.

Even so, she knew she would be glad of his knowing touch working over the marks that Weissman and Mustafa inflicted, and when he led her naked onto the bed she certainly did not fight as he rubbed aromatic oils into her aching flesh, nor argue when almost an hour later he covered her with heavy white towels and let sleep claim her.

As dinner approached Chang left her to rest, and later brought a tray up for when she awoke.

As darkness fell Dr Casswell was surprised to hear a tapping at his bedroom door. Chang had already told him that Sarah, exhausted by a combination of the oppressive heat and her encounter with Mustafa, had fallen asleep in the adjoining room. Had he wanted her she would have come, but it would be unlike her to appear at his door without being summoned.

It had been a long evening. After coffee and liqueurs out on the terrace with Uri and Anna, Casswell had also pleaded exhaustion, which gave him a chance to re-read the extract he had been working on all morning.

The tapping started again but was more insistent this time. Annoyed at being disturbed, Casswell opened the door a fraction and peered out into the gloom. What he saw astonished him. In the doorway were two of Uri Weissman's burly housemen dressed in long white robes and fez. Between them they were carrying a roll of bulky carpet.

The taller of them, speaking in thick, almost incoherent English, said, 'We have brought a gift for you.' The words were so mutilated that Casswell asked him to repeat what he said. He had obviously learnt the introduction parrot fashion.

Casswell stared in amazement as they carried their burden in; a female was wrapped up inside, and as they unrolled the intricate weave she fell in a tumbled heap at his feet.

'Anna?' he said in disbelief.

The blonde stood up very slowly and offered him a deep curtsey. She was dressed in the costume of a harem concubine. Veiled, her blonde hair was covered in sheer black silk, and her ample breasts were snug in a sheer silver and black bra that pressed her heavy orbs together and thrust them forward like a ripe banquet. Each pinkly flushed nipple was tipped with a silver bauble. Her midriff was bare and she was wearing a pair of tiny black panties, tied on each hip, under a pair of sheer black harem pants. To complete the ensemble she was wearing black and silver felt slippers.

In appearance Anna Weissman was every inch the willing slave girl, every inch except for the expression in her eyes, which far from being coy and submissive was open and expectant, not to mention deeply excited.

Casswell looked her up and down appreciatively.

'I am yours to command, master,' she said with a stifled giggle.

Casswell could not contain a smile; nothing could have been further from the truth.

'Uri keeps telling me that you understand women, Rigel, what women truly need. I've come to find out if that's true.' Her tone was flirtatious.

Casswell waved the words away. 'To be honest, Anna, I don't think you're ready for what I can offer,' he said without rancour.

'Please, Rigel,' she whispered seductively, 'come on. Please show me.' It seemed events of the previous day had whetted her appetite.

Casswell looked her up and down again. It was tempting. She was slim and very beautiful, with delicious breasts, her body lithe and exquisitely formed, but unlike Sarah he doubted Anna would ever fully respond to training. She most certainly was not naturally submissive, just deeply curious.

'Please,' she said again, and he could see the excitement mounting in her eyes.

Picking up a little brass bell from beside his bed, Casswell summoned Chang. His servant appeared instantly and took up a stance by the double doors, legs parted, arms behind his back. Anna looked puzzled and was about to dismiss her servants when Casswell caught hold of her wrist.

'Oh no, Anna, that isn't how it works. Here in this room I am the master. You have no power; you give yourself to me entirely and do as I say. If you want to do this then you must understand I command and you obey. There is no going back. No half measures.'

Anna reddened furiously. 'But they are my house staff.'

'Not now – at this moment you are the slave here. Now get on your hands and knees.' Her colour deepened, and he could see she was about to protest. 'You heard me,' he added; this time his tone was harder and without a shred of humour, and if Anna Weissman was about to say anything else, she thought better of it.

Casswell looked at the two men who had carried Anna in. Both of them, he could see, were delighted by the turn of events. He beckoned to the taller of the two. 'Lift your robe.'

The man stared at him in complete amazement, but after a life term spent in service, did as he was told.

Casswell looked down at Anna, now on all fours at his feet. 'You know what he wants, don't you? What he has always wanted? He wants you to suck his cock, to take him in your mouth and suck him dry. Press those beautifully painted lips around his shaft, lap at him with that tongue that has given so many orders, until he comes, until your mouth is full of the taste of him. Pleasure and obedience, every slave has to understand that.'

Anna gasped, her eyes bright with indignation and astonishment. 'But I thought it would be you,' she began.

'I'm not going to do that for a servant... not a servant, Rigel.'

Casswell's expression did not falter.

Slowly the man began to lift his robe. Beneath it he was naked, his cock already hardening at the prospect of his mistress's lips tight around it. Casswell wondered how many times the servant had fantasised about such a moment.

'I can't do this,' she said, shaking her head and clambering to her feet. 'It's madness.'

Casswell shrugged. 'Then you will be beaten until you can. Chang...' Casswell's man moved towards her. 'You want to understand what I do, Anna, how I make women feel. Therefore you shall.' Anna's eyes widened with horror as the little oriental grabbed hold of her wrists. 'Or perhaps you would prefer to leave now... there's the door. All you have to do is tell me and you can go now. Say it after me, Anna. Say, "Rigel, I want you to let me leave now".'

They stared at each other for the briefest of instants, and Casswell walked over to the side table and poured himself a brandy, contemptuously unmoved by her dilemma. He had seen it a hundred times before.

Anna reddened. 'I can't do this,' she shrieked, struggling furiously to free herself. But they both knew she had chosen. Chang was totally unmoved by her efforts and with the practise he'd acquired over the years, there was no way the blonde was going to get away from him unless Casswell commanded it.

It seemed as if Anna Weissman was not the first slave girl to need correction in Casswell's suite. Above them, set into the ceiling, was a large metal eyelet. With deft hands, Chang tied the blonde's wrists together with a leather strop and then aided by Anna's servants, soon had her secured and tied to a rope suspended from the ring, her arms stretched taut above her head.

All the time it was obvious to Casswell that Anna was still torn between outrage, fear and curiosity. It was an expression Casswell recognised, though he suspected that when this evening was over it was not an experience Anna Weissman would be likely to repeat.

'All right,' she said, breathing hard. 'You've had your little joke, Casswell, now let me down and we won't say any more about it.'

Casswell watched her with interest. 'But you begged me a moment ago to show you how this felt. And you know what you have to say.' He smiled thinly and ran his hands over her exquisite body. He could see in amongst all the other emotions Anna Weissman was almost crazy with excitement.

'Bastard,' she hissed, between those exquisitely painted lips.

Under his exploratory touch Anna began to relax; perhaps the blonde felt she might win him over, but any feelings of success were short-lived. With two deft movements Casswell ripped away first her veil and then her sheer silk top. Anna shrieked, straining furiously against her restraints, but before the sound had stopped echoing Chang handed Casswell a thick leather paddle and without breaking his stride, Casswell drew it back and struck Anna Weissman hard across the creamy cheeks of her bottom.

The blonde woman screamed with a mixture of shock and pain, then spun and hung for a moment on the rope, gasping for her next breath. 'Rigel?!' she shrieked, as if she could not believe what she had experienced.

Before she could gather her wits, Casswell laid the paddle on again with a deadly accuracy. She squealed and swore furiously. He then hit her again, higher this time; her slim body convulsed with pain, heavy breasts jutting forward, her nipples – now having lost their spangles – gathered into florid crimson peaks. She looked absolutely exquisite.

The two housemen looked on in complete astonishment, eyes alight, as Casswell lay on the paddle with an ease that came of experience. One, two, three more, each stroke making their mistress weep and beg him to stop.

Casswell hit her one more time, and then said in a voice barely above a whisper, 'Do you understand now, Anna?'

Breathing hard she glared at him, her eyes as bright as flares. 'I won't do it, do you hear me?' she snapped, glancing at her servant. 'I won't do it.'

Casswell drew the paddle back again. 'Oh, you will,' he said, in a low, even voice. 'I will beat you until you do.'

Anna Weissman's expression fell as she suddenly realised he meant every word, and she gasped with terror. 'All right, all right,' she gabbled. 'Enough. Please Rigel, no more. Cut me down.'

'You will obey me, you understand,' he said, and it was not a question.

She nodded. 'I will obey you.'

Casswell signalled at Chang to cut the rope. She fell like a sack to the floor, but even so her eyes did not leave Casswell's. He looked towards the serving man, and this time without so much as a murmur Anna crawled slowly across the floor towards him, her bottom livid with the weals from the kiss of the paddle.

Without a word the man lifted the hem of his robe, higher and higher, revealing his swollen erection.

Anna flinched, as if the sight of her fate was more than she could bear, and then without another word she rose to her knees and took his engorged purple crown between her lips, eyes closed, her elegant hands cradling his distended balls, tongue and mouth working along his shaft.

The man gasped with surprise and delight, closing his eyes as the pleasure took hold.

Casswell looked across at the other servant, who was an altogether smaller, slower looking man sporting a day or two's growth of beard. His lips were slack and wet, big brown eyes wide with excitement as he watched Anna and the serving man. It was quite obvious that he hoped to have a turn, too.

'Remove her trousers, Chang,' Casswell said casually, pouring himself another brandy. 'I believe this gentleman also has need of Miss Weissman.'

Without a word Chang stepped up behind her and ripped away the thin voile of the harem pants. Expertly he unfastened the side ties of her knickers and pulled them away. Although she stiffened for an instant, Anna Weissman offered no resistance as her other servant knelt between her legs and ran his hands appreciatively over the plump wet contours of her quim, that gaped between the curves of her raw and reddened buttocks.

She moaned as he found those tingling, throbbing places that pleasured her, and as her body opened for him, Casswell settled into an armchair to watch the performance. Behind him Chang stood by, completely impassive and unmoving as Anna Weissman brought the two men closer to what promised to be a breathtaking climax. Casswell allowed himself the narrowest of smiles. Their hostess was a far better pupil than he could have possibly imagined; her progress and submission, even if they were short-lived, were truly magnificent.

In the adjoining bedroom Sarah had woken from her sleep with a start. She sat bolt upright in bed trying to get her bearings, and realised that the sound of a woman's voice had woken her – a woman crying out in torment and excitement. Sarah clambered out of the bed, grateful that since they had arrived in Turkey Chang had dispensed with the wrist chains that normally secured her to the bed frame at Casswell Hall.

As she pulled on a thin cotton robe there was another cry of anguish – and then another.

Sarah could not work out where it was coming from. As quietly as she could, she tiptoed across to the door that connected her room to Casswell's. Turning the handle she realised it was locked, so pressed her ear to the wood and then, on her hands and knees, peered through the keyhole. She could see very little but believed the cries were coming from within.

It then occurred to her that perhaps the noise was not coming from Casswell's room at all. What if some woman was in genuine trouble? Sarah picked up a robe and hurried out onto the landing, trying to find someone to help. The house was dark; the only light came from the stairwell that led down into the sitting room.

As Sarah got halfway down the stairs she heard male voices from somewhere below, and was about to call out when intuition made her stop. She peered down, and stretched out on one of the sofas, Uri Weissman and another distinguished grey-haired man were sitting in the open doorway to the terrace. They both looked and sounded slightly drunk.

A couple more careful steps and Sarah could now overhear their conversation.

'So we can speak freely?' said the older man, sipping from a brandy balloon. 'How is the translation coming along, have you any idea?'

Weissman waved away whatever anxieties dogged him. 'Don't worry,' he said, sniggering softly, 'I've made sure

Casswell is well occupied this evening. And as for the transcript, you'll just have to be patient, Piers. He has only just begun. You know what Rigel Casswell is like, that mix of dogged determination and inspiration. The man is a genius and completely obsessed. I've already told you, you'll have the book as soon as it's done. I promise.'

Sarah was puzzled. It did not add up. As far as she knew Casswell's brief was to take the translation back to Oliver Turner in England, the man who was funding their trip.

Perhaps the newcomer was part of the committee that Oliver headed. She wondered if she ought to talk to Casswell about it, but just as she turned to creep back upstairs the mystery female cried out again, much louder than before, the tortured sob echoing through the house, and to her horror she lost her footing and stumbled forward. Reaching desperately for the banister but unable to regain her balance, she tripped out of her seclusion in the shadows into the light on the landing.

Uri Weissman looked up… and then smiled. 'Ah, Miss Morgan, good evening,' he drawled. 'How are you?'

Sarah struggled to regain her composure. 'I – I couldn't sleep,' she stuttered feebly. 'And the noise…' as she spoke there was another shriek, '*that* noise…'

Weissman smiled, although it did nothing to warm his expression. 'Ah yes, your master has such a talent, and my sister has always been such a wayward creature.'

Sarah looked down at him in amazement, totally stunned. 'Anna?' she gasped, looking back up the stairs.

Weissman laughed again. 'Oh yes, she was so very curious about what it was that Casswell had to offer. Seems to me that she is finding out first hand.'

He waved her down to join them, and aware of her nakedness beneath the robe, Sarah reluctantly descended the stairs; she could see no easy way to refuse.

'Would you like a drink, Miss Morgan?' Weissman gushed. 'Have you met Mr Heinman, by the way?'

Sarah shook her head to both questions, and then took the hand that Weissman's guest offered, although as their eyes met she realised he was far more interested in the way the contours of her body showed through the thin cotton wrap than any pretence at social pleasantries.

Weissman handed her a glass of champagne. 'We were busy celebrating your master's arrival.' His eyes held hers. 'He is your master, isn't he?'

Sarah reddened furiously. 'Yes... yes he is, amongst other things. I work for Dr Casswell as his PA.'

Piers Heinman drained his glass and chuckled. 'Oh, I am sure you do, and I am sure you are very, very diligent in your duties.'

Uri Weissman smiled, his eyes glinting as he very gently traced the curve of her breasts through the fabric with a single finger. 'I think Mr Heinman would like to see exactly what it is that Casswell and I have enjoyed,' he said. 'Undo the robe.'

Sarah stiffened. 'I'm sorry?' she blurted.

Uri Weissman's expression hardened. 'Oh please, don't be coy. You heard me, my dear. Or would you prefer me to call Casswell down and tell him you disobeyed me?'

Sarah shook her head, hesitantly placed the champagne flute on a nearby side table, and slowly untied the wrap.

'Off,' snapped Weissman, as if there was some doubt that Sarah would do as she was told.

Sarah let the wrap fall to the floor, and now she was naked, Piers nodded and to her surprise pulled her close to him. She shivered as his hands crawled over her body, but her treacherous nipples hardened under the touch of his enquiring fingers.

'Turn around,' he ordered. 'Bend over, I want to see the rest.'

Blushing, Sarah obeyed and leaned forward in front of him, over the coffee table, giving Heinman an even greater view. He grunted as he slipped his hand between her thighs, seeking her sex, thumb sliding in and out of her quim while his fingers stroked at the tight puckering of her rear passage. Sarah felt a great rush of humiliation rising from low in her belly.

'Hmm... good and tight,' Heinman grunted appreciatively. 'Have you any oil there, Uri?'

The Austrian nodded, and from a cabinet produced a small bottle. Heinman poured a few drops into his palm, and Sarah closed her eyes, guessing what was to follow as the old man very slowly eased his finger past the tight closure of her bottom. The sensation took her breath away as her body surrendered to him.

Again Heinman grunted and then pulled out. Smiling at Weissman he poured more oil into his palms and worked it back and forth over Sarah's flesh. 'Would you like to share her with me, Uri? How about it? It's been a long, long time since we had such a lovely creature between us.'

Weissman smiled, chuckled, and drained his glass.

Upstairs, under the watchful eyes of Casswell and Chang, Anna Weissman rolled exhausted onto the floor between her two house servants, although before she could have time to recover, the taller of the two crouched between her legs and parted her trembling thighs. She made no attempt to resist his advances. Lifting her body up to him, the man began to lick at her sex, lapping his own seed from the depths of her quim. Under his eager ministrations Anna began to writhe, gasp and cry out as he brought her closer and closer to orgasm. The blonde was lost in the intense medley of sensations; perhaps it was the ultimate humiliation to feel such intense pleasure at the hands of the two lowly ruffians.

Casswell smiled, beckoning Chang closer, asking him to go next door and wake Sarah. Once Anna had left he wanted her brought to him so he could enjoy her.

Chang reappeared a few seconds later, looking concerned. 'She's not there, doctor,' he announced.

'Not there?' Casswell stared at him in surprise.

'Uri Weissman has her downstairs,' Chang informed him.

Casswell's expression hardened. Weissman was a bully, and although Casswell had known him for years, he still did not consider him a friend or close associate.

Meanwhile Anna Weissman, utterly exhausted, what was left of her costume torn to shreds, finally got back onto her hands and knees. She looked up at Casswell, her icy-blue eyes bright with knowledge. There was nothing left for the woman to say; she had finally experienced and understood the things that had whet her appetite and excited her curiosity for so long.

Casswell smiled and waved her away. 'Go back to your room, Anna,' he ordered, and without another word the slim blonde did exactly as she was told. Casswell waited until she had left and then dismissed the house servants, immaculate again in their long robes, standing to attention either side of the double doors as if nothing had happened. All that remained to mark the events of the last hour was the rich Turkish carpet on the tiled floor.

As soon as the two men had gone Casswell hurried from his room. From the landing where Sarah had hidden he looked down into the sitting room below.

Sarah was crouched on the floor between the two men,

her eyes closed tight. On her knees, she was straddling Uri Weissman, his cock driving in and out of her tight wet sex, while Piers Heinman was pressed hard into the tight confines of her bottom. It was a heady image.

Sarah's body worked back and forth between the two men. There was no escape from them, nor relief from the intensity of the sensations. Beads of perspiration clung precariously in the valley between her pert breasts. She was breathing hard. All three of them moved in fluid unison, the two men quite obviously relishing the moment.

Sarah gasped at the feeling of fullness as Weissman and Heinman pressed home. Her body eager and hungry to reach the place of no return, dipped and twisted so her throbbing clit ground against Weissman's root, each stroke taking her closer and closer to the edge of oblivion. Covering her, Heinman was snorting like a stallion sliding deeper and deeper into that dark tight place, while beneath her Weissman strained to fill her to the very brim.

As the intense pleasure built, spiralling up through her tummy, Sarah struggled to remember that she needed to talk to Casswell about what Heinman and Weissman had been saying.

Heinman's hand then slipped from her hip, his fingers moving down to the throbbing rise of her clitoris. Uri Weissman roared and then bucked like a wild animal, forcing himself deeper still, his cock throbbing as orgasm washed over him, and as if his ejaculation was like lighting a fuse, the sensation flared and then exploded through each of them.

Casswell went back to his suite. Sarah never disappointed him. He smiled; once she returned to her room he would have Chang bring her too him.

Chapter Five

The next morning in the vaults of the museum, Sarah sat alongside Casswell, working in silence as they so often did. Sarah's body and mind ached, but it felt good to be back into their usual routine. She replayed the conversation she heard in the sitting room the night before. Maybe she had misunderstood what Weissman said; after all, she only caught a brief moment of the conversation.

It was almost lunchtime and the morning's work had gone well. Glancing up at the clock, Sarah wondered whether by some miracle Mustafa Aziz, the museum curator, had forgotten about the second part of the bargain struck by Anna Weissman. It seemed unlikely, even though he had not appeared all morning, although neither had Anna Weissman. Sarah wondered fleetingly what Anna had made of her initiation.

But now, for the first time since arriving in Turkey, Sarah felt cool and relaxed, and it was a real sense of relief that her concentration could return to the computer screen. Reading Beatrice's account of daily life at the castle was a delight, like catching up at long last with an old friend – a friend whose life was also not running as smoothly as she would have liked.

...I do not know what to do. I fear that our lives here are about to change forever. This morning my master told me he has been greatly honoured by the king. His visit was to judge if he was worthy of the honour. At first I thought my master meant by gift of land, or perhaps a title to add to those already held by him, for he is indeed a true and loyal subject. He said no. It seems that the king's cousin, the Lady Cassandra of Villon, so very recently widowed by a man twice her age, feels in need of a new husband and that husband it seems is to be my master. Although this is a political alliance, gossip in the castle yard already has it that the Lady Cassandra has a reputation as a woman of great passion and plans to be a wife in every sense. None of these things bode well for me. I sense my master is torn by this strange turn of events.

His majesty has gone so far as to grant my lord a divorce from his first wife so he can fulfil his part of this obligation, although I suspect from my lord's demeanour that however great the honour, he is not delighted by the news. I suspect he knows this is yet another marriage meant to secure his position within the court and assure the king of his loyalty, as if his actions and oath of allegiance were not enough already.

The whole household has been instructed by his lordship that we are to make ready for a visit from his betrothed before the month is out. I fear for what is to become of me. In the absence of there being a lady of the house I have taken on many of those duties, including seeing that my master's children are schooled and cared for and that the house is run in a manner befitting a man of his station. I hoped that one day he might take me for his own – but perhaps it's true that this is a foolish thought...

Sarah read on through Beatrice's feverish preparations for the Lady Cassandra's arrival, on through tales of cooking and cleaning, until it seemed Beatrice would drop from the work heaped upon her.

...And now I know that I am undone and there truly is no

future here for me. Lady Cassandra called me to her chamber within a short time of her arrival in the quiet hours before the great feast that I have worked so hard to prepare in her honour.

When she arrived, Cassandra was welcomed at the gates by my lord and master who could, with the best will in the world, hardly mask his disappointment that his new fiancée is so unpleasing to the eye. As he formerly introduced her to all those in the household he looked in my direction not once, but twice. I saw her ladyship follow his gaze with interest, and knew in that instant that she saw me then not as a servant but as a rival for his affections. No sooner had I returned to the preparations for the great feast than I was summoned to go to her freshly prepared rooms for a private audience, but also, I feared, to discover my fate.

Lady Cassandra is indeed an austere woman with coarse black hair, shot through with grey, heavy jowls and an even heavier body and spirit. I cannot imagine my beloved master sharing a bed with such a woman as this, nor wish to imagine his handsome body alongside so dour, unfeeling, and cruel a woman, although this is her obvious intention.

As I entered the suite of rooms I saw she had ample servants of her own, as is to be expected of a woman of her station, but as our eyes met I knew it was not the running of the house that interested her. I knew for certain by the icy look that I was undone. I saw the dislike and the distrust in her eyes. She dismissed her servants and spent no time on such niceties as might have been expected.

'I need you to know, Beatrice de Fleur, that I am mistress of this castle now, and I will have you know and understand it, you little whore.' It was a harsh and unnecessary thing to say to me.

I curtsied low to show respect, although I fooled no one. 'Yes, m'lady,' I said.

'You are a viper in the nest, wench,' she continued. 'You are little more than a slave in this household. I can see the way you have ensnared my betrothed and have heard stories of your part in the downfall of the previous mistress here. Trust me, girl, I will not tolerate such behaviour under my roof. The king warned me that you were a dark influence on an otherwise godly household.'

My cheeks flared red with indignation, for I am obedient to all who command me and am regular to church. Had I not warned my master against a plot by his first wife that would have killed him? Had it not been me who warmed and readied this very room this woman was in now? Had I not spread the floor with fresh rushes, making preparations for a feast in her honour? She looked me up and down with contempt.

'You were from a good family?'

I nodded, anxious not to antagonise her further.

'And now you are a bonds woman here?'

Again I nodded.

'So truly little more than a slave, then?'

I refused to be provoked. 'My services were gifted to the household from the abbey and I serve as his lordship commands me,' I said as humbly as I could manage, though the words stuck in my throat.

Cassandra snorted. 'I have heard how he commands you from the father abbot here. I have ways of teaching creatures like you to obey and what is expected of a decent god-fearing woman.'

I looked up straight into the eyes of the tall man dressed in the garb of a priest. I realised with a start that this was the man who had beaten and taken me so fiercely when the king had last visited us, and who not more than a month before I believed to be the king's son. Now, hiding behind the grey habit of a holy man, he leered at me. With a growing sense of horror, I realised this was not the king's legitimate son at all, but his bastard, born the wrong side of the blanket, found a sinecure in the church, who had abused me.

'Indeed I have seen, good lady,' he said with mock piety, eyes crawling shamelessly over my body. 'She is a truly devilish creature who would be best kept on a very short leash if she was ever to serve you well.'

I was about to protest when Cassandra smiled. 'I shall take your counsel, Brother Jacob, and take note of your cure.' She turned back to me and said, 'The gown you're wearing, where did you get it from, girl?'

I blushed, for it had been a gift from my master from the dowry of his former wife, and was indeed a fine robe now that it had been cut to fit me. I explained as best I could, but with an icy expression she bade me take it off lest it was spoilt.

'Spoilt?' I said with surprise.

She nodded and continued. 'I will stand for no division of loyalties in my house. You will serve me alone and serve me true, as my maid in waiting, here in my chamber. Once I am settled in the house I shall appoint my own servants to the positions of housekeeper and steward.'

'But I serve my master,' I began, the words out before I realised what a mistake I was making. Cassandra's cruel eyes darkened, but I saw that they were tinged with a look of triumph; my words had condemned me.

'Of course, if you do not like the arrangements you may leave now. So tell me, girl, will you serve me in whatever way I see fit?'

I was caught in a trap. If I did not agree to her terms I would be put out in little more than I wore, and where would I go to then? To whom would I turn? I have no family, nothing save those people in the castle. Since Father Orme went on a pilgrimage in the spring I have no one but my master to protect me. At least if I agreed to serve Cassandra I might remain in the household, and I prayed that my master would not forget or abandon me.

'Well, what say you, child?' snapped the woman.

I lowered my gaze. 'Yes,' I said unsteadily.

'Yes, ma'am,' she snapped back. 'Father Abbot, perhaps you can teach this little creature some manners. I believe she has gotten above herself, sleeping with my betrothed, running the household, commanding the staff, giving herself airs and graces as if she was mistress.' Cassandra spoke with an icy derision that made my flesh crawl.

'Indeed, ma'am,' he said, and with a grim sense of foreboding, I realised I was in for more of the treatment he meted out when the king visited us at the castle.

The abbot picked up a short crop from the table and flexed it into an arc. I shivered and began to protest, but I understood what was asked of me. I had no need of a beating to show me obedience. I had put on no airs – there was no need for this – but before I could say anything, the abbot caught tight hold of me. Without giving me a chance to remove the beautiful laced gown, he ripped the front open from neck to waist, the fabric biting into my flesh. I cried out in fear and tried to cover myself but he didn't listen, instead he forced me down over a side table.

I knew what would follow, and an instant later I heard the crop cut through the air and explode across my back like a thunderbolt. I screamed, knowing there was no mercy to be found. My body contorted with the pain, thrust forward, my flesh glowing white-hot as another blow found its mark. Tears filled my eyes and I screamed as he hit me again and again. This time there was no king to prescribe how many blows should be struck, just him and his strong right arm.

Lady Cassandra watched with a strange glazed expression on her face, her dark eyes fixed on mine.

The head of the whip bit again, surging through my body like a forest fire. After a stroke or two more my mind was almost lost, the pain a distant shadow on my thoughts as I tried mentally to hide from the vicious cut of the whip.

As I stood trembling and weeping, the odious abbot dragged the rags of my fine dress to the floor and hit me again, making me cry out in pain and humiliation.

Finally, when he was breathing heavily, he stepped closer and pushed my legs wide open and forced me lower down over the table, fingers cramming into the wet confines of my sex. Lifting the hem of his priestly robes, breathing hard, he stabbed his loathsome cock into me. I wailed in pain as he breached me and the rough cloth of his robe rubbed at my back and buttocks. Dragging me back onto him, hands clawing hungrily at my breasts, twisting and pinching my nipples, I thought he might tear me apart with the animal vigour of his desperate coupling.

His mistress looked on in amusement as her precious abbot came closer and closer to his discharge. On and on he pressed, finally I felt him shudder, his thrusts grew more ragged and then I felt his cock twitch and he gasped and roared and thrust deeper still, filling me to the very brim, filling me with his seed, and at last he was done, wheezing hard, leaning heavily on my poor battered body.

It was a few minutes before the abbot composed himself, and then the Lady Cassandra, who had been staring at me throughout, said, 'I intend to rest before the feast your master has prepared in my honour. Come here, girl, and help to undress me.'

I looked across at her in amazement. I was naked, sweating, beaten red, and already I could feel the trickle of the despicable abbot's spent lust running down the inside of my thighs, and yet she wanted me to wait on her? What manner of woman was this? Had she no mercy or shame? I looked around for the rag of my gown to cover my nakedness, and began to speak, but Cassandra would have none of it and growled furiously at me.

'Come, wench! Have you not learned what happens to those who disobey me?'

Unable to speak, I crept to her as naked as the day I was born, my whole body crying out in discomfort.

Standing before me she indicated the fastenings on her bodice, and with shaking fingers I slowly began to undo them. She watched me, those dark eyes darting back and forth across my body, and did not resist as I pushed the rich fabric back off her broad shoulders. As I stepped back she stroked my breast, her finger lingering on the engorged nipple. As our eyes met I understood everything; Cassandra wanted me as much for pleasure as for pain.

After a second or two my nipple hardened under her attentions and she bent forward to lap at it, drawing it deep into her mouth. 'You poor broken little bird,' she murmured. 'Serve me well and I will treat you well... cross me and I will *break* you.'

I was stunned.

Moving away, she turned her attention back to the grovelling abbot, who stood watching his mistress in awe. 'Make yourself useful, man; see if the water I asked for is ready. I will have my new maid bathe me and help make me ready for the great feast tonight.'

She had not even called me by name, and yet I knew that before the day was out I would know this terrible woman in the most intimate of ways. She caught hold of my hand and guided it up to her heavy breasts, and without any more encouragement, for now I understood the nature of this bargain, I began to stroke her distended nipples, rubbing them and tugging them gently until they rose into hardened peaks. I did not resist as she drew me close so that I might suck on them. The Lady Cassandra moaned with pleasure as my lips closed first around one and then the other, cupping them as I lifted them to my lips.

In an adjoining room her house staff busied themselves preparing a bath in front of a great log fire, and it was there Cassandra ordered me to complete her disrobing. I saw no choice but to comply. First the remains of her blouse and then the heavy brocade of her skirts and soft embroidered folds of her petticoats, last of all I took off her pantaloons, open at the crotch so that she could make water easily into a chamber slipper brought by one of her maids.

Finally naked in the soft glow of the candlelight, Cassandra stood straight to show herself off, though I was unsure whether this was for me or for the abbot's benefit. Although she is a person of great power, she is truly no beauty, a great lumbering ox of a woman she has thighs like tree trunks, her sex a great bulging mound topped with a thatch of coarse dark hair, and no waist at all, her breasts huge and pendulous, her belly hanging down in folds. But even so, eyes averted I helped her into the wooden tub full of steaming water, perfumed with rich oils and unguents, and kneeling alongside, soaped her heavy frame. She moaned as I touched her white flesh, obviously relishing my touch as I worked over her and then, after a while she pulled me close, and grabbing hold of my wrist guided my hand deep between the fold of her thighs.

As I brushed the mat of hair that trimmed her quim she opened her legs and pressed my fingers into her. I closed my eyes and shivered. Her sex was wet, warm and hungry; folded back and forth like a complex chamois leather bag. Under her guidance I found her pleasure-bud nestled like a great gooseberry between the heavy outer lips of her quim. It was already large with passion, and as I ran my finger back I could see I had discovered what the Lady Cassandra truly wanted from me. Not to pleasure the master, but to service the mistress.

With one hand working between her legs I soaped her breasts, still teasing and circling her nipples, and she began to writhe under my touch and shiver under my ministrations to her quim. I let my fingers slide in and out of her, feeling the depths of her body tightening around me like a hungry mouth as she got closer and closer to coming.

Then Cassandra gripped my wrist and bade me cease my touching. Freeing herself of my caress she ordered me bring the candelabra closer. I thought this was perhaps to see more clearly the path of her passion, but instead, as soon as it was within striking distance she got to her feet and grabbed one of the candles in a meaty fist. Still standing, Cassandra guided the candle deep inside her gaping sex, moaning with pleasure as she did so, the heavy lips clinging to the tallow shaft as she began to move it in and out of her quivering body.

I was kneeling still beside the bath and she caught hold of my hair and pulled me back towards her. Still working the candle in and out of her throbbing quim with one hand, she splayed the lips of her sex with the other, revealing the great bud of her pleasure nestled like a dark pearl in amongst the folds.

'Here, girl, suck me,' she roared on an outward breath

and pulled my face up against her belly. I gasped at the odour of her body; even bathed she smelt rich and musky, and ripe of the ocean. My lips closed around the swollen hooded peak and as bidden I sucked and lapped and kissed and circled that most magical spot, until I knew she was so close to the very edge that I was amazed she could hold back.

The candle slipped in and out, dripping wet now with her juices. The smell of her body was almost overpowering. Above me Cassandra writhed and twisted, and now that I was holding her quim open, her other hand cupped and squeezed her breasts until finally with a guttural yell she drove the candle fully in and thrust her hips towards me so I almost drowned in the rolling depths of her flesh.

'Yes, *yes*,' she hissed in delight, head thrown back, eyes closed, the great mare sweating now, glittering beads dripping off her chin and running down in the mountain valley between her heavy breasts.

I shook from exhaustion and shock as the woman finally plunged down into the water to refresh herself. After a moment or two she handed me a cloth.

'Now finish washing me,' she said, settling her bulk back amongst the rapidly cooling water. She closed her eyes as I completed the job, then a tapping at the chamber door was heard and gradually grew more insistent.

Finally Cassandra opened her eyes and looked at the abbot. 'Go and see who that is,' she said. 'Tell them I do not wish to be disturbed.'

The abbot returned a few seconds later and looked down at me. 'It is a message from the lord of the house, your ladyship, asking if Beatrice might go to help make ready for tonight's festivities. He is anxious that all goes well for the feast in your honour.'

Cassandra looked triumphant. 'Tell him to come in and see me. Perhaps like Beatrice here, his lordship needs to understand who is lady of this estate and who the slave.'

As she spoke, Cassandra glanced at me and I tried hard to suppress a shudder of revulsion…

Sarah nipped the bridge of her nose, and although she was looking at the computer screen her heart and her mind were deep in the castle with Beatrice. She was about to proceed to the next page when a movement caught her eye. By a run of shelving Mustafa Aziz was eyeing her work, and what had broken her concentration was him mopping his brow with the grubby handkerchief. Knowing he had been seen, the Turk smiled, and Sarah shivered under his undisguised and repulsive lechery.

'Good day, Miss Morgan,' he drawled, as their eyes met. 'Come along, my pretty, Miss Weissman is already waiting for you.'

Sarah looked across at Casswell. His expression was closed and totally unreadable. With a shudder Sarah got slowly to her feet, and in complete silence followed Mustafa Aziz through the shelves and maze of corridors towards the fetid little cell she had been taken to the day before.

Chapter Six

'Well, fancy seeing you here,' Anna Weissman said sarcastically, as Sarah drew level with her; the statuesque blonde was framed in the open doorway of the cell. She raised perfectly plucked eyebrows and looked Sarah up and down. Dressed in a crisp white blouse and tailored blue skirt that emphasised her shapely hips, Anna seemed totally out of place in the grubby little room She was wearing thick gold bangles like manacles around each wrist and high-heeled court shoes. To complete the look, she was beautifully made-up, her long fingernails painted scarlet to match her full lips. She looked as if she would have been more at home in an uptown department store than in a cellar at Mustafa Aziz's beck and call.

Sarah shivered at the thought. The tiny windowless cell was no more inviting than when she was last there, although somebody – presumably Mustafa – had thrown a white sheet over the cot bed to hide the stained and filthy mattress.

'Don't talk,' Mustafa snapped from behind them. 'I am in charge here and you will do as I say. That was the bargain. You understand me?'

Sarah understood only too well the kind of obedience the fat Turk demanded, but wondered if Anna Weissman had any idea what she was letting herself in for. Mustafa directed them to the centre of the room and settled down on the battered armchair. For a few seconds he looked the two females over as if he'd rehearsed this moment a thousand times in his head.

Finally he said, 'I want you to undress each other.' As he spoke he lit up a cheroot. 'But be gentle and slow – you know, like real lovers, kisses and touching and everything. I want you to touch but it is very important that you kiss. Here, put this on.' He handed Sarah – who was wearing the barest minimum of make-up – a hand mirror and a tube of scarlet lipstick. 'So you look like real whores.'

Sarah glanced at her reflection in the fly-blown glass. Her skin was flushed from the heat and her hand was shaking. After a second or two Anna took the tube from her. 'Here,' she said gently, 'let me,' and drew a dark slick oval around her lips. Surprised by the other woman's compassion, Sarah looked in the mirror. The effect was startling – from secretary to siren in seconds.

Anna looked Sarah in the eye, a flicker of mischief played around her mouth and she threaded her fingers into Sarah's dark hair and pulled her closer. Sarah was too surprised to resist, as Anna kissed her and she could taste the strange rose-flavoured lipstick on her tongue.

The touch of the blonde's lips was a revelation. Anna Weissman's tongue was a delicately invading pressure, encouraging her to open and then delving deeper. Sarah was still astonished at her tenderness, and even more surprised to feel her body responding to Anna's delicate caresses, a little flicker of desire and expectation igniting low in her belly. This was not what Sarah had expected at all.

Anna embraced Sarah, pulling her closer still, fingers locked in her hair, Anna's lips working enthusiastically on her own. Against all the odds Sarah felt her apprehension beginning to recede, replaced instead by a real desire for the Austrian woman. Her resistance may have begun to fade, but she had not forgotten that it was Mustafa Aziz, not Anna Weissman, who was in charge of what went on. Opening her eyes for an instant, she caught sight of the fat Turk watching them, his dark eyes glinting maliciously.

Anna began to unbutton Sarah's blouse, her strong hands pulling the thin fabric aside, cupping Sarah's pert breasts, teasing the nipples into peaks with her carmine painted fingernails. Sarah groaned in spite of herself as the woman nipped them between her nails, making Sarah shiver with pleasure. Her kisses were becoming more and more animated, lips working harder, tongue working deeper and deeper. Sarah instinctively returned the woman's kisses, her hands moving as if they had a will of their own to undo the blonde's elegant blouse.

Underneath Anna was wearing a white silk bra. Trimmed with delicate lace, the fabric was so fine that her nipples jutted through. Anna let out a throaty chuckle as Sarah's fingers found the hardened peaks and began to stroke and tease them. Pulling away for an instant, Anna unfastened it so Sarah could take her bra and blouse off.

Returning almost at once to compelling kisses, Anna guided Sarah's hands, encouraging them to explore her body. The blonde's creamy white skin was as warm and smooth as silk, the strange almost liquid weight of her exquisite breasts cradled in Sarah's palms increasing her desire with every passing second.

'Oh yes,' Anna murmured as Sarah began to circle her nipples with her thumbs. They stiffened instantly. Shifting position, Anna bent to draw one of Sarah's nipples deep into her mouth, her pearly-white teeth nibbling and nipping at the delicate bud.

Sarah closed her eyes, every cell absorbing exquisite feelings. It felt amazing. Her whole body began to glow with a soft but undeniable hunger. Caught up in the sensations, she had to remind herself again and again that Mustafa was watching them. If she listened beyond the sounds of her own rapid pulse, beyond Anna Weissman's soft suckling and moans of desire, Sarah could hear the Turk's heavy breathing and smell the rancid scent of the cheap cheroot polluting the stifling air.

Even so, against all odds she could not hold the thought for long, as Anna's palm slid down over her thighs and cupped the front of her skirt, instantly igniting a flare of need, rubbing her quim through the thin fabric, her fingers brushing and seeking out the seat of Sarah's desire. Sarah knew she was already wet, her sex glowing with expectation. As Anna's fingers brushed against her clitoris Sarah gasped in delight and thrust forward to chase the sensation. Anna Weissman smiled knowingly, and Sarah was stunned at just how good the Austrian was making her feel.

With deft fingers, Anna unfastened Sarah's skirt and eased it down over her hips, while her tongue and lips were still working their magic on Sarah's throbbing breasts. Beneath her clothes, in line with Casswell's express orders, Sarah was always naked. Shaved and oiled, her sex was as tempting and vulnerable as a ripe peach.

As her skirt slithered to the floor it seemed the Austrian had finally found exactly what she wanted. Moaning with delight she slid a finger between the folds of Sarah's naked quim and eagerly returned her lips to Sarah's mouth, her artful tongue in tandem with artful fingers, working up a medley of pure bliss.

Through misty vision Sarah could see Mustafa's eyes widening as Anna's fingers pressed deep inside her. Sarah's body opened like a flower and Anna commenced a slow but compelling rhythm, in and out. The woman knew exactly what she wanted and exactly what she was doing.

Sarah began to move in time, impaling herself more eagerly on the woman's fingers, but it seemed that for the Turk the seduction was not happening fast enough.

'You have to undress her too,' he snapped at Sarah. 'Now, come on, I have not got all day. Get her clothes off. I want to see her too, see you both – skin to skin. Now.' He rubbed his hands together, mimicking two bodies touching.

Reluctantly Anna Weissman pulled away, and despite her anxiety, Sarah was stunned to find she was trembling with excitement and expectation.

The little room was oppressively hot, and Mustafa was still watching them from the chair, his cock pressing up like a tent pole through his stained cream chinos. He mopped his head and face with the filthy handkerchief, eyes firmly fixed on the two of them. Anna looked at him with disgust and undid her own zip, dropping her skirt to the floor.

Underneath she was wearing a white G-string, her lean legs and pale skin a stark contrast to the bleak little cell. Sarah was suddenly nervous of the statuesque blonde, but as Anna turned in response to a gesture from Mustafa, she was stunned to see that her back was marked with a row of fresh weals.

Sarah had no doubt now that it had been Anna in the bedroom next to her own on the previous evening. Strangely it made her heart tighten with tenderness and empathy; it seemed that Anna Weissman truly understood now what it was to be a slave.

Mustafa inspected Anna and nodded his approval. 'Come here and let me feel that body of yours. You think you are so very special, so very important. I want to smell you on my fingers.'

Sarah saw a flash of anger on Anna's beautiful face,

and then without hesitation the blonde stepped closer to him, almost defiantly. Hands on hips, legs apart, her eyes alight with hatred, she tipped her pelvis towards him. Sarah wondered how on earth it was that the blonde had agreed to the deal with the Turk, and wondered how much her brother had to do with arranging it.

Mustafa grunted as he wrapped his fingers under the wisp of fabric that covered Anna's quim, his fist tightened, and he tore it away. Anna flinched as the ripping fabric bit into her flesh, but he merely sniggered at her discomfort, and his nicotine-stained fingers parted her sex lips. Leaning forward he ran his tongue over the wet folds, snuffling and grunting inside her like a pig rooting for truffles. As he lapped at her pleasure-bud, his fingers drove into the depths of her body.

Sarah could see the revulsion on Anna's face and was relieved when Mustafa finally pulled away, and licking his lips, he waved them both towards the camp bed.

'You taste very good today, Miss Weissman,' he said, wiping his mouth with the back of his hand. 'Lay down on the cot... and you,' he waved towards Sarah. 'I want you to straddle her, sit on her face and I will watch her lick you. And then when she is done with you, you stick your pretty little tongue deep inside her here, like this...' and he drove his fingers through his clenched fist, the gesture incredibly obscene. 'I want you to make her cry out for mercy, and then trust me, I will fuck you both. Here...' from his pocket he pulled the thick white dildo that Sarah had used the day before, and handed it to Anna. 'Use this on yourself while you lick her.'

Sarah shivered as the man ran a slug-like tongue over his lips again.

'I see finally you have felt the kiss of the whip, Miss Weissman,' the odious man continued, goading them. 'I regret not being there when you were beaten. Who was the lucky man? Was it the good doctor? It would be nice to see you brought to your knees. Tell me, did you cry out? Did you beg for mercy? I would have paid almost any price to have watched him lay the whip on you.'

Anna Weissman glared at him, but without another word she settled down on the cot bed, her legs parted on the narrow mattress, dildo held tight in one hand. She looked like some astonishing erotic sacrifice. Mustafa grunted his grudging approval. 'Very nice, Miss Weissman, but I want to see that little toy working away inside you. And you, Miss Morgan, do not just stand there, get on top of her. I want to be paid for my part of the deal. You have to earn the right for your master to work on the manuscript.'

A few rooms away in the relatively tidy crypt Rigel Casswell collected together the remains of the morning's work, assisted by one of the museum staff.

For the first time since they arrived he was deeply aware of his surroundings. The shadowy crypt felt oppressive. Although it had once been a magnificent place, the huge vaulted room was lit by a series of fly-blown bulbs, plaster had fallen from the ancient walls, and the paint was flaked and peeling. Every available surface was stacked with labelled boxes and files and piles of papers, some of which evidently had not been touched in decades. The air was dry and dusty and full of the smells of decadence and decay.

Casswell stretched. He was ready to go back to Weissman's house to avoid the heat of the day, and although his face did not betray a flicker of emotion, he was concerned about Sarah's whereabouts. He knew the details of the deal struck by the curator and the Weissman's, but that did not mean he was happy about it.

Until arriving in Turkey, Sarah's sexual awakening, in fact her whole erotic education, had been in his expert hands, and when she hadn't been under his direct supervision she was in the hands of men he trusted implicitly to take care of her. Men of integrity who understood the roles of submissives and their masters, men who knew the unwritten code of behaviour that governed the dark and pleasurable game.

Casswell slipped the documents he had been working on into his briefcase and glanced around the room, wondering where Sarah was. He had no real idea what kind of man Mustafa Aziz was, but every instinct told him the man was not to be trusted.

'Do you know where the curator is?' he asked as casually as he could manage, still packing his briefcase.

The man, who had just finished locking Beatrice's diary back in its protective case, looked across at him with a bemused expression. Casswell wondered how good the man's English was when he turned and grinned, revealing a large gold tooth.

'You want Mr Mustafa?' he said conspiratorially. 'He is not far from here, he have his own special place. You like to go and watch him, maybe? I can take you there. Mr Mustafa he not know that we know about his very secret place. I get you a good view, yes? A good seat?' As he spoke he held out a grubby hand.

Casswell looked his would-be guide up and down. It seemed that here at the museum everything had its price, even betraying your employer. Casswell took out his wallet and placed a note on the assistant's palm. The man pulled a face, but Casswell refused to be intimidated. It was this or nothing.

The man held up his hands in a gesture of surrender. 'Okay, okay, you drive a hard bargain, Englishman. Come,

I show you where he and your woman are...'

The man waved Casswell to follow him through a labyrinth of narrow passages beyond the room where they were working. Finally, just as Casswell suspected he might be being taken on a wild goose chase the man pushed opened a low door into what looked like a tiny storeroom. The interior was bathed in deep shadow, although what hit him before the sight was the smell; the air inside was hot and heavy with the acrid stench of bodies and sweat. One wall of the room was studded with a series of peepholes bored through the crumbling plaster, and in front of each hole was a chair. Other men, all of whom looked as if they might be on the museum staff, already occupied three of the chairs.

They looked up momentarily, blinking in the light, and then returned to whatever was going on in the room beyond. It seemed as if Casswell had inadvertently stumbled across the port's contingent of voyeurs.

His guide indicated a chair and then pulled the door to. As he settled, Casswell wondered if he could trust any of the men to guide him back out of the dingy underground maze and into the daylight. But before the idea took root, he glanced through the peephole closest to him and to his surprise saw Anna Weissman stretching up to run her tongue across the shaved and open quim of dear Sarah. The floor of the storeroom was set well below that of the cell beyond, and seen from this angle it was a revelation. Both female's bodies gleamed with a gloss of sweat, and Sarah's sex flushed scarlet, the inner lips slick with sheer pleasure.

She was crouched on all fours over the blonde's face, her eyes closed, her hips moving backwards and forwards over Anna's busy tongue. He knew her well enough to know that Sarah was extremely excited, her body taut and expectant as the blonde's tongue and fingers brought her closer and closer to the edge of orgasm.

Sarah moaned and writhed, struggling for breath, struggling to hold on. What was even more remarkable was that with her other hand his student of the night before, Anna Weissman, was driving a dildo deep into her own sex and was obviously close to the edge too. It was a stunning tableau. Both females were totally consumed by the fire of passion. Watching from the comfort of his armchair, Mustafa Aziz was also sweating hard and enjoying the spectacle, his erection like a mountain in his stained clothes.

Crouching above Anna, Sarah suddenly began to buck and threw back her head, crying out in ecstasy, spine arching as the woman beneath her lapped on and on, driving her through into a shuddering orgasm. As if she was afraid to miss one second of the delight, Sarah ground her wet quim down onto her companion's face, chasing every last sensation, every glittering moment of delight, and then suddenly it was done, all over. Unable to take any more, Sarah fell forward onto the cot, breathing hard.

Mustafa Aziz got slowly to his feet and applauded, almost as if he was watching a cabaret. 'That was good, very good,' he gloated, running his hands over Sarah's glistening flesh. 'Now,' he said, gripping the back of her neck before she had time to catch her breath, 'I want you to kneel on the floor, and do the same to Miss Weissman. Quickly, while she is so very close to coming. Now, do as I say.'

Sarah winced as the man's grip tightened, but did not resist as he dragged her off the bed onto the filthy floor. Kneeling there between Anna's open legs, she tentatively kissed the woman's flat belly, her tongue slowly tracing a path down from her navel to the rise of her sex. Anna was still working the dildo in and out, lifting her hips in time with the penetration. Sarah hesitated and then very gently kissed the wet junction where Anna's sex lips divided, encircling her clitoris and sucking gently on the swollen scarlet bud.

Anna Weissman whimpered and lifted up to give Sarah greater freedom. Sarah sucked and nuzzled again at the plump, fragrant folds. As they began to find a rhythm, Sarah caught hold of the dildo, easing it from Anna's glistening fingers and took control of its passage, losing herself in the act of pleasuring the blonde. It was a compelling image. Casswell felt the breath catch in his throat. Sarah and Anna looked exquisite, lost in a sea of rapture.

Standing above them both, lips slack and wet, eyes dark with a shark-like hunger, Mustafa ran his hands over Sarah's shapely hips. At first she barely seemed aware of the Turk, and then her eyes widened as he roughly pushed her thighs apart and ran a hand up into the engorged opening between her buttocks. Casswell saw her whole body stiffen for an instant as he unzipped his fly, and grabbing hold of her hips, guided his raging cock deep inside her.

Sarah shrieked as he pressed his unwieldy shaft home, his hands catching hold of her breasts, fingers twisting and pinching her erect nipples. Deeply and securely embedded, Mustafa Aziz hunched over Sarah's shapely frame like a slavering, rabid dog, frantically forcing himself deeper and deeper while beneath them both Anna Weissman cried out in pleasure as Sarah brought her to the shores of oblivion.

In the gloom of the tiny room, Casswell's companions were deeply appreciative of Mr Mustafa's erotic little cabaret. Next to him one of the men had his cock wrapped tight in his fist and it was obvious that he might well come along with the three figures in the cell. He grunted, swearing furiously, eyes glazed as he started to twitch and snort. Casswell looked away.

Back in the cell beyond the peepholes, Sarah's part in the sordid arrangement was over and done with now, and Casswell vowed to take her back to Weissman's house as soon as he could, to get her away from Anna and the pig Aziz. The Turk rocked back onto his heels, mouth slack, his shrivelled cock nestled in the grimy folds of his trousers, slick with the rich juices of desire, spent and flaccid. Sarah had slumped down onto Anna and looked as if she was asleep.

Casswell rose and made his way back to the cellar and the stack of ancient treasures, and didn't have to wait long for his pupil to arrive. He smiled; Sarah Morgan was a truly extraordinary girl. She was tidily dressed, with her hair brushed, looking as if she had just spent the previous hour taking dictation.

Chapter Seven

When Sarah got back to Weissman's house she was grateful that Casswell dismissed her. She hurried upstairs to shower. It seemed to her that so far the trip to Turkey had been punctuated by encounters with Mustafa. She had no idea where Anna had gone after leaving the museum, and Chang was nowhere in sight either. In some ways it was a relief, but in others she felt abandoned, dirty and abused. The dried evidence of Mustafa's lust was still on her thighs, her body was sore from the way he had fucked her, and her nostrils were full of the stench of his sweat and breath.

A sound disturbed her thoughts, and she swung round to see Chang watching her intently. 'Dr Casswell said you might need me,' he said, and to her surprise, Sarah's eyes filled with tears.

Chang shook his head. 'Don't cry, Miss Morgan; you understood that total obedience was part of the arrangement if you were to remain in Dr Casswell's employment.'

She nodded, afraid to speak. How could she tell him of the humiliation she felt as Mustafa abused her, when so much had happened since she first arrived at Casswell's house?

Chang looked her up and down. 'We all learn our place, and it seems that while you are here it is to be at Mustafa Aziz's beck and call. But things will change. Bathe, wash your hair, and rid yourself once again of the stench of the filthy man – we won't be here much longer. If it is any comfort to you, Dr Casswell is not easy here either – something's wrong.'

Sarah nodded, still too unsettled to speak. It was totally unlike Chang to confide in her.

When she emerged from the shower, Chang had turned back the bed and set a tray on the bedside cabinet.

As she crossed the room she noticed there was a pile of Casswell's notes stacked by the computer. Seeing the neat white bond covered in her master's distinctive hand was oddly comforting; despite everything else, whatever happened to her, Beatrice and her adventures and her loves, passions, and pain were still there to guide her through. She knew Casswell already had more work for her to transcribe, so after a rest she would get on with typing it up, restoring some sense of order.

Naked, her hair still wet, Sarah picked up Casswell's manuscript and settled back among the pillows and began to read the diary. Within seconds she was drawn into the girl's life at the castle and her troubles, and suddenly all thoughts of Mustafa Aziz and Anna Weissman seemed to fade into insignificance.

...So much has changed since the night the Lady Cassandra arrived at the castle. His lordship was in a difficult position – if he questioned her decision or refused to let her have me as her servant, he would be acting disrespectfully to the king and this Cassandra knew only to well. He certainly could not choose me over his betrothed.

He praised me to her, saying I had given fine service in the house in the years I had been there. At this Cassandra smiled, although the expression had no truth or warmth, and said, 'I know the service she has provided for you and how well you like it, sir. I'll have no division of favour under my roof. Either she stays and serves me or she goes. She told me she was given by the church; if we cannot reach a compromise then the church shall have her back. I know the perfect spot. What say you, father abbot?'

My master caught hold of her hand and said gently, 'Beloved, let us not argue and begin this marriage under a cloud, particularly not over something so insignificant as the fate of a serving wench. If you wish to have her in your service then so be it, I have no objection, I am happy that she will be of some use to you.'

I knew he said it to save me, but I also knew that Cassandra understood exactly what he was doing.

The next few days went badly, the whole of the household in uproar as Cassandra made her mark on its running – she was not slow to lay on the rod, nor her cruel and cutting tongue. As for me, I was given charge of her bedchamber, although my duties extended far beyond those of cleaning and mending. I dreaded the end of each day and the coming darkness – each night she would call me to undress her and then take me to her bed to perform all manner of unnatural acts under the watchful and lustful eye of the king's bastard.

She bade me sleep on a cot in her room in case she needed me during the night, and often she did. Many nights would I crawl into bed with the taste of her sex on my lips and fingers. It seemed there was not a minute for me to call my own. When Cassandra had done with me, the abbot would creep up to the cot, cock hard and ready, eyes dark with desire, and use me, holding me down, a hand over my mouth so I should not disturb his slumbering mistress, and although there were no more beatings, these cruel and jealous couplings with me hunched beneath him like some wounded animal were almost more painful.

And then, a month or so after her arrival, on the Sabbath, while I was attending her ladyship at the chapel, I caught sight of my lord and master kneeling by the altar rail. As he stood and turned to go back to his seat, our eyes met and my heart leapt. It was all I could do to stop myself crying out to him.

I prayed that my Lady Cassandra had not seen the impassioned look that passed between us, and when the service was done, I scurried from the chapel, gaze demurely on the cobbles, tucked tight in at her wide, while my heart beat like a drum in my chest.

After we had broken fast a page came to the chamber and bade me follow, saying one of his lordship's children – whom I had not seen since Cassandra's arrival – had been taken sick with a fever and was calling for me. Even Cassandra could not deny the call of a child, and so I followed the boy up to the nursery. I was anxious for the children, whom I have always held in particular affection.

But as I reached the first landing the master stepped out into my path and grabbed tight hold of me. Without a word he took me in his arms, and pulling me into the shadows kissed me fiercely, and I cannot deny I returned his passion with an equal vigour. I hungered for his body and firm touch. There was no time for finesse, no time for more than we had. Eyes dark with desire, body fierce and strong he pushed through an open doorway, holding me tight against the frame, his lips on mine, body pressed close to me, his hands on my breasts, lifting my skirts with haste, seeking my sex.

I caught tight hold of him, my hands eager to hold his manhood. I was already wet for him, eager and hungry for him. As my fingers closed around him he was already hard, throbbing, ready for me. For an instant I froze in case I had overstepped the mark, and he groaned softly and turned me in his arms so that I could bend over the stairs, and then he fucked me hard and true, driving again and again into my tight and tender quim, the very fury of his passion taking my breath away.

It did not take us long to make an end to it. We both burned red-hot with lust. I mewled and cried, driving my hips back into his belly, matching him stroke for stroke and he plunged again and again, crying out with pleasure.

At last he collapsed on top of me, whispering words of tenderness and such love that it took my breath away, and it has been these memories of all that passed between us, more than anything else, that has kept me going these weeks since that fateful day.

Back once more in Cassandra's chambers she bade me how faired the child. I hesitated – I swear for no more than the barest of an instant – for lying comes hard to me. And then she smiled slyly and beckoned me closer. As quick as lightening her hand was up between my thighs and, too slow to resist her, she pressed home into my private parts. Triumphant she pulled away, her fingers slick with seed and the remnants of my pleasure. She sniffed her stubby fingers thoughtfully, eyes fixed on mine, her face a mask, and then said, 'What is this then, girl, an assignation? On the Sabbath?'

I reddened and looked away.

'So tell me, wench, who fucked you this fine morning. Which of the household has been this way?' She snatched tightly my quim through the folds of my gown. 'Tell me now or I will have you beaten soundly until you do.'

I shook my head, for I dare not speak.

Undeterred she caught hold of my hair and pulled my face close to hers. Her breath was foul, her touch unmerciful. 'I shall have an answer or I shall have you beaten until you confess, now tell me who has rutted and rolled with you this morning, girl.'

Still I could not speak. Face contorted with anger she ripped away my Sunday gown.

'Tell me!' she shouted. 'I will have an answer! Was it perhaps the man who has yet to share my cot? The man betrothed to me, promised to me in marriage who still chooses to share his favours with another? A man who even before his wedding vows are spoken betrays me thus with a serving girl?!' Her voice rose in volume as she raged, and I feared for my life.

Finally she threw me to the floor, picked up a birch from the hearth and cracked it viciously across my back. It was a cruel blow and it felt as if I was cut in two by it, but before I could protest or appeal to reason, she hit me again and again, one stroke after the other in a blind and terrible fury.

No man was she, versed in the arts of the whip, but a wild and furious banshee. The birch caught my neck and face and as I rolled over to protect myself, it caught my breasts and belly and arms. No part of me was spared, and all the time she beat me her eyes were wild with fury and what seemed to me the most awful jealous rage.

'I will not be shamed!' she roared. 'There is but one mistress in this house, and you will understand that, girl. Do you hear me?'

'Yes, my lady, yes!' I sobbed and shrieked, trying to roll away from her.

At last, when she had all but exhausted herself, she cried out, 'Father abbot?!'

The king's bastard must have been waiting close by, perhaps – for his tastes are cruel – he had be watching or listening to what passed between us, for he appeared in Cassandra's chamber as if by magic.

She threw down the birch and said to him, 'Make

yourself ready, father, and take this miserable creature out of my sight, to the place we have spoken off. I shall prepare a letter for the abbot there. I want her gone today, before the sun is set.'

And so I found myself on the road to the Abbey of Saint Joseph.

Dressed in little more than rags, cold and afraid, barefoot and no more than a chattel, I can see no way out of my present dilemma save the intervention of heaven itself. Oh, how easily it seems I have come to this, fallen and lost. Settled in this evil place, each night I am expected to wait on the abbot and the debauched and depraved women who call themselves sisters of the church. I in my turn serve each of them, as a bedmate, as a slave, as a maid. Worse still, if by chance a traveller happens by and calls here for hospitality, then I am sent to warm their bed and next day am expected to confess my sins – if sins they are – to the abbot and his harpies, and beaten for my lusts and desires. If my tale is too innocent, if the man refused me, then I am beaten for lying, yet if it is too debauched they lay on the rod for my eager fleshly passions.

The journey to this dark and ungodly place was arduous – my body still torn and bruised from the mistress's beating. The abbot would not take a wagon for it would slow him down. He was afraid, I think, to be too long from Lady Cassandra's side, lest another should take her favour, so we rode. I on a mule, dressed in a manner befitting my station, for the irony is that through all of this, though I am a slave to Cassandra and my master, I am considered highborn and even in my disgrace I left the house dressed well from the dowry chest of my master's previous wife.

Once out on the road it is hard to tell who had the more beatings, the mule or myself, as we made our way through the harsh winter landscape. The Abbey of St Joseph is several days' hard ride from the castle. Each night when we had eaten, whether we stayed in an inn or camped out under the sky, the abbot would call me to him.

'Girl, you are truly the spawn of a worldly devil, tempting a man from the straight and narrow with that body of yours,' he would say, looking me over. 'All day long as you ride alongside me the dark forces who inspire and rule you enter my head and set off such imaginings. Such possibilities, even the smell of you on the breeze, turns my thoughts away from the godly to the fleshly.'

I looked at his face, slack with overindulgence and wickedness. Could what he said be true? I thought not; surely it was the darkness in *his* heart that fired those thoughts. As a man of the cloth was he not supposed to fight such lusts and hungers that teased him away from the paths of righteousness?

But he would have none of it. He would have me stand by the hearth or the fire, regardless of how bitter the night, and take off my clothes. Naked, on my hands and knees, I would beg for mercy as he took off the thick belt he wore around his outer robes, and leathered me.

When he'd thrashed me he would lift the hem of his robe and have me take him in my mouth, sucking dutifully at his manhood, worshipping him in the most base and ancient of ways, and then he would spill his seed on my breasts or in my hair, or at the last moment pull away and drive without mercy into my quim.

Cold and badly fed, riding as little more than a camp follower to the abbot, my spirit was all but broken on the long ride to the abbey. I was never safe; all day long I felt the eyes of the men who accompanied us on me. They were part of Lady Cassandra's retinue, no better than rogues and ruffians, and liked nothing better than watching me with eyes that burned with animal hunger. I am sure they heard what passed between the abbot and me at night. And on the one evening the abbot rode into a town to find better sport, they took it in turns to take me there amongst the earth and ashes.

But worse was to come.

At last, in the distance, we spotted the Abbey of St Joseph. It stood alone on a hillside, a bleak desolate place, and as we approached I had a sense of great foreboding.

The gates were manned by a novice monk, and dressed in the grey habit of his order, he was an ugly, twisted, hunchbacked boy who could barely speak, but what he lacked in words he more than made up for with the expression on his face. He eyed me with such a lust as I have ever seen on the face of one so young, his gawking made all the more noticeable for one supposedly in the service of the church.

I thought perhaps it was an oversight. Perhaps he had never seen a girl, perhaps his simple mind made his thoughts all the more obvious – but once taken inside I could understand why he behaved so; here at the Abbey of St Joseph it seemed that all appetites and lusts were indulged.

It was early evening as we rode into the beaten earth yard. The rush torches were lit and a small group of men were gathered in the doorway of the main hall. At first I believed they were supplicants or penitents, perhaps on a pilgrimage to one of the many shrines in the district.

As we were shown further in to the hall, I saw that they were watching some kind of tableau, and as I picked out the details my blood chilled.

There in the circle of men, their bodies picked out by firelight, were two females, engaged in an act of unnatural lust. They were sitting up on their knees. One was a large plump woman, blindfolded with her hands tied tight behind her back. Slick with sweat, her ample body was the colour of new milk, her hair a fiery red and her breasts, like plump pillows tipped with large nipples, were currently being manhandled by a slip of a boy who drew first one and then the other into his mouth. As he sucked hard and long the other female was servicing her from behind with a great carved phallus. Above them a raddled monk wielding a stick encouraged them on, with a crack across their ample buttocks if it looked as if either might be flagging.

At the far end of the hall, sitting on a raised dais, the father abbot of this den of iniquity looked down on the spectacle with delight while between his legs a young man crouched, avidly sucking his master's raging cock. They were picked out by the flickering light from the fire and torches, which made it seem like a scene from damnation's cradle.

Was this the abbey that the Lady Cassandra believed me so ideally suited to?

The abbot – an old man with thick grey hair – waved the boy away as we reached the platform, but not so far; no doubt as soon as our business was concluded the boy would be back to suck him. To one side of the old man stood a sister of the church. Dressed in a grey habit she was as thin as a whippet, her skin the colour of bad suet, her features dour, eyes haunted and unreadable and lips narrow. The way she looked me up and down made me shiver.

The abbot took the goblet she was holding and beckoned me closer. His eyes were glazed from a mixture of desire and wine. He took the letter proffered by the king's bastard and read it slowly, lips moving as he deciphered the words. It seemed he was not altogether surprised by our arrival and greeted the king's son in a manner that suggested they were old friends. He read Cassandra's missive through once more and then dropped it to the floor, grinning. The nun retrieved it without a word.

'So you were gifted to your master's household by the church, eh girl? Her ladyship seems to think it is high time we took our gift back.' He lifted a hand to encompass the hall. 'Here we serve the community in whatever ways the community demands. For example, the good people of the town like nothing better than to come and watch the sisters hard at their work.'

On the floor of the hall the crowd, oblivious to our arrival, bayed and cheered the two women on.

He looked at me encouragingly, but I knew better than to speak.

'They pay well, very well, for the privilege,' continued the abbot, after a moment or two. 'We, of course, distribute money to the poor and support our little community from the gifts and donations the faithful are kind enough to give. And from what my dear cousin Cassandra says in her letter, you would appear to be the perfect novice to join our little community, talented in all those ways that goodly women have, and versed as you are in the ways of obedience.'

The king's bastard smiled, and taking a goblet of wine from one of the servants, added, 'Aye, but not chastity.'

The abbot leered slyly, although I guessed from the way he looked at my tormentor that there was little love lost between the two men.

'As you say, brother, but we all serve in our own way.' He looked at me. 'Come here, and let me see what you are made of.'

I moved closer. He looked me up and down. All the while behind him I could feel the icy eyes of the sister upon me.

'Not bad at all, although she smells from the road,' the abbot concluded. 'I would like to see her undressed.'

The king's bastard prodded me with his crop, as if I might be too deaf or too stupid to understand what was required of me. Nervously I unlaced my bodice and slipped my skirts to the floor. The abbot grunted and cupped my breasts in his wrinkled palms, weighing them thoughtfully as if they were good fruit. The treacherous teats hardened almost at once, and he grunted his approval, then ran a hand down over my waist and flanks and then over my belly and buttocks. His touch was not unkind, but much as a farmer might handle his stock. He slipped his hand between my legs, one finger seeking entry into my quim. He breached me and at once my body tightened around him.

He nodded appreciatively. 'Seems that your Lady Cassandra is a fair judge of female flesh. She is a comely wench; small built, but there are those with a taste for something a little leaner than Sister Mary and Sister Therese.' He indicated the women still writhing in the sawdust. 'I am certain we can find a way for her to earn her keep here.'

On the floor below us the two women were coming to a noisy climax, but before they could collapse they were pulled apart by the monk, who pushed the one with the dildo onto all fours and with both hands settled on her ample hips and drove his cock deep inside her. His penetration of her sent a roar of delight through the assembled crowd, while her companion was rapidly handed over to one of the watching rabble.

The sister standing behind the abbot then stepped forward. 'I shall see to it that she is bathed and dressed in a manner more befitting our order,' and as she spoke, she tucked the letter into her purse.

The abbot nodded. 'Aye, Sister Judith, a fine idea.' He turned his attention to the king's bastard. 'Have you dined, brother, or would you care to join us for a little supper? I can rustle you up a girl or a lad if you've a mind to indulge yourself once you have dined.'

Meanwhile Sister Judith grabbed my arms, giving me no chance to gather my clothes, and without thinking I began to protest.

'Silence!' she snapped, dragging me down off the dais. 'Trust me, girl, you'll need nothing here, and if you fight me I will break you like a twig. Perhaps you don't know who I am, but I know very well who you are, Beatrice de Fleur. It seems at last my prayers have been heeded.'

I turned to look again at the hag, and for some reason she did look familiar, but I was certain I had never met her before.

Her expression hardened under my unguarded inspection. 'Have you no idea who I am, girl?' she hissed.

I was almost afraid to say no, but she continued. 'Your master's first wife, she who is now banished and disgraced because of your word, your betrayal; she was my sister. Now do you recognise me?'

I stared at her in horror, remembering only to vividly the plot to kill my master, and felt an icy claw close tight around my heart. I knew I had to get away from the abbey or this crone would make my life a living hell – if indeed I lived at all.

Piled at the door to the hall were many cloaks and robes, left there by the revellers. Without thinking, as we reached them I grabbed the first I could, pushed my captor away and ran headlong out into the bitterly cold night, wrapping myself in the heavy woollen cloak as I ran.

I was fast and nimble, and although naked I had not

removed my boots. In the torchlight I make out the fine grey stallion the king's son rode – as yet it had not been unsaddled or stabled and was tied to a rail. Unfastening the reins and grabbing tight hold of the mane I leapt up onto the horse's back, and slipped my feet into the stirrups.

With my hand locked in the reins I turned the beast towards the gate, while behind me Sister Judith staggered out into the yard and shrieked, 'Stop her, stop her! Stop her now!'

Hunched over the beast, the sound of her voice distracted me and the horse, who was lively despite a day's journey, skittered and frisked across the slippery clay yard. It was just enough to undo my bid for freedom. I did not see the figure moving towards me through the shadows, but as I reached the main gate I was astonished when the hunchback boy leapt out at me and grabbed the animal's ornate halter. Startled, the horse reared and I was unseated, losing my grip, and before I could recover rolled helplessly down into the filth.

Sister Judith and the boy were upon me in an instant, dragging me to my feet.

'Defy me would you, you little bitch?' she snarled, breathlessly shaking me. 'Try and make a fool of me by escaping? I shall teach you a lesson you'll never forget.' Dragging me, she and the boy pulled me through the stable yard, yanked off the cloak and strung me, without ceremony, between two of the stable supports.

And there was no mercy to be had. I cried out in terror and fought like a wildcat to stop them from tying me, for I knew that this woman wished me nothing but malice. But it was hopeless; the boy was unnaturally strong and the crone driven by pure evil. I could neither resist nor escape them.

'You will learn the error of your ways,' she snarled, 'or be broken in the process.'

I cried out, begging to be cut down. The boy, meanwhile, had picked up a whip and encouraged by his mistress laid it on with a vigour that was terrifying.

My cries must have been louder than I thought, for moments later as I twisted and shrieked against my restraints, trying to avoid the kiss of the whip, I saw that we were no longer alone – men from the hall had filed out into the cold night to witness my disgrace.

'I'll have her when you're done,' called one, supping from a flagon of ale. 'Don't mark her too bad, sister.'

Judith growled her reply and I felt the whip's cruel touch again and again on my delicate flesh, making me twist and weep, while behind me I could hear the men's excitement growing, until at last I could feel nothing.

Finally, harsh unfeeling hands cut me down. I felt them on my breasts and belly, wrapping me in a coarse blanket, and then I was dragged across the yard, where the boy opened the doors to a damp cellar and threw me down into the darkness. Afraid and alone, cold and lost, I curled up under the foul blanket in the hay and straw and let night claim me.

And so it was I found myself prisoner at the Abbey of St Joseph...

Chapter Eight

Sarah Morgan lay the pages down on the bed, her heart racing. Was this terrible imprisonment to be the fate of her alter ego? To be enslaved at the hands of a cruel and bitter woman?

Sarah glanced around the bedroom, wishing that Casswell had finished the rest of the translation so she could find out what happened to Beatrice.

Finally, still feeling agitated, she settled back amongst the fragrant pillows and covers and was about to sleep when she heard the door open. Chang stood in the open doorway. 'Tired from your exertions?' he asked, and Sarah roused herself as he continued. 'You will accompany the doctor to dinner this evening. He's been invited to meet the museum trustees.'

Sarah nodded, imagining the social constraints of a formal dinner party, although it would not be the first occasion she had appeared as Casswell's companion. Any such notion, however, was short-lived.

'It seems you have already met one of the guests. Herr Heinman?' Chang's expression remained impassive, but Sarah guessed he knew the form her encounter with Heinman had taken. Sarah felt the heat in her belly as she remembered the long hours spent downstairs with Uri Weissman and his eager friend. She nodded.

'And of course that filthy Turk will be there, although tonight it's likely he will be there as a minion, and you as one of the VIPs. A fitting reversal of fortune, don't you think?'

Sarah looked at Chang; they both knew that whether she was invited as a guest or not, it would make little difference to her fate. In the unique and very private circle of sexual connoisseurs in which they moved, if Dr Casswell gave her to one of the guests to use as he willed then she had no choice but to comply.

Chang beckoned her to follow him. If she was to arrive on Casswell's arm then she had to be prepared and look the part. As Sarah slipped out from under the sheet and got to her feet, the little oriental moved closer and slid a hand speculatively between her thighs. It was the intimate gesture of one who knows he is in control.

'It seems a long time,' he murmured, sliding a finger into her.

She certainly knew better than to resist, and Chang with his odd combination of kindness and cruelty knew her body more intimately then any lover. He knew she was wet; the diary had ignited a dark need in her and it was almost a relief to have a way to ground the fear and the desire that Beatrice's words had evoked.

Chang smiled inscrutably as he slid a finger deep into her, and without thinking Sarah moaned as his finger brushed her clitoris. He nodded his approval; in some ways she was as much his as Casswell's. 'Bend over,' he said.

Sarah did as she was told, turning and bending over the side of the bed. For a few moments she stood there, knowing he was examining her. She reddened, wondering what would follow. 'Have you been touching yourself?' he asked, sliding his finger into her again. She shook her head. 'Keeping for yourself what you are promised to share with my master?'

'No,' Sarah whispered.

A single finger slid higher to brush the ridge of her clitoris, and she moaned softly.

Chang laughed. 'You are such an alley cat; no wonder that Aziz wanted you so badly.' Sarah shivered as he withdrew his hand. 'You need to be reacquainted with some of the rules.'

She wondered what he meant, even though in the time she'd known him he had punished her on many occasions. She swallowed nervously, and then he moved closer, bringing his hand down sharply and spanked her. It was a complete shock. The blow sounded like a pistol shot and she yelped in pain. Her skin glowed as he smacked her again. She wriggled instinctively to try and avoid the blow but he smacked her again and again, building up a mesmerising rhythm. Sarah felt the pain and the heat course through her bloodstream, mingling with pleasure.

Then just as she began to relax Chang nudged her legs wider apart, and rubbing his hand up between her thighs, spread her juices out over her delicate flesh.

Still dressed, he moved closer and against her, thrusting hard, cupping and stroking her breasts, anointing them with the perfume of her body, so that as Sarah moved all she could smell was her own excitement. The rich musk and his touch excited her intensely until she was thrusting back against him, eager for the feel of him inside her, eager for the pressure of his body against hers, and eager for whatever pleasures he might give her.

Chang's fingers moved back – back to her anus. Sarah shivered; this was the place Chang preferred, so tight and dark and forbidden. He pressed a finger in to the hilt, her body opening under his knowing exploration, and unlike her encounter with Mustafa Aziz, seemed to welcome the unnatural invasion.

The sensation made her gasp. Slowly Chang withdrew his finger, but before she could regain her composure he drove his cock deep into her quim, thrusting so hard it took her breath away, while at the same time easing his finger back into her anus, stroking his throbbing cock through the thin wall of membrane that divided one pleasure from another. With his other hand he pressed on her clitoris, riding her every thrust and twist. It was all too much; her mind was overloaded with exquisite sensations, rendering her capable of nothing but surrender.

Chang filled her completely, her body at his mercy as they began to move together. He rubbed the engorged ridge firmly, stroking the delicate hood of her clit again and again. He knew exactly how to touch her, exactly the pressure and speed that drove her wild. The pleasures were overwhelming, driving away all reason. Knowing the way Chang's mind and desire worked Sarah could submit willingly, giving herself in a way that came from a perverse sense of trust.

He slowed the pounding of his hips, fingers echoing the change of pace, and as he did Sarah felt the first waves of orgasm swell through her like a tidal surge, and before she had time to consider it, found herself drowning in a swirling well of pleasure and pain, her eyes closed as she drank in the coursing tumult of passion.

'Tell me you want to get out of here,' Uri Weissman whispered to Sarah under his breath. The evening with the museum trustees was far duller than anyone had imagined it would be.

Casswell adjusted the cuffs of his dress shirt; it was a gesture, Sarah knew, that indicated he was bored. But it seemed, despite Weissman's suggestion, that there was no way they could easily make an escape. Dinner had been convivial enough, even if the company and conversation a little boring. Their fellow guests seemed to mainly consist of local worthies and their wives, and the connoisseurs and masters were keeping their predilections for pleasure and pain well hidden from those on the guest list with less broad tastes.

Mustafa Aziz was there with his wife, a plump woman who quite obviously wore the trousers in their household, but that did not stop him from leering salaciously every time he caught Sarah's eye. It made her shudder with revulsion, as she remembered him pawing her. Fortunately there were sufficient other guests so their paths barely crossed, and she noticed that if there was any possibility of him sidling close, Casswell skilfully guided her away.

After dinner everyone was shepherded into a room where there was a long and very dry presentation on behalf of the museum.

As everyone settled into their seats, the muted and polite conversation died to silence, and Sarah realised she was beginning to expect every encounter, every social gathering to rapidly deteriorate into a debauched sexual banquet. Tonight at least, it seemed, she was wrong. Up on a podium one man waxed lyrical about the trustees' plans to extend and expand the museum collection and buildings, and he was followed by another showing slides of artist's impressions of what the planned extensions and improvements might look like.

Sarah adjusted her dress; a simple yet stunning sheath, black trimmed with silver, low cut and expertly boned to show off the enticing upper slopes of her breasts, her deep cleavage, and her narrow waist. Several of the men in the audience were clearly far more interested in the dress and what it contained than listening to the speakers, and Sarah felt both flattered and unnerved by their avaricious glances.

She tried hard to concentrate on the presentations. None of the board seemed in the least aware of the erotic treasures they had hidden away in the museum vaults, or if they were they were being very careful not to reveal any detail that might excite interest amongst the assembled patrons. Once or twice the host referred to 'our distinguished guests', indicating Casswell and Weissman, who were sitting with Sarah to one side of the room near open French windows.

The Austrian was getting gradually more agitated, and Sarah felt a hand touch her thigh. He leaned a little closer and his fingers squeezed. She shivered, struggling not to react, and hoped that no one could see.

'Faint,' he whispered. She looked at him. He smiled slyly and leaned closer still. 'Come on, we have to get away from here before we all die of complete tedium – you and me and your precious master. I know the perfect place. A ten minute drive from here is somewhere much more to your taste.' He paused, eyes alight with lust. 'And mine.'

Boldly, almost defiantly, Sarah met his gaze.

'Come on,' he pressed. 'You know you want to.'

Sarah glanced around the assembled crowd. No one would think it odd if she fainted, for despite being next to the French windows the room was hot and airless, so she put a palm to her brow and swayed very slightly on her chair. It was not altogether pretence, because the atmosphere was oppressive. Casswell looked at her anxiously, but Weissman winking conspiratorially at him allayed any concern. And then it was done, eyes closed she let herself flop gracefully into Weissman's waiting arms, and he was on his feet in an instant.

'Excuse me, excuse me, I'm terribly sorry, please do carry on,' he said officiously to the speaker, then carried her out onto the terrace, unable to resist clutching her around the waist tighter than was absolutely necessary, and 'accidentally' touching her breast.

Casswell was a yard or two behind, wearing a concerned expression despite the fact that he knew it was a ruse to let them escape. Once out in the slightly cooler air and away from prying eyes, Sarah staged a miraculous recovery.

'Well done,' said Weissman with a grin, leading them down to where the cars were parked. 'I know a very interesting little club nearby that is much more fun.'

Casswell looked back towards the building. 'But what about you precious trustees?'

Weissman laughed. 'Have no fear; those who are interested will join us later, no doubt. The club isn't a particularly well-kept secret.'

Sarah guessed exactly what Casswell meant, but stayed quiet as they climbed into the waiting limousine. Once settled, in the darkness, Weissman leant closer and renewed his exploration of her body. She knew better than to resist, and if Casswell objected, he said nothing.

Weissman eased the straps of her evening dress off her shoulders and stroked her breasts, tweaking and twisting the nipples into flushed peaks. Almost instantly Sarah felt the first flicker of pleasure ignite low in her tummy.

'How much will you take for her?' Weissman asked Casswell, as he gently nudged Sarah's legs apart and slid a hand beneath her dress and down between her thighs, cradling her naked sex.

Casswell took a cigar from his jacket pocket and lit it before shaking his head. 'I've already told you, Uri, she is not for sale. She is far too valuable to me.'

In the shadows, Weissman's fingers sought entry. 'Oh come, come, Rigel; everything has a price.' His eyes flashed lecherously as her body opened to him. 'And I am a very wealthy man. Tell me what you want. Name your price.'

He pressed a finger deep between the lips of her sex, and Sarah shivered as another joined it, while his thumb circled her clitoris. Without thinking she began to move with his touch, and opened her legs wider to allow him unhindered access.

Casswell watched her wordless compliance, and smiled. 'From you, Uri?' he mused. 'Nothing. She is beyond price. Besides, Sarah and I have a great deal to do before we go back to England.'

Weissman's expression hardened, his touch growing more and more intense. Sarah gasped for breath and as she felt the sensations building, wondered as her body began to move against him whether all modesty and all shame had now gone. She was wet and eager, already longing for whatever it was Weissman had in store for her.

'But Casswell, look... she likes me,' Weissman protested in a mocking tone.

Casswell's smile did not falter for an instant. 'That's where you're wrong Uri; she is well trained and obedient: she is the perfect slave.'

Weissman snorted and pulled Sarah even closer, and she knew what he wanted. He unfastened his fly and she straddled him, with one hand guiding his cock deep inside her.

'Well trained indeed,' he grunted appreciatively, as his erection speared up within the succulence of her sex. He looked up into Sarah's eyes. 'Now I want you to fuck me; show me just how obedient you can be,' he hissed, and with that he stabbed his hips upward, making her gasp and her sparkling eyes widen as he filled her aggressively.

As though in a dream she began to move against him,

obediently riding the rigid column that impaled her.

Weissman snorted with delight. 'Won't you join us, Casswell?' he goaded. 'I'll ask my driver to slow down. Come along, why not share her with me? Why not share your precious little slave girl?'

Sarah tried to turn to see Casswell's face, but in the gloom she heard him chuckle. 'That's my whole point, Uri,' he said. 'I don't need to share her. Whatever she does for you or with you, she will always be mine, and at the end of the evening and the end of this expedition I will take her home with me to Casswell Hall.'

Weissman grunted, but Sarah could see that his thoughts were less and less on what Casswell was saying and more on his mounting ardour. She ground against him, riding down onto his shaft, her body engulfing him, contracting around him, her pleasure building. So sensual were her movements that it took mere minutes, no more, to take them both to the point of no return.

As Sarah shuddered and gasped, thrusting against him, Weissman snorted and buried his face into her welcoming cleavage, and she felt him shudder, felt his cock convulse deep inside her, and knew it was over for the moment. As she slumped in his arms and lowered her head to his shoulder, exhausted, she noticed the driver's dark eyes watching her closely in the rear-view mirror.

'So tell me, what is your pleasure this evening, gentleman?' said the sycophantic proprietor, showing them to an unoccupied table close to the stage of the seedy club.

'Champagne,' Weissman told him.

The man nodded. 'Of course, Herr Weissman,' he said greasily, and beckoned one of the waiters over and babbled the order to him while staring quite openly at Sarah, eyeing her with lurid interest. Other shady eyes had turned to admire her, too.

There was one other girl in the club, but she was hooded and on the small stage, her hands and feet manacled to an ornate wooden frame. The owner's crawling gaze, however, ignored her and remained firmly on Sarah, making her feel horribly uncomfortable.

'Yours?' the greasy man said to Weissman. 'A new acquisition?'

Weissman shook his head. 'No, unfortunately not.'

'Oh, my apologies, Mr Weissman,' gushed the man, with an obsequious nod of his head.

Weissman waved a hand indifferently. 'That is all right, she is with...' he paused, as if teasing, '... she is with my good friend here, Dr Rigel Casswell.'

Instantly the man's eyes lit up, and he bowed. 'Dr Casswell?' he fawned. 'I have heard of you. You are translating the maid's diaries, are you not? It is my pleasure – no – my honour, to welcome you into my humble establishment.' He quickly uncorked the champagne handed to him by the waiter, and handed them each a glass. 'I have heard so much about you. I am honoured to welcome you here; you must have this on the house – I insist.'

Weissman appeared to be deeply uncomfortable with the subservient man's enthusiasm, and his inside knowledge of Casswell's mission in Turkey.

Casswell nodded an acknowledgement of the exaggerated plaudits and murmured his thanks, clearly wanting no more, so the proprietor returned his attention to Sarah.

'And this is one of your pupils, yes?' he said, drooling over her even more appreciatively than before.

Sarah sensed that Weissman was about to protest, but Casswell nodded in response to the question. The man leered. 'Quality becomes its master,' he slavered. 'May I?'

Without hesitation Casswell nodded, and understanding what was required, Sarah obediently sat still so the man could admire her at his leisure.

Casswell nodded towards the girl on the stage. 'And is she one of *your* pupils?' he asked. She was slightly more heavily set than Sarah, with riper breasts and hips. She stood so still that she could have been a statue, and what gave her away was the twinkle of an ornate ring that pierced one nipple and caught the light as she slowly breathed. The girl was a compelling sight. Her large breasts were framed by a tight leather harness, which went around her neck and down over her belly, and as it crossed her sex it split in two, running down so a thin strap encircled each thigh. Her pubic hair was dark and sleek, clipped into a tiny triangle that neatly framed her sex pouch.

The man smiled. 'Indeed, she is,' he said. 'We keep a small stable here for the use of our clientele. She is quite new – a good girl, though. I bought her from a dealer in Marmaris.' He glanced again at Sarah.

Casswell smiled thinly; he had seen the look of avarice and interest many times before. 'So what is it that you have in mind?' he said, sipping his champagne.

The man sniggered. 'Am I so very transparent, Dr Casswell? Well, since you ask, I thought perhaps we could exchange a little favour. My girl, as you see, is ready to be beaten, I have already a volunteer, one of our regulars – but perhaps we can come to some other arrangement.' He paused, eyes alight. 'Perhaps you would like to do the honours?'

Sitting beside Casswell, Weissman smiled calculatingly. 'No, I have a much better idea,' he interrupted, and it struck Casswell that the Austrian could not bear to be upstaged by him. 'How about your slave girl beats his slave girl, Casswell?' Weissman went on. 'Let's see how she is on the other end of it.'

Sarah looked at them both in horror, but the club's proprietor seemed to be both impressed and intrigued by Weissman's suggestion.

Casswell's smile did not falter. 'Certainly, but won't your volunteer be disappointed?' he said.

The host shrugged. 'It is of little consequence. There will always be other nights.'

On the far side of the stage the identity of the volunteer was beyond any doubt. A heavily set red-faced man in evening dress was watching the bound girl like a cat surveying a mouse.

'He has paid me well, and I will ensure he does not suffer unduly for his loss. But it would be good if he did not use the paddle tonight. He is a good man but heavy-handed. I am certain he will not mind if the show is good. It will be something a little different.' He looked at Sarah again, and then added, 'Although, of course she cannot work dressed like that.'

'Strip her, then,' said Weissman flatly, draining his glass. 'I'm sure your volunteer would be only too happy to give a helping hand.'

Despite the fact that Weissman was overstepping the mark, Casswell indicated that Sarah follow the proprietor up onto the little stage, and an odd hush descended over the club's patrons as she climbed slowly up alongside the bound girl.

Casswell knew Sarah well enough to recognise that she was nervous, her pulse fluttering in the bowl of her throat as she tried to swallow her apprehension. The club owner stepped up alongside her and invited the man – the volunteer – to come and assist in Sarah's disrobing. He needed no encouragement and clambered up to join them, eyes bright and eager. Wiping his mouth with the back of his hand he circled Sarah a few times, like some feral cat waiting for the moment to pounce.

'Come on,' he hissed, encouraging her to undress for him and the waiting crowd.

Sarah's eyes had darkened with apprehension, but very slowly she began to push the shoulder straps of her evening dress down; too slowly for the impatient volunteer, and he dragged them down to her waist in one violent move.

Casswell saw her flinch, her eyes flashing with a mixture of fury and fear. Even so, she looked exquisite in the lamplight, nipples pert and flushed, crowning her mouth-watering breasts. A faint murmur of approval rippled through the watching audience while the man ran his hands over her, hungrily almost, as if she was something edible.

Sarah shivered, and then he dragged the dress lower still, down over her hips, over her thighs until finally it fell to the floor. As he pulled it down he moved with it, falling to his knees, following its tantalising journey, and pressed a kiss to the flat plains of her belly and then the mound of her sex, tongue easing her labia apart.

Sarah gasped and closed her eyes as he bit and nibbled at the delicate flesh.

Casswell glanced around the audience. There was not a man who didn't envy him those exploratory kisses or the fragrance and taste of her body on his lips.

After a few moments, the host very gently eased the man away and back to his seat before turning to Sarah and handing her a flat leather paddle.

At once Casswell saw the conflict in her face. She was reluctant. It was not in Sarah's nature to inflict pain. The man lifted an eyebrow questioningly. The sense of anticipation on the room rose a degree or two, although Casswell did not doubt her obedience for a single moment. She would do exactly as she was instructed.

'Come on, give the thing to me,' the volunteer shouted from his seat. 'I'll show her what to do with it.'

Sarah stared at him; it was obvious he would thrash the bound girl cruelly, so very slowly her hand closed around the handle of the leather implement and she turned to face the captive girl.

Beads of sweat had lifted on the other girl's chest and trickled down between her breasts. She was trembling with anticipation. Casswell wondered how much the girl could hear through the mask. It appeared that she was straining to try and catch some clue to let her know what was going on.

Sarah then took up a position behind her and drew back the paddle. There was a tangible sense of excitement in the audience. The first blow was hardly more than a tap, but both girls squealed with shock and surprise.

'If you do not beat her properly, then our friend over there will be only too happy to take over from you,' the owner of the club warned.

Sarah bit her lip anxiously and drew back the paddle once more. This time the blow was harder and the bound slave girl jerked forward and let out a strangled cry of pain. The audience were totally entranced by the events on stage. Sarah struck again, her breasts swaying as she swung the paddle back and struck the tied creature. The girl shrieked. Sarah hit her again and then again, harder still, the crack of the leather against her delicate pale flesh lifting a blotchy red area. The girl moaned and hung limp as Sarah laid the paddle on again and again.

Now she had found a rhythm, and perspiration shimmered on her face and breasts. The girl in the harness writhed and twisted against her restraints, her nipples engorged and flushed with the intensity of the beating.

After six more strokes the proprietor smiled and took the paddle from Sarah's trembling fist and leaning close, whispered something into her ear. Casswell saw her stiffen, and then blush anxiously. He could not hear what was said, but Sarah hesitated for a moment, and then moved around the bound girl and dropped to her knees in front of her. It was a breathtaking moment.

The girl was panting, hanging still in anticipation of whatever might follow. Sarah hesitated again, and then held the girl's thighs pulled her close. Gently she began to lick the girl, her tongue working its way into the fragrant folds, her fingers exploring the slick depths.

The girl began to move, but this time her gyrations were of pleasure, not pain, and as she writhed in time with Sarah's tongue and lips, the owner of the club released her ankles by unlocking the manacles. It was then that Casswell understood what was going on. The man who had earlier volunteered to beat the girl clambered back onto stage, his erection clear in his evening trousers. As he walked across the little stage he undid his shirt and unfastened his fly. Standing behind the bound girl, he encircled her waist with one arm, pulled her back to him and without prelude drove his cock deep inside her. Then, withdrawing for a moment, he lifted her and thrust his cock into Sarah's mouth. She gasped, the girl's juices coating her chin as he fucked her mouth, then he withdrew from her and drove again into the girl sandwiched between them.

Caught up in the lewd performance, Sarah lapped at the junction where rigid cock penetrated the succulent quim, nuzzling and sucking at their throbbing flesh.

It was a stunning image; Sarah kneeling, covered in a

gloss of sweat, crouched between the legs of the bound girl while from behind the man fucked her long and hard.

It did not take long for another of the guests, at the invitation of the owner, to clamber onto the stage, drop to his knees and thrust his cock into Sarah, his fingers circling her waist to seek out her pleasure-bud.

Casswell refilled his champagne glass and looked around with a satisfied smile. His lovely pupil had done him proud, and there was not a man in the room who did not envy him.

Sarah was relieved when the club's owner showed her through to a backroom behind the stage where she had the chance to shower and get dressed. Her masked companion appeared to have been taken elsewhere, so that someone else could enjoy her favours.

The atmosphere in the nightclub was now electric, and with the 'cabaret' over, several other girls had drifted down from an upstairs room. Sarah and the other girl had clearly been an appetiser for the patrons; the champagne was flowing and they were eager to savour the arriving girls' attentions. Amongst the mêlée Casswell and Weissman were surrounded by a small crowd, and the proprietor was eager to introduce their honoured guest.

It was less than fifteen minutes later when Sarah emerged from the dressing room, but as she stepped into the dingy passageway someone caught hold of her arm.

'This way,' he said.

Sarah jumped and looked up into the eyes of Uri Weissman's driver, too surprised to resist him. He was a tall guy and well built, and he met her enquiring look with a surly smile.

'I've come to collect you,' he told her, guiding her towards the back door. 'I have to take you back to Mr

Weissman's place. His orders.'

'But what about Dr Casswell?' Sarah began, looking back towards the bar area, but rather disturbingly, she could not see any familiar faces now amongst those gathered closest to the door at the end of the passage.

The driver shrugged. 'I've no idea. I'm like you, I just do what I'm told and don't ask questions.'

Outside, Weissman's limousine was parked in the shadows of a warehouse. As they set off across the car park the driver, uninvited, put his arm around her shoulders. It was an oddly possessive gesture, and not one Sarah much cared for. And away from the noise of the club, she had the distinct and unsettling sensation that a pair of eyes was following her. She glanced back anxiously over her shoulder, saw a dark silhouette by the back door of the club watching her, and new it was Uri Weissman.

Sarah Morgan was a real find, and the Austrian was annoyed that Casswell would not part with her, but as he watched her slip elegantly into the back of his car, casting a nervous look back in his direction as the driver closed the door for her, he smiled thinly.

Chapter Nine

A few hours later, back at Weissman's house, Casswell stretched, slipped off his evening jacket and then poured himself a brandy over ice from the tray beside his bed. He thought about calling for Chang to give him a massage, and then decided against it; it was very late.

The doors to the balcony were open and the drapes fluttered in the warm night breeze, which carried the smell of the sea and the sound of distant music. It had been a long day and he was looking forward to relaxing with the latest transcripts of Beatrice's diary before going to sleep.

The meeting of the museum trustees and then their sojourn to the club had proved interesting. And not just because of Sarah's performance on stage, although it had been quite stunning. He was delighted with his pupil's progress; she never ceased to enchant and surprise him. Sarah Morgan had come a long way since those first tentative steps back at Casswell Hall.

During her performance the bar had filled with more patrons, amongst them several of the guests from the museum party and, once everyone had partaken of some drink, Casswell had learned more about how it was that Beatrice's diaries ended up secreted away in an isolated little Turkish port town.

He glanced at his watch, wondering whether Sarah was asleep. She would be intrigued to hear how the books were brought to the port by an uneducated monk who believed he was taking sacred documents away for safekeeping, and the friar who rode with him, who knew exactly what it was the books contained and hoped to use them to secure himself a fortune once he settled in the port. It was the friar who had first started the secret society that flourished just beneath the thin veneer of normal port life. A cadre of educated, well connected men who understood the pleasure of the whip; men who kept slaves and harems of their own. Casswell received several interesting invitations during the few hours he spent at the club. The men he had spoken to were all fellow connoisseurs who were waiting for the completion of his translation with bated breath.

Weissman's mood had improved, too, over the course of the evening. Casswell had been concerned that his refusal to part with Sarah might jeopardise not just their relationship, but also his mission in Turkey. Uri Weissman was most certainly not a man to be crossed.

A soft knock at the door broke Casswell's chain of thought. It opened, and Anna Weissman stood there, dressed in a fine cotton chemise that did very little to disguise the curves of her exquisite body.

'I thought you might like a little company,' she said, not waiting to be invited in. 'I can't see why I could not have gone to your stuffy dinner party.'

Casswell smiled. 'You would have been bored senseless. Do you want a brandy?' he offered.

Anna nodded.

'No servants to deliver you tonight?' he mused, adding ice to her glass. 'No games? No magic carpet?'

Anna took the drink her offered her and laughed. 'No, not tonight, Rigel. Just me and my curiosity. I want to have more… a lot more.'

It was Casswell's turn to laugh. 'Now you see, there is the rub, Anna. The true submissive would never dream of asking for more. You just want to experiment and explore a little. This is lust, not submission.'

She took an elegant sip of the brandy and moved closer, seductively. 'Is that such a bad thing?' she purred. 'Rigel, I need a guide. I need someone who knows. I can hardly ask my brother, now can I?'

Casswell eyed her thoughtfully and indicated the ottoman at the foot of the bed. 'You know lesson one; total obedience, and total trust.'

'Haven't we already done that?' she said, pouting. 'The other night?'

Casswell's expression hardened. 'And total silence.'

Without another word, Anna sat on the blanket box, drained her glass and set it aside, held the hem of her chemise and pulled it over her head. There was no getting away from the fact that she had a quite magnificent body.

Casswell picked up the expensive little sliver of fabric from the floor and ripped a strip off the hem. Anna's eyes widened in shock, but if she was planning to protest she wisely thought better off it.

Casswell blindfolded her. He could see that she was apprehensive, her breath fast and shallow, little beads of perspiration dampening her brow. He smiled; it was time Miss Weissman experienced a little fear.

He settled her back on the ottoman, and ripping more of her chemise he tied her wrists to the legs of the chest and then, having slipped a cushion under her hips to make her body more accessible, secured both her ankles. She whimpered as he tightened the ties.

She looked quite exquisite – a luscious feast. Casswell stroked her pensively, and then taking an ice-cube from her brandy glass, slid it around the dip of her toned belly. Anna gasped and shivered. Very slowly he circled each nipple in turn, and watched them hardened and rise like rosebuds. Her whole body trembled in anticipation of what might follow. With deliberation Casswell poured the last of his brandy over her quim, and then began to lap at it while his fingers pressed into those silken sex lips – lips that were getting wetter and wetter with every passing moment.

Just as Anna began to relax and move with him, Casswell palmed the remains of the ice-cubes into his mouth and then pressed hard against her tight pussy.

Ice and fire. Anna Weissman's body flexed, and she mewled in shock and delight as he returned his attentions to the swollen ridge of her clitoris.

'You... you *bastard*,' she gasped, trying to wriggle away from his tormenting caresses, but Casswell merely used his tongue to push the ice deeper still.

Writhing beneath him, Anna Weissman cried out in a heady mixture of pain and pleasure as he brought her to the point of orgasm again and again, but skilfully denying her the final prize. He applied a pair of silver nipple clamps to the exquisite peaks that tipped her full breasts, making her mewl and gasp all the more earnestly, brushing them, making her cry out as the pleasure and pain coursed through her veins. As she lifted herself to try and ensnare him, to try and drive him over the edge, he took another little something from his box of toys, and slid an anal plug into that tight dark space that as she writhed against him just begged to be filled.

Anna gasped as it popped home, and relentlessly, Casswell teased her supine and bound body, expertly brushing her clitoris with his thumb so that shards of pleasure spasmed through her. It was such a shame that she was Uri Weissman's sister, for the more he saw of her the more potential she showed. It crossed his mind, as she moved against his knowing touch, to take her back to England. He had enough contacts to have her placed with someone who could deal with her wilfulness and bring out her full potential.

Beneath him Anna was deliriously begging for satisfaction.

'Please, please,' she sobbed, almost in tears, trying desperately to lift her hips to his touch, to take her to that all-consuming place, completing the sensual arc he had begun.

Then Casswell slipped his hands under her taut thighs, lifted her towards him as much as the bonds would allow, and drove his cock deep inside her, making her scream in delight, and at the same time his educated fingers renewed their attention, circling the throbbing scarlet bud that lay between those succulent lips.

This time there was no going back. Anna Weissman began to buck and twist, pushing herself hard onto his cock, crying out again and again as the waves of orgasm crashed over her. As her climax finally engulfed them both her quim closed tight around his cock like a hungry mouth and pulled him with her down onto the shores of oblivion.

At the door of Casswell's room, Sarah hesitated for a moment. She wanted to go in and tell him that she had increasing suspicions about Weissman's motives. She also longed to feel the comfort of his arms, the reassurance that only a master could give a slave.

She stood by the door for a moment composing herself and her thoughts, agonising over how to broach the subject of his associate – it certainly was not going to be the easiest conversation she'd ever had.

There was no reply to her tentative knock, so she tried again – still no reply, but some part of her knew it was important that she told Casswell about her concerns regarding Weissman. So against her better judgement, she opened the door and pushed it open.

And what Sarah saw was not Casswell alone or a sleep, but hunched over the tied body of a woman – a woman she instantly recognised only too well as Anna Weissman, who was even now in the throes of a very animated orgasm. Casswell's expression was taut with pleasure, his cock buried to the hilt in the female as he rode her bucking form.

Sarah tried to suppress her squeal of dismay, and took a step back. The lurid tableau hit her like a body blow. She felt lost, both betrayed and alone in a world that had no place for her.

As she was about to turn and flee to the temporary sanctuary of her room, Casswell looked up at her. 'Sarah?' he grunted, his teeth clenched with the effort of fucking the woman.

She did not wait to hear what else he had to say, if anything. Instead she ran from the room as fast as she could, along the landing to her room and slammed the door shut, leaning back against it and panting heavily. With a racing heart she was not altogether surprised to see Chang waiting by the bed.

'Where have you been?' he asked.

It was all too much for Sarah. She burst into tears and through the sobs told him, and then unable to hold back, described her intense feelings at discovering Anna Weissman in the arms of her master.

Behind her blindfold, still bound tight on the ottoman, Anna Weissman struggled to catch her breath, gasping as the tremors of passion slowly ebbed away. It felt amazing to let go, to let another take control completely; unable to object or to resist the advances of her lover, she'd had no option but to submit and drown in a sea of ecstasy. Her whole body ached with it; her mind was awash with the intense bliss that had roared through her at the approach to and point of orgasm.

And Casswell was *so* good. She needed to find a way to have more. It made her every previous sexual experience fade into insignificance – his knowing mastery of her mind and body almost driving her to the very shores of madness.

As he began to untie her she wondered about Sarah. She thought back to her overwhelming moment of climax, and how he had called out his slave girl's name. She was not offended; it seemed even when he had been making love to her, his mind was on his darling girl.

How very touching.

Chapter Ten

'What on earth did you mean, bursting in on me like that?' Casswell's tone was icy cold.

Sarah looked up at him tentatively. She knew that this was not the way she was supposed to behave, however much she was provoked. Surely her time at Casswell Hall had taught her that, if nothing else? Total obedience was expected. Wasn't that the very first thing Dr Casswell had taught her?

She did not know whether to apologise or stay silent, and a single tear meandered down her cheek.

Casswell saw it, and despite his annoyance, his expression softened. 'If it makes you feel any better,' he said, 'I know you don't like it here, and I no longer trust Uri Weissman, so as soon as we've finished with the diary we'll leave. We'll go home. Will that cheer you up a little?'

Sarah sniffed, nodded, and gave him a weak smile, the tears sparkling in her wide, hopeful eyes. He stroked her cheek, smudging away the tear with his thumb, and although the touch was tender, nothing could quite disguise the fact that he was comforting a possession.

'How very touching,' said Weissman, wandering into the breakfast room. 'So what is this – a little heart to heart?' He was dressed in a long robe, with nothing on his feet. 'Hardly what I'd expect to see between master and slave, Rigel,' he added, somewhat derisively. 'Anyway, how did you enjoy the club last night?'

Casswell smiled and settled at the table. 'Fine, thank you, Uri.'

'And how was my sister?'

Casswell's expression remained unchanged. 'Also fine, thank you.'

Sarah glanced warily across at the Austrian, detecting an edge in his voice. As their eyes met he attempted a smile, but fooled nobody. Sarah knew without a doubt that he was jealous of Casswell, both professionally and socially, and that made him dangerous, and she sensed they had to be careful.

Weissman waved the waiting houseboy over and had him pour the coffee. 'Good, I'm so pleased,' he went on. 'But all work and no play makes Jack a dull boy. Isn't that what you English say? So,' he continued without pausing for a response, 'I have arranged for us to go out on a boat. A little sightseeing, a little bay hopping, and then a barbecue on a beach in a cove a few miles up the coast. One of the museum trustees, who is particularly keen to ingratiate himself to you, has offered us his yacht for the day.'

Casswell sipped his coffee. 'That's very kind, Uri,' he said, 'but I'm afraid that Sarah and I have to work today – I'm sorry.'

Weissman smiled without mirth. 'Oh, don't worry, I am aware of your schedule, Rigel, and it has not been overlooked. The plan is to leave early this evening.'

Casswell nodded graciously – what else could he do? 'In that case, we'll accept,' he said. 'And now if you will excuse us, we must prepare to leave for the museum.'

As they went back upstairs Sarah could not help but wonder what the cruise might entail, and was overcome with a bad feeling. The increasing mistrust between the two men was becoming perilous, and she suspected that Uri Weissman had a few tricks up his sleeve to get what he wanted.

After the events of the previous day and evening it was absolute bliss to be back in the cool dark vault sitting beside Dr Casswell, piecing together the events that surrounded Beatrice, and as Sarah began to transcribe the notes her thoughts rapidly drifted away from Weissman and back to Beatrice de Fleur, currently incarcerated in the isolated abbey far away from her lord and master.

...It seems that I am alone now, lost and cold and at the mercy of the abbot and his debauched and cruel womenfolk. Sister Judith is proving true to her word. Every day here I pay for what she sees as my transgressions. I sense that she plans to break me and make me pay for my part in her sister's betrayal, whether I deserve to be treated badly or not.

Here in the abbey I am expected to be at the beck and call of whoever shouts the loudest, and whomever I cannot serve has reason to punish me for failing them. I am so tired and so lost.

For weeks now I have longed for word of my master, praying that he would send for me, praying that he would have a change of heart although knowing, hope against hope, that it could not be true; who am I, a mere servant girl compared to the Lady Cassandra?

Each day I wake in the bed of whoever has had use of me the night before. Oft time it is the abbot himself, who although he has a taste for boys sees me, quite slim built and still young and fresh, as the best of both worlds. He likes it most when I let him take me from behind, invading my bottom, his gnarled and veined old cock buried to the hilt while he mauls my breasts and bites my neck and shoulders. For such and old man he has an insatiable appetite. Each morning he wakes ever eager for more, always hungry, his manhood stiff and ready he pulls me to him to suck his cock, or ride him until his seed and passion is spent. He tells often that morning pleasure sates the aches and base desires that plague a man of the cloth, and relief before morning prayers means he can turn his thoughts to higher things and allow him to go about the more normal duties of a man in his position with a clear and lucid mind.

It seems that only after dark is the rest of the abbey a den of debauchery such as I saw on the night of my arrival. During the day we are expected to carry on much as any other holy order – although I feel that nothing can quite disguise the taste and flavour of lust that lingers here in the walls like the taint of smoke.

Each day when morning prayers are over Sister Judith puts me to work, cleaning and washing and doing such menial tasks as she feels might break my spirit.

Often she will call me to attend in the visitors parlour if travellers and pilgrims happen by, my body barely covered, dressed in little more than rags. The reputation of the Abbey of St Joseph is widespread. Some travellers come miles out of their way, far from the normal pilgrims' route to take advantage of our hospitality. Most have heard of the goings on and come to sample the buxom charms of the sisters Mary and Therese. While the sisters ply their trade, one working on each other with tongue and fingers and that great carved phallus, inviting the pilgrims to join them, I am there to wait on table, bringing in wine and such victuals as are required, and when the watchers are heated from the show to be used as they see fit.

Sister Judith has had my hair hacked short, so I look more like a youth than ever. I am dressed in a simple unbleached shift that does little to flatter my body, but little to hide me either. It seems that lost as I am there are men who prefer the submission of a true slave to the bawdy charms and demands of Junoesque sisters.

'Come close, little one,' they whisper, as I hurry by with my tray or basket or jug of beer. Moving closer – for it seems I am ever under the watchful eye of Sister Judith, and know I will be beaten if I upset the pilgrims or deny them what they crave so badly – I close my eyes as they slide their coarse hands up under my robes to seek out those secret places. Some wish to fondle my breasts, or slip their hand between my legs, fingers seeking entry, some cold and brutal, some gentle, and all shades in between.

And then, when their blood is up, they look towards Judith who for the price of a few coppers or a bottle of brandy or some trinket that catches her eye, directs them to take me out to the stables. My body is bought and bartered and used for coppers. Out in the stable they mount and take me like some domestic animal, a beast of burden fit only for one thing.

But Judith will not break me, I have sworn that. I may be a slave here in the abbey, but I have known love and joy and the great passion of true desire. I know the way my master's face lit when he saw me, I know the feeling in my heart, and in my belly as he called me to him and as he took me to his bed. Even now, in the dark of the cellar, I can smell his body and feel the weight of him moving against me and feel of his cock pressing home. Nothing Judith can ever do to me will or can take those feelings and memories away.

During the day I turn my hand to more domestic matters, and while I work I dream of life back in the castle with my master. I had thought to make friends with the hunchback boy, but his mind is too muddled by lust and too simple to hide it. He frightens me, although I have tried hard to win him over with kindness and gifts of food, but even so, I am loath to be alone with him for he is strong and rough. He likes to touch me and Judith does little to discourage it.

Many come this way, and every traveller who comes through the gates, every man who takes me out to the stable, every woman who bids me lay with her and show her delights that no man could match, I have asked them all after the fate of my lord. I hang onto every scrap of news however small, however unlikely its truth. I have passed those things through my mind like a miser counting his hoard. I heard tales of good harvest, of festivals and hunts and fine feasts. But then today came the news that I had dreaded, from a monk travelling with a party of merchants and their ladies.

I was taking ale through to the main hall and caught him between the rigours of his devotions and heading for what I suspect he already knew would be high jinx in the hall.

'So know you anything of his lordship?' I asked, replenishing his mug from the jug of ale I carried. I had already told him that I'd served in that household caring for and teaching my master's children.

'Aye, indeed I do,' said the monk, cheerfully. 'We are on our way to that very castle now,' he embellished, 'for the wedding celebrations of the man of whom you speak and the Lady Cassandra. Would you like me to pass on your good wishes?' His words were a spiteful joke, for what was the worth of good wishes from a slave?

But the joke was lost on me as my heart sank like a stone – if only he knew how far. I shook my head and thanked him, but my good wishes, even if they reached their destination, would cause only more trouble.

My eyes filled with heartfelt tears just from the very thought of it.

It was late, the merchants' ladies had retired after dinner and the rigours of the day, so only the men and those who lived in the abbey were gathered in the great hall. Drunk from ale they began to call for an entertainment, and of course Sister Judith and the abbot were only too happy to oblige. For a price.

As I walked in with the ale Judith caught hold of my arm. 'Come, girl,' she said. I had spent most of the evening in the kitchen and was surprised she called me, as it was always the sisters of the abbey who put on such entertainment if it was to be had. It was this that the abbey was famous for.

On the dais the abbot waved to one of the monks, Brother Joshua, who helped him with all the affairs both godly and base at the abbey. The man banged his staff on the floor to catch the attention of the revellers.

'Tonight, gentlemen,' he announced, 'as you are all men of means, we are to have an auction of our more saleable items for the poor of the parish.'

'We don't want t'pay no more money for no more relics, nor more prayers said for our mortal souls, no more old bones,' heckled one drunken voice from the pit, and those gathered laughed.

The monk laughed too. 'Tis a good thing, for none are on offer, brother. What we had in mind was the sale of revel; a little pleasure.' As he spoke Judith pushed me further onto the dais.

'Ah, here we are,' said Brother Joshua, catching my arm and pulling me into the light. 'Here we have a fine example of the very thing I mean. Our first lot; what am I bid for a night with this fine and comely wench.'

There was a low babble and murmur of unrest from amongst the crowd, but Joshua was not thrown. 'Come, good gentleman, a girl such as this – for the night – what will you pay? Surely such gentlemen as you know what to do with a willing wench after dark, or am I mistaken? Would you prefer that I drag out old Sister Agnes to sing to us and strum a little on her harp? Come, who would like to plant a root in his fine furrow?' As he spoke, Brother Joshua grabbed me around the waist and cupped my sex. I tried to pull away but he held me tight.

'Don't fight me, girl,' he hissed, from behind a fixed smile. The men laughed, and it seemed then and only then did the good burghers catch the monk's drift.

In an instant I felt all eyes in the room turn on me. I reddened furiously, and Brother Joshua unhanded me and then said, 'Come along, no need to be coy. Show the gentlemen what is on offer, girl.'

My colour deepened further still, but I could see the thunderous expression on Sister Judith's face, so gathering my courage I was about to bend and catch hold of the hem of my shift when the hunchback boy leapt onto the stage and, snatching the open collar of the shift, ripped it off me. I screamed, and in shock tried to cover myself, but the men bayed with drunken delight. I can only imagine that Sister Judith ordered him up onto the stage, for I cannot believe he would have done it without encouragement.

'She's a little too coy for my tastes,' called a red-faced hulk of a man from the floor. 'I prefer my women a little more compliant.' He chuckled rudely. 'Warm and willing.'

Brother Joshua smiled. 'Oh, don't be fooled, good sir, she is more than willing,' he said. 'Turn for us, girl, and let the good men see what it is they are bidding for.'

I turned slowly, feeling the avaricious eyes of every man upon me.

'Who would like to come up here and inspect the goods?' Brother Joshua offered, and the fat man was on his feet almost before the monk's words had done.

'I sir,' he said, and clambering onto the dais he began to inspect me. Running his hands over my flesh, touching and mauling my breasts, hands crawling up over my thighs and into those most secret places between my legs. Each touch brought a whoop of delight from the other men in the crowd, and I looked down at the floor, too ashamed to meet the man's eye.

He grunted, 'And what do I get if I buy her, sir?'

The monk grinned. 'Anything she has, good sir. Take her just as you will from now until the cock crows.' He sniggered evilly, and added, 'Or your cock gives up the ghost!'

'And then, if you can think of nothing else, get her to service your wife!' another yelled from the floor.

There was a great roar of laughter, and although the big man laughed, I noticed there was no warmth in his eyes.

'Anything?' he qualified.

'Indeed, anything.' Brother Joshua nodded obsequiously. 'Anything at all. Pay the price and beat your peers and you shall have her.' Then turning his attention back to the other revellers he called, 'Now, who among you will start the bidding?'

The big man settled back on a bench. 'I'll give you a gold piece for her,' he announced proudly.

There was a hush amongst the other men; it was a high bid and one I doubted would be topped by any of them for the sake of a little sport.

'Start lower, Bay,' complained the man who had heckled him moments earlier, 'so's we might all have a little fun – otherwise there is no sport in this. One bid, one call – where's the enjoyment in that?'

The man Bay's belligerent countenance did not falter. 'I don't want sport, I want pleasure,' he gruffly pointed out. 'My own pleasure, not yours. If there are no more bids to be had then I would take my prize.' He looked towards me and my blood ran cold.

'Indeed, Master Bay,' grovelled the monk. 'Are there any more bids? No man among you can top him?'

There was not a murmur in the hall, and Bay looked triumphant. 'There we are, then, the matter is settled. Here is my money for your precious poor.' He dropped a single gold coin onto Joshua's greedily open palm. 'Now I would liked her tied, blindfolded and taken up to my chamber.'

The monk lifted an eyebrow. 'As you will, sir, but what about your lady?'

Bay's expression hardened further. 'It is no business of yours, monk. She does as she is told. I paid a fair price for her too, and that bargain was not just for the night.'

Brother Joshua nodded, clearly not wanting to antagonise the brute. 'As you like,' he snivelled.

The hunchback boy grabbed me and practically dragged me from the dais, as onto it from the far side stepped the buxom Sister Therese. The men instantly forgot my fate and whooped and cheered and stamped. It seemed that her reputation preceded her.

Back in the shadows, Sister Judith tied my wrists and blindfolded me with a cotton rag, while the boy held me tight. Watching her face in the instant before she covered my eyes, as she glanced around the crowd, I thought then that the vicious crone knew this man, Bay, and had specially arranged for me to go on stage first. The thought made my blood run cold.

Once I was tied the hunchback picked me up and threw me over his shoulder as if I was no more than a sack of feathers. By the time we reached the merchant's chamber I was sick with fear, and with the jolting and banging of my body against the boy's twisted frame. It seemed to take an eternity, as we slowly climbed dark and cold steps, and then ahead of us a door opened and I guessed we had arrived. The boy set me down, thankfully on my feet.

In the chilly darkness and the silence my mind reached out to try and piece together such clues as there were about where I was and whom I was with.

'Well,' said a male voice that I recognised instantly as belonging to Bay. 'What think you of her, my pretty? Here, would you like to touch her, or would you prefer that I set her to work on you now? Or shall I make sure she understands that here I am the master and that what I say is the law. What say you?'

I heard not a word in answer, but instead he pushed me onto my knees. Unable to save myself from the aggressive thrust my head hit the floor and I cried out in pain and shock, but to no avail. He ran a hand over my shoulders and back, locking his fingers in my hair and lifting my face towards his unseen companion.

'What do you think, my dear? Pretty enough?' Still I heard no reply, and then he continued his exploration, his coarse and heavy hands working up over my buttocks, sliding down between the cheeks, exploring the secret places that lay between. 'Young, tight, and willing,' he said. 'Perhaps I shall leave you here in her place and take her with me. What do you think, precious? Would that please you, to live a slave's life?'

For an instant there was stillness. I felt the glow of the log fire warming my flank, and then over the crackle and the hiss a more unpleasant sound, something that sparked a memory that for a moment I could not quite place, but an instant later I knew exactly what it was. A broad belt or strap hit me hard across my back, making me cry out with pain. All thoughts were lost as the sensation roared through me, making me scream and instinctively try to crawl away.

Before the second blow struck Bay hauled me to my feet, and grabbing hold of my wrists, jerked them high above my head. He was a man of immense strength, and I could not resist him or fight him. With an arm around my waist he lifted me bodily and hung me from something, so that my feet just rested on the floor. As I twisted to find a sort of balance my face brushed against heavy fabric, and I realised he had hung me from the bed frame.

And I paid the price for my fear and that attempt to crawl away. The next blow caught me high across the back, curling around me like a lick of fire, and before I could recover there was another blow, a loud crack, and another and another, each as hot as a flame. I cried out as the pain gripped me, and then realised I was not alone. Another voice begged for mercy in the darkness beside me – another female voice.

'Stop, my lord, please stop,' she wept. 'Do not beat her any more. I will do exactly as you ask… I will, I will!'

Bay sniggered, again without humour. 'What, lady, you want me to stop? Then will you take her place, my dear? Would you like to feel the kiss of the strap across that delicate flesh of yours?'

There was silence, and the belt found its mark again. I pulled and twisted against my restraints.

'I will do as you bid me,' she said. 'Stop, please, I am yours, sire, to do with as you will.' The voice was firmer now, and it made me wonder if this was a game they played.

Another excruciating stroke, and my body contorted under the belt's cruel kiss.

'Oh, you will do as I bid, pretty one, even if I have to

tie you myself. In fact, perhaps I will. 'Twill be a pretty picture, my sweet young wife bound to the bed, legs open, so that she might be serviced by the tongue of a slave girl. What say you, my sweet?'

I heard a whimper, and then the same gentle voice said, 'As you will, my lord, as you will.'

'Then that is what I will,' Bay chuckled. 'Take off your petticoats, lady, lay down and defy me not.'

As I hung there, sore and bruised, I heard his woman as he worked, sobbing. And then minutes later he cut me down and freed my hands, and I already knew full well what he expected of me.

Still blindfolded, he guided me down onto the bed and there I found her, this wife of his, her skin as smooth as alabaster, and she trembled as I gripped her calf to steady myself. He pressed me onto my knees.

'Come on, girl, do not pretend that you don't know what I want from you,' he snarled. 'I want you to give this debauched lady of mine those unnatural pleasures and caresses that she shared with the good sisters at the convent, that taught her to value them above my cock. Or would you prefer the kiss of my belt to the kiss of my wife's lascivious body?'

Slave or no slave, the lash is a cruel mistress, and so it was I began a steady progress of pleasuring his wife's body, and did all that I was ordered, my hands seeking the curve of her breasts and the soft narrowing of her waist.

Although she was slim her breasts were heavy and firm, the nipples small and tight like the bud of a flower, making me think she was young too.

But it seemed that this tenderness was not what Bay wanted, or at least not this alone. I drew one of her nipples deep into my mouth, and the girl groaned and writhed as

I began to play and suck at those peaks – for we knew this oral work, this delicate tracery and teasing was the forerunner and pattern of my lapping and sucking and fingering of her sex. In the darkness behind my blindfold all was reduced to pure touch, my fingers becoming my eyes.

While I held one breast to my lips my other hand traced a pattern down over her flat belly to the gentle rise of her sex mound. Her hair there was like a glossy pelt, smooth and silky under my fingertips. I wondered as they bade entry what tenderness this girl had ever known as wife to so cruel a man.

But it was no business of mine, and Bay had other things on his mind.

'Get your face there, girl,' he ordered, 'I want you to make this frigid bitch cry out with desire, make her weep and wail for me to fill her sweet little cunt with my seed. Let me tell you, girl, you are the tease for the stallion.'

I did as he demanded; I kissed a path down where my fingers had been just an instant earlier and pressed my lips to her quim. She was as soft and fragrant as new mown hay and eagerly lifted up for me to have use of her. As I slipped a finger inside she was wet and hot with excitement, and I wondered again if perhaps it was his cruelty that made her ready for the fray. Bay gripped my head and pushed me closer still. My tongue lapped and pressed home at those places that make a woman writhe with joy.

As she began to twist and buck under my ministrations I felt a hand sliding between my legs. It seems that the stallion wanted not just his own filly but the tease as well. Then he mounted me from behind, driving into me, sinking his fierce cock well home. My back was raw from his strap, my mouth full of the flavours and excitement of his wife, and my sex full of his cock.

He groaned as my body closed around him, and he bucked and drove into me all the harder, making me cry out with pain and pleasure. His fingers agitated my pleasure-bud, and then grabbing my hand he pressed it up between my legs so that I might pleasure myself as well.

It was a potent mix, him driving deeper and deeper into me, his wife lifting herself that I could lick her all the more avidly, her juices so plentiful that they trickled down my chin.

And then, just at the moment when I felt she and I and Bay could hold back no more, he dragged me bodily from his wife and drove full tilt into her. She screamed out in a mixture of shock and delight, and as I rolled away and pulled off my blindfold I saw him riding her like a cock stallion, fingers pressed tight up against her quim to bring her to the end of that long ride.

She was young indeed, and as pretty as a picture. It stuck me, looking into her face, flushed and tight in the throes of passion, that we could easily have been sisters.

'Here wench,' Bay grunted, when the tremors of passion had left them both. I crawled up onto the bed alongside them. The girl, heavy-eyed, tired and sweating from her exertions, rolled me onto my back amongst the tangle of bedclothes and took the place I had so recently abandoned. It seemed Bay was right; she had certainly learnt well from someone how best to pleasure a female, and with her tongue and knowing fingers she brought me to a lovely climax. And it was enough to rekindle the fire in Bay's great belly, and he fucked me soundly.

And so it was all night long that one lust would lead to another, until at last, in the wee small hours, we curled up in each others' arms and slept that way until morning…

In the shadowy gloom of the museum vault Sarah looked up from the pages she had been reading and putting onto disk. Next to her Casswell was still hard at work, his expression focused, eyes and hands working in perfect harmony as he scanned down the page of the book, translating as he went, recording the words in his distinctive handwriting.

He had already begun another page, another entry, and Sarah wished with all her heart that she could read the script for herself so she could find out what would become of the girl she saw almost as a reflection of herself. Their fates seemed somehow inexplicably interwoven through the mists of time.

Chapter Eleven

Later that evening, Casswell waited at the handrail watching Sarah climb the gangway of the yacht that was to take them out for the short cruise. The day, which had been oppressively hot, was thankfully cooling. Work had gone well, and despite his niggling anxieties about Uri Weissman's motives, Casswell felt in need of relaxation, although he was still far from certain about the company they were in.

Weissman and his sister were standing by the stern rail with their host, and were watching Sarah's progress too. Casswell had instructed Chang to accompany them; he was feeling it was becoming increasingly important to have more than one pair of eyes with him, and certainly Chang's loyalty and commitment to Casswell were never in doubt. The oriental followed Sarah up onto the yacht, his face as impassive and unreadable as always.

Across the bay the sun was slowly setting in the cloudless sky. A refreshing wind whipped across the tiny harbour, stirring the sails and rigging of the boats moored alongside the quay, lifting the sea into tiny white peaks, while gulls and other seabirds hung in the thermals, spiralling lazily in the early evening sky.

Casswell looked back towards the town. White houses in a mixture of Moorish, Ottoman, and Turkish styles clung to the steep hillside, glowing unnaturally in the fading light. The trip to Turkey was not going as he had anticipated. Whilst the translation was proceeding well, he knew with increasing certainty that he could not trust

Weissman. It still surprised him, for Uri had been in his circle of associates – part of an elite group – for many years, and Casswell had always prided himself on being a good judge of character. Although he and Weissman were not close, he had most certainly never considered being betrayed by him. But then, jealously and envy were a volatile and dangerous combination.

Sarah's expression softened as she looked at him, and then she paused at the top of the gangway to take in the view from the deck, the sea breeze teasing anyone lucky enough to look at her, by moulding her delicate dress to her delicious breasts and her shapely thighs.

The little cove wrapped its rocky arms tightly around a shallow saucer of dark blue sea, giving shelter to a mix of pleasure craft and fishing boats. It was a beautifully clear evening, golden light rippling across the water, fractured by the swell. Casswell and Chang were no more than a few steps away, and she was glad they were there; with them both onboard she felt much safer.

It seemed they were the last to board, for she and Chang were barely up the gangway before some crew began to make ready to sail.

'We've been waiting for you,' said Weissman impatiently, heading towards them. 'Let me introduce you to our host. Casswell, you remember Fredo, you met him at the club last night.'

Anna Weissman, sipping champagne, smiled enigmatically in Casswell's direction. 'Don't let him bully you,' she laughed, lifting her glass in welcome.

Sarah looked down, a part of her not wanting to meet Anna's eye, for the last time she had seen the blonde was in Casswell's room, tied down and in the throes of an explosive orgasm. Beside her, Casswell politely extended his hand to their host. She remembered seeing the man at the club, although she had not known his name or been introduced. Fredo was an elderly, balding man of indeterminate race, whose eyes where little more than dark slits in an oddly reptilian face.

Sarah glanced around while Fredo explained to Casswell and Weissman the finer points of his yacht. The main deck was covered with an awning that created a pool of shade and a windbreak, and it was here that several of the other passengers were being served cocktails and *hors-d'oeuvres* by uniformed stewards. Sarah recognised several of the faces from the dinner of the museum trustees, and others from the club.

She was delighted to see that Mustafa Aziz did not appear to have been included on the guest list. Fredo's conversation was dull, and Sarah's attention continued to wander. A uniformed steward handed her a glass of champagne while she casually watched the other guests amble about and mingle.

'Don't tell me you're bored already, darling,' said Anna Weissman with a sensuous smile, gaining a fresh glass of bubbly as another steward-born tray passed by. 'Our little pleasure trip has hardly begun.'

Before Sarah could reply Weissman turned to join them. 'So, are you enjoying your time in Turkey?' he asked Sarah, and his arrogant smile did not falter as his voice dropped to a purr. 'You know I will have you, Sarah, by hook or by crook. Your beloved master is only human, everything has its price, and I am a very determined individual.'

He stared at her, quite obviously enjoying her discomfort, and then catching hold of her arm he said, 'Come along, let me introduce you to some of my friends.' And then in a quieter voice he added, 'And Anna, why don't you go and rescue the good doctor? I'm sure he would appreciate being saved from Fredo's clutches.' Sarah was about to protest, but Weissman's fingers tightened around her upper-arm and he guided her towards a group of men gathered by the starboard rail.

The crew were making ready to leave the shelter of the port. The engine, that had been barely idling since they came aboard, the sound no more than a backdrop to the gentle music and light chatter and laughter, began to work more earnestly as the captain slowly manoeuvred the boat out of the little bay into open water.

As Sarah obediently exchanged social pleasantries with the other guests, Weissman at her side, she was aware of the way he looked at her – and he was not alone. Her exhibition at the club had obviously stayed in the minds of the audience and whetted a few appetites.

Although at first glance the other guests appeared totally at ease, eating and drinking and chatting as the yacht glided through the waves towards the open sea, there was a real and very tangible hint of expectation in the air. It was something Sarah was beginning to recognise; that thrill, like the smell of smoke gathering in the air that held the promise of the fire to come.

Not that she and Anna were the only female guests. Several girls wandered around the deck, barefoot and wearing skimpy dresses or little crop-tops and shorts, showing cheeky glimpses of toned, sun-kissed flesh.

Sarah tried very hard not to be intimidated by the undisguised interest of the men she was introduced to. Their gaze lingered a little too long on her breasts, and then crept down over her shapely frame as if she was a luxury item on display. She had no idea where Chang had vanished to, and Anna was deep in conversation with Casswell and Fredo. With Weissman at her side, she felt far from safe or at ease.

Beside them, leaning against the guardrail, was a middle-aged man, talking to one of the girls. He was dressed in casual but obviously expensive clothes. At first glance the couple just seemed to be chatting – but there was something indefinable simmering just below the surface that suggested an awful lot more was going on.

Sarah found it impossible to look way from them, and watched furtively from the corner of her eye. The man leant a little closer, and the girl did not move away. Sarah could feel the unspoken sexual promise building between the two of them. As she watched the man very slowly stretched out his hand and stroked the girl's face. She had large brown eyes and long plaited hair. She looked down demurely as he stroked her again, ever the perfect slave, and then, as if defining his mastery over her, he began unfastening her blouse. She did not resist him, allowing herself to be undressed and fondled and used, as he desired. He eased a hand inside her blouse, pushing the fabric back to reveal first one and then the second small but perfect breast.

Sarah glanced anxiously at Weissman, who appeared oblivious to what was going on so close by, while her attention was drawn instinctively to the girl and her older companion. The rest of the passengers and crew, and even Casswell, seemed to have faded into insignificance.

The girl's creamy skin was as pale as a new moon, in contrast to the man's suntanned and rugged hand. In his grasp her breasts were hardly more than delicate upturned peaks, tipped with tight scarlet flowers. The man smiled, his eyes bright and predatory, as he rolled one nipple between his thumb and forefinger, as one might an expensive cigar.

The girl's expression glittered with suppressed pleasure. She was awaiting instructions from her master. His other hand moved to join the first and pushed her top back off her shoulders. Her petit body could have been sculpted from creamy white marble, and as his hands reached her shoulders she leant back against the handrail, readying herself for whatever it was he wanted.

The man's eyes narrowed with pleasure as he ran his hands over his prize, the girl not resisting. Her compliance was total, her expectancy as tangible as the sea breeze. Sarah held her breath, and thought she heard him moan with delight as he moved even closer and bent over the delightful creature, sucking one of the peaks deep into his mouth.

The girl shivered and closed her eyes. Sarah finally tore her gaze away, feeling the sensation of the electric touch echo through her own breasts and belly. She had been unaware that Uri Weissman was watching her watching them, but as she looked away she felt his hand slide up over her hip.

'This is exactly what they mean when they say a pleasure cruise, don't you think?' he whispered, pulling her closer, his hand creeping down to surreptitiously cup one of her buttocks. 'Fredo's stable is legendary. He picks most of his girls from the Far East, and some from Eastern Europe.' As he spoke he swooped, pressing his lips to the curve of her neck, just below her ear. He inhaled her delicate perfume and then lifted his face again, looking down at her, his nostrils flared. 'But after last night's performance at the club, I'm sure you will be just as popular as anything else he's got on offer,' he murmured.

Sarah stared up at him and saw herself reflected in his hungry eyes. 'I…' As popular? The words dried in her throat as she realised what Weissman was saying, and she knew there was no way she could escape him or whatever the cruise might hold in store for her.

Around them the crew were busy raising the sails, and Weissman's gaze fixed on her, dark and feral. 'And before you cry off or head back to your precious master, Casswell knows the score here as well as anyone else,' he said, taking the unfinished glass of champagne from her lifeless hand.

Around the deck, couples, two's and threes and foursomes were already shaping up. From beneath the awning an elderly grey-haired man smiled at her, and at some level Sarah knew that she had been promised to him. Standing with him was a much taller, extremely attractive young man, dressed casually in cream chinos and blue cotton shirt, his laidback manner in sharp contrast to his companion's upright and very military bearing.

'Uri, my dear chap, I'm so pleased to see you again,' the elderly gentleman called, looking pointedly at Sarah, who felt her colour rising. 'Perhaps you would care to join us for a drink.'

Weissman smiled. 'I'd be delighted, Granger, but let's be frank,' he called back, guiding Sarah over to them. 'I'm not who you really want to be with, am I? May I introduce Dr Casswell's delightful assistant and companion.'

The man's expression sharpened as he laughed at Weissman's candour, and the expression gave him a sly, fox-like quality. 'The name's Granger – Granger Hall,' he introduced himself to her, extending a rather bony and limp hand. 'And this is my friend, Rupert Carlisle.' He indicated his tall companion with an equally effete gesture.

Sarah glanced over towards Casswell. He looked at her, and she guessed he had been watching her progress around the deck. He indicated his consent with a barely perceivable nod of the head, so she turned back to the elderly man and his companion, and smiled nervously.

'Well trained indeed,' Uri Weissman snorted derisively, spying the signal. 'Like one of those silent whistles.'

Without the courtesy of asking whether she'd had enough champagne, the elderly man took Sarah's glass, and then said in an authoritative tone that alarmed her, 'You will join us below deck. There we can relax, and get to know each other a little more… intimately…'

His demeanour chilled Sarah, and she could see from the expression on his face, thin lips and cold narrow eyes, that this man was ruthless and used to being obeyed without question.

'It's less windy below decks,' his companion, Rupert, continued before she could respond, somewhat stating the obvious, 'and as we leave the harbour's protection it is going to be quite cold once the sun is fully down.' His accent was pure English public school.

Granger smiled and squeezed her hand possessively with skeletal fingers. 'What did you say your name was again, my dear?'

Uri Weissman chuckled. 'She did not, and you don't have to worry about her name, Granger,' he said. 'As agreed, she's all yours – eager and very, very talented. And believe me, that is a commendation born of personal experience.'

'Oh, I do hope so,' the elderly man ruminated, with a calculating glint in his eye. 'Now, Rupert, be a good chap and take the young lady below, would you? We'll follow you down in a short while.'

Rupert nodded and took Sarah by the elbow, and she threw Casswell one final nervous glance, but he merely lifted his glass in a silent acknowledgement of what was happening as she was guided down the steep steps into the yacht.

'Granger doesn't like to waste his time with what he

perceives to be unnecessary preliminaries,' the younger man candidly informed her as he led her through the plush lounge area, Sarah cringing with embarrassment and hoping the few guests socialising there could not hear what he was saying, but suspecting they could. 'He no longer has the stamina or the inclination to indulge in such things. It will be my duty to get you prepared for him... if you understand my meaning.' The conversation was so frank that Sarah's cheeks reddened furiously.

He took her along a short and narrow passageway, opened a door and politely showed her into a small cabin. It was stunning and elegant, a luxurious combination of maple and red-veined marble with gold fixtures and fittings. And there was a double bed, covered with a crisp white sheet.

Then, with no further formalities, he faced her, held her close, and trailed a fingertip along her jaw-line, toyed with her earring for a moment, and then traced down the elegant sweep of her throat, along her shoulder, then down to the curve of her breast. There his fingers lingered again, savouring the feel of her, barely touching her softness, and then he continued and circled her nipple, which hardened instantly under his knowing touch.

'Granger likes to watch,' Rupert crooned. 'He likes me to be a little rough, and then he'll want to fuck you.' He smiled as Sarah looked anxiously back at the beautiful polished wood of the closed cabin door. 'Actually,' Rupert went on, gently placing his fingers against her chin to make her face him again, 'we both will, but he always likes to go first. Not that I'm complaining, of course. Who could complain about having to perform such pleasurable duties?

'He won't speak to you...' Sarah barely heard his words any more, '...he likes his girls obedient, submissive, and above all, totally silent.'

The polished cabin door opened and Sarah glanced around anxiously. There was definitely no going back now, for Granger had followed them down.

'Have her undress,' he ordered curtly, his manner brusque and at odds with his urbane demeanour above deck. 'You know I don't like to be kept waiting. Let me see what she has to offer.'

Rupert positioned a chair for the elderly man, who sat and looked expectantly at the uncertain girl. 'Take your clothes off...' Rupert instructed her.

Facing Granger in the slightly cramped surroundings, knowing she had no alternative but to do as they told her, Sarah began to undo her dress. Lifting her hands behind her back to lower the zip, she saw and felt Granger's eyes absorbing the sight of her dress stretched tightly across her breasts, caused by her innocently sensual movement. His rapacious expression made her shudder inside. Very slowly she slipped the dress off her shoulders, and wriggling very slightly, allowed it to slide down, the material whispering promises to the two men as it peeled off her hips and fell in a shimmering pile at her dainty feet. Underneath, due to Casswell's instructions and the heat of the country they were in, she was completely naked. Her skin had just begun to tan, offering a lightly golden hue to her smooth flesh.

Sarah stood meekly, her arms impotently by her sides, wondering what exactly would happen next.

Rupert had poured Granger a brandy, and the elderly man sipped it as he sat back with apparent satisfaction and studied her beauty. Then he nodded, his alert eyes never leaving her, and Rupert moved close, pressing himself to her back.

Sarah held her breath and waited, watching for any

reactions from the sitting man, but there was little evidence of any. Apart from the expectant sparkle in his eyes, he appeared cold and detached.

Then she trembled slightly as Rupert's hands rested on her hips for a few seconds, and then rose, over her taut tummy, and up to her breasts. He cupped their ripe firmness, and his thumbs teased her nipples, which instantly and treacherously stiffened in front of the old man's eyes. She could feel the warmth of Rupert's body enveloping her back, radiating through his clothing. His nose and lips nuzzled into her hair, and he audibly breathed her scent. Then he slowly lowered his face and kissed her ear, then down to her neck, muttering graphic descriptions of what he was going to do to her, and what she was going to do for the both of them. With more urgency his hands cupped and possessed her breasts, which filled his hungry palms as her slow breathing deepened.

Then one hand moved again, down over her tummy, barely touching her flesh, making her tense and her senses tighten, and he cupped her sex mound. Sarah gasped involuntarily, and his fingers worked between her pussy lips, peeling her open, exposing her shamelessly for the man sitting nursing his brandy, contemplating her with little emotion.

Rupert bent her forward, and from behind he eased his fingers up inside her, making her gasp again with shock and shame. Between them, the two men were rapidly reducing her to a sexual commodity, but despite her chagrin she instinctively began to move against the invading fingers, and the warm lump she felt rising against her bottom, strangely excited by his impersonal attentions.

'Bring her here, closer,' Granger demanded, his voice low and expressionless. 'I want her closer.'

Rupert moved, one arm around her waist, his other hand still wedged between her thighs from behind, his fingers still inside her increasing wetness as he shuffled her over to where Granger sat, and with his toe he nudged her feet apart so that the old man could see every succulent detail and what his fingers were doing inside her.

Granger placed his brandy glass on the occasional table beside his chair, craned forward and ran a hand down over her hip, and then pressed a single finger up inside her, alongside Rupert's. His touch was as cold as ice, and made Sarah close her eyes against the humiliation and visibly cringe. He chuckled huskily, clearly relishing her shame, then slowly withdrew his finger, closely studied the glistening juices that coated it, turning his finger this way and that with a deliberation that utterly humiliated her, and then fed it between his dry lips and imbibed of her essence. After a moment or two, as if he were the connoisseur of some priceless and exotic vintage wine, he nodded.

'She's certainly a prize specimen,' he concluded, and nodded at Rupert, indicating that his young associate should proceed.

Up on deck Uri Weissman drew deeply on his cigar and then looked at Rigel Casswell. 'You want to come and watch your girl in action?' he goaded. 'What about you, Anna; you want to join us, or are you going to seek out a little fun of your own?'

The majority of the passengers had already drifted below, including Fredo, their host. The yacht had caught the edge of a stiff breeze that was eagerly driving them hard along the rugged coastline, and behind them the port had already vanished from sight.

Casswell nodded; he wanted to keep an eye on his girl,

even though he had the security of knowing that Chang was looking out for both of them.

Once below, Weissman directed Casswell through the lounge and along the narrow passageway. Quietly he unlocked and opened one of the cabin doors, and silently indicated that Casswell should sit on one of two chairs, strangely positioned side by side facing the beautiful wood panelling of an inner bulkhead. Having closed and locked the door from the inside, Weissman then settled on the chair beside him.

Beyond the small unblinking eyeholes Sarah was already naked, stretched out on the double bed, while Rupert crouched between her parted legs. As Casswell's eyes adjusted to the vision he realised the man was rubbing oil all over her body; over her breasts, her arms, her shoulders and up the arc of her neck, and down over her belly. His palms and fingers were working back and forth, lingering for a few seconds on her sex mound, between her limp thighs.

And Granger observed, apparently unmoved by Sarah's preparations. Rupert reached for a small bottle and poured a little more oil into the palms of his hands, and began to rub her again. Sarah was visibly relaxing. His strong hands swept up over her slim body, leaving a gleaming trail in their wake. It was a compelling image, although Casswell sensed her apprehension along with her growing excitement. She looked stunning lying submissively under the man's touch, her sleek body supple and toned and shimmering in the seductive lighting. Her nipples had hardened into dark nubs. With her eyes closed, her mouth opened slightly and perfect white teeth nibbled her lower lip, and she frowned as her confused emotions caused her inner turmoil. She moaned softly, allowing her body to flow with the soothing strokes, lifting her hips fractionally to meet him as he leant forward. He traced a finger down between the lips of her sex, making her stiffen and gasp softly, the oil making her flesh glisten like wet silk He added a little more lubricant, and then bent forward, very slowly and deliberately, to lick her. Sarah shivered, almost flinching, as his clever tongue found her secret spot.

'Open yourself up for me...' he ordered, his voice almost hypnotic. 'Hold yourself open for me...'

There was the slightest hesitation, and then Sarah's fingers moved downwards and held her moist pussy lips apart as commanded. Her whole body stiffened as Rupert licked and sucked, his tongue flicking around the engorged ridge of her clitoris, concentrating on its sensitive hood. He pushed his hands under Sarah's buttocks and lifted her up towards his mouth, so that no part of her was concealed or beyond his reach.

Casswell guessed what would follow; he had seen Chang work often enough. The man's fingers gently worked the oil down over the sensitive bridge of flesh that lay between her sex and the tight little closure between the cheeks of her bottom. It was Chang's favourite place, and apparently one of these men's too.

Casswell wondered if Sarah would protest as the fingers traced the contours of the deep valley between her buttocks, seeking her tight rear opening, but his tongue was keeping her occupied, working diligently across and around the bud that lay between the open lips of her sex.

Rupert moved away fractionally and Sarah moaned, lifting herself so as not to miss one single stroke, one single pass of his clever, clever tongue – and as Sarah lifted clear of his open palms Rupert slid a single finger up into the snug dark depths of her bottom with admirable precision.

For an instant Casswell saw her stiffen, her body resisting, eyes flickering open. But Sarah knew better than to protest, and Rupert renewed his attentions to her clitoris, this time moving lower so that as her hips sank to chase his tongue she lowered herself further and further onto his rigid, waiting finger, accepting it deep inside her most secret channel.

From the darkened cabin beyond the panelled bulkhead, Casswell silently acknowledged that it was a skilled and cunning strategy.

Rupert's thumb slid into her vagina, impaling her again and again, both finger and thumb working in tandem now to bring the supine girl to the very edge of orgasm. Sarah bucked and writhed. The muscles in her neck and jaw tightened – and then, as the man's tongue executed another scintillating pass over her labia, she began to move with him, oblivious now, lost to everything but the compelling ride out towards release... but just at the split second when her orgasm seemed inevitable, Rupert pulled away.

Sarah moaned, her hands blindly searching him out, but she was to be denied; Granger was on his feet and unzipping his trousers.

His younger associate climbed off the bed and out of the way. Granger, his cock jutting and bobbing out in front of him like a gnarled trunk, crouched between Sarah's open thighs and, as if manoeuvring a doll, hoisted her hips up towards him. Her body tensed, still instinctively seeking Rupert's continued caresses, and at that moment Granger took her weight on his hands and drove his cock fully home with one aggressive penetration.

Sarah screamed and then convulsed with pleasure as he breached her, her body straining and arching to draw him in. She was so close to the edge that Casswell wondered if she had noticed the change of partner.

Desperately she began to thrust onto the rampant cock of the older man, fighting for her prize. The fingers of one hand gripped like talons into the white sheet, while the fingers of the other, still holding those slick lips open and so close to the seat of her pleasure, sought her clitoris and began to caress it frantically in an attempt to keep the flame burning. And then Casswell saw the first wave of pleasure hit her, sweeping away all reason as she was engulfed in the ecstasy of orgasm.

Above her, Granger strained forward, his face reddening, gaunt features contorted with pleasure as Sarah's tight, wet pussy sucked his desiccated penis deep, deep inside her.

But there was more. As the elderly man pulled out of her, his tight chest wheezing, his seed spilling onto her thighs and pooling in the dip of her quivering belly, Rupert, now naked, clambered back onto the bed and held the limp form of Sarah around the waist. Her body was so enmeshed in the aftershocks of her orgasm that she seemed almost liquid, and unable to resist she gave herself over to the younger man to do with as he pleased.

So with little effort he turned her over onto her front and pulled her up on all fours, her face pressed down into the mattress. With one hand he renewed his attention to the tight little entrance between her buttocks, smearing it with the mingled juices of their mutual desire and the remains of the slick oil, while his other hand strayed back between her legs, stirring the fading fire back into a bright flame.

Even through the bulkhead Casswell could just hear Sarah's muted moans, the intense sensations igniting a mixture of protest and pleasure.

'No, no, please... oh, please...' she gasped, trying without conviction to wriggle away from Rupert's invasive touch. He moved over her, and as he pressed his finger home, Sarah's body opened.

Granger seemed equally eager to see Rupert's needs answered, to see his associate fuck Sarah's bottom, and in an apparently spontaneous and bizarre gesture of encouragement he massaged some of the oil into the length of the younger man's throbbing erection. It was an incredible action, and Casswell saw Rupert gritting his teeth, and knew that he too was close to the edge and that the old man's touch was taking him perilously closer.

Clearly Rupert's touch had found the magic spot for Sarah, for she, oblivious to what was going on behind her between the two men, was straining back, and as she pressed onto him he slipped his finger out of her prepared anus and Granger aimed the pulsing erection in his skeletal fist and pressed the spongy, purple helmet against that same tight opening.

Sarah's body resisted for a few seconds, and then Rupert renewed his attentions to her clitoris, lunged with his hips, and she was lost.

Casswell could not suppress a feeling of pride as he watched his delightful girl bravely accept the man into her rear and heard a moan – part protest, part passion – sigh from Sarah's open mouth. Rupert ran his hands over her slick flanks, his touch meant to still her for a moment, to allow her time to acquaint herself with the feel of his length and girth stretching her rear passage, and then very slowly, gradually getting faster as his climax approached again, he began to piston in and out of her, his groin slapping noisily and rhythmically against her raised buttocks.

Sarah, exhausted and weak, rocked on her forearms and knees in the middle of the bed as he rutted against her, until he came deep inside her, his face red and his jaws locked in a grimace of undiluted passion.

It was the early hours of the morning when the yacht finally docked again at the port. Sarah leant against the handrail and watched the lights of the harbour drifting closer and closer in the darkness. Casswell stood beside her, and she was glad of his presence. She felt far from home and longed to be back in England, realising that she now thought of Casswell Hall as her home.

Around them couples talked and dozed on the seats and recliners, while below decks an occasional sound of passion still carried up through the fresh night air.

Chapter Twelve

'So how is it going with the diary, Dr Casswell?' asked Mustafa Aziz the following morning. The last time Sarah had seen the fat Turk was at the dinner party for the trustees, which seemed like an age ago. She looked up from the computer screen into his unshaven face. He was standing so close that she could smell his aftershave and his bodily odour. Casswell looked up too, his expression impassive.

'Very well, thank you,' he said, setting aside the magnifying glass he was holding.

The curator smiled, and Sarah sensed that something else was playing on the man's mind. Mustafa moved a little closer, his tone conspiratorial. 'You know, doctor, I have heard – no – I know, that there are other works. I know there are other books that were brought by the monks to the area. They are quite close by.' He grinned, and it was obvious the existence of these other books was something that excited him. He leaned a little closer and spoke shiftily. 'Maybe with my help you might be able uncover the mother lode?'

Sarah glanced across at Casswell, and saw instantly that Mustafa had his full attention.

'You know where there are more of these diaries?' Casswell asked. 'Are they here in the museum?'

The fat man shook his head. 'If only it were that easy. No, unfortunately not, and there are no more of the girl's diaries – at least, I do not think so. I have not had the opportunity to catalogue or examine the books I am telling you about fully. But I truly think that they would be of interest to you, doctor. As I said, I believe they come from the original collection brought here by the abbot who brought that to this area…' he indicated the bound book lying on the desk before Casswell.

'The current abbot,' he went on, 'has in his possession the remains of a collection of books, manuscripts, even some scrolls and papyrus in the original box, which is held at the little abbey in the mountains. It is perhaps half a day's drive from here. I have tried my hardest to get the old man to part with them and let us take care of them for him, but unfortunately he is reluctant in case somehow the story of his predecessors' taste in erotic writings gets out. This new man is very devout, very pious. But…' Mustafa paused, his dark eyes alight with excitement.

'But what?' Casswell urged impatiently.

'But I spoke to him this morning, and he is eager to meet you. Since your arrival here it seems that word of your mission has spread far. He rang me on the pretext of some other matter regarding an obscure relic, but the main thrust of his conversation was you, Dr Casswell. It seems that after all these years he would finally like to know what it is that he has hidden away in the box, and would be happy for you to take a look at them.'

Casswell nodded. 'It sounds very interesting,' he said. 'We would be foolish not to go.'

Mustafa shook his head, glancing at Sarah as he did. 'No, unfortunately it cannot be "we" – just you, Dr Casswell. It is a closed religious order, therefore no women are permitted within the abbey precincts.'

Casswell hesitated for a few seconds, and then said, 'Very well, I understand. Have you any idea when the abbot can see me?'

'I can phone him back now, if you would like me to.'

Casswell nodded. 'Fine,' he said, and then turned his attention back to the page he was working on.

The brief exchange over, Sarah looked back at the screen, wondering what the books might be; Casswell's well-disguised interest had whetted her own curiosity.

Only a few minutes later the heavy silence of concentration was broken by the sound of the curator's shoes hurrying across the stone floor, and Mustafa looked triumphant.

'He says he can see you today,' he announced animatedly. 'In fact, if you leave now he has said you may join him for a late lunch. This is a tremendous honour, Dr Casswell. This current abbot knows a great deal about the man who founded the original community and brought the diary with him. But unfortunately if you cannot go today it will be another two weeks before he can see you; some strange edict that means that after today they take a vow of silence as part of a cycle of prayer and abstinence.' Mustafa paused while Casswell deliberated, and then after a few seconds the Turk added, 'I can arrange a car for you, if you like.'

'Yes, okay, fine,' Casswell decided, and turned to Sarah. 'I'll ring Uri Weissman and arrange for Chang to come over and pick you up at lunchtime. Maybe you can get to do a little sightseeing while I'm gone.'

Sarah nodded; she knew it was too good an opportunity for Casswell to miss, but before she could say anything Mustafa interrupted them. 'No need for you to phone Herr Weissman, doctor,' he said. 'I will arrange for a car to take your assistant home, have no fear. She only has to give me the word when she is ready to leave.'

As he spoke, Sarah was overcome by a sense of foreboding, and even Casswell hesitated for a moment. 'You won't be coming up to the abbey with me, then?'

He sounded surprised.

Mustafa held up his hands in a gesture of apology and regret. 'Unfortunately not, I am much too busy today to spare the time, but my assistant will be happy to accompany you. He is a good man and will help to translate for you. The abbot speaks some English, but it would be an opportunity wasted not to take a translator with you.'

Casswell nodded his agreement, and began to gather his things together as the niggling uncertainty in the pit of Sarah's tummy was growing, and although she carried on working, the idea of Mustafa offering to look after her was ridiculous and unsettling; it was like a lamb being minded by a starving wolf.

She tried to concentrate her attention back to the work on the desk before her. As far as Sarah was concerned, she had honoured any bargain with the Turk that the Weissmans had arranged. She did not particularly want to go back to their house, either; at least here in the museum vaults it was cool and relatively safe.

Careful not to catch Mustafa's eye, Sarah made a show of continuing to type, and was relieved when after she and Casswell had said their goodbyes, Mustafa accompanied him up and out of the vaults to a waiting car.

The work that morning had gone really well, and there were pages and pages of Casswell's distinctive script to continue putting into the computer, so Sarah turned her attention to those.

...Days at the abbey have passed slow and heavy, knowing that somewhere out in the country beyond the mountains my master is preparing for his marriage to the Lady Cassandra. Whereas before I have managed to keep my spirits up with thoughts to freedom and returning to the castle and to my life with him, it seemed in truth that all was lost. Until, that is, until this very morning, when my salvation came in an unexpected form, and all that I have known over the past few months appears to have been turned on its head.

It is the custom of the abbey to open its doors to travellers after morning prayers, to those true pilgrims who want a place to water their animals. 'Tis only later in the day that those who know the true nature of the abbey come looking for more sport than simple prayer and water from our well. So when in the noon daylight I saw a party making its way slowly up the track to the abbey, I was unsure as to the nature of their stopping. Did they want water? Or perhaps alms? Or was it the debauchery that began when the shadows lengthened that this fine party sought?

Sister Judith had set me to work in the laundry this morning, and so the first I saw of them was hanging out the linen, and then a while later when I went out with another basket I heard a familiar voice in the main courtyard. It stopped me in my tracks.

It was a voice from my past – a voice that was both a joy and a curse. When first my master made me his own he had staying with him a distant cousin, Lord Usher, a rich man whose tastes in pleasure and pain where similar to those of my master. Listening now to his cultured voice on the breeze, I remembered in an instant the day we had first met.

I had been minding my master's children when my lord sent for me. He was waiting a little distance from the castle, in the old walled garden down beside the river. My heart quickened with desire as I saw my master standing there amongst the trees, although I blushed as our eyes met, ashamed to feel so brazen, so wanton, but even so I hurried across the rough grass towards him.

I sensed a brooding hunger in the way he stood, the way his gaze settled on me. It excited me beyond all measure that my lord's eyes were dark with desire. I knew that I wanted nothing more at that moment than to do as he bade me, whatever it might be – my body was his alone to command. My sex moistened at the thought of his touch, his lips, his kisses, the cruel bite of his whip on my pale flesh as I writhed, bound and helpless, waiting for his pleasure.

By all the saints, such demons, such devilry, such desire has filled my thoughts and my dreams since he took me that day in his apartments, I cannot tell you. Even my humiliation had done nothing to stem the flow of fire that bubbled in my veins.

'You are late, girl,' my lord snapped. 'What kept you?'

I began to protest, and only then did I realise that he was not alone. Until that moment I had not seen that deep in the shadows stood both the old priest who attended my master, Father Orme, and another; an unknown nobleman, who watched my approach with equal interest. T'was Lord Usher, the man who even now was dismounting in the courtyard of the abbey.

'Lift your dress, wench,' he had ordered me in that distant garden. I slowed my step and hesitated for an instant.

'Do as the Lord Usher says,' said my master, and, seeing the look of approval and encouragement on my master's face, I did exactly as I was told. But even as I lifted my heavy skirts Lord Usher's expression hardened.

'What folly is this?' he growled furiously, indicating my undergarments to my master.

My lord turned to me. 'Take them off, Beatrice. I would have you naked under your robe from now on. No more of these foolish pantaloons and petticoats. Take them off; have I not explained to you, you are mine? Mine as and when I command, not held at bay by linen and wool. Now take them off, at once!'

I blushed, eyes downcast, and nodded. I understood that he meant for me to be always at his beck and call, always ready be touched by him and others if he so chose. I slipped off my petticoats. He nodded his approval and then indicated that I should hold my robes all the higher so that his compatriots might examine my nakedness.

The stranger stepped a little closer and ran a hand over my belly, and then down through the soft dark curls that framed my sex.

'Would you have me undo her bodice for you, cousin?' asked my lord. 'A finer pair of sweet breasts you'll have trouble to find this side of the city.'

The man snorted and shook his head. 'Nay, here in my hand I have the only thing that truly interests me.' His fingers tightened on my quim. 'I would wish that our maker had had the good sense to strike the whole of the female sex deaf and dumb so that I could fuck them all without having to worry about talking to them or wooing them or other such pointless posturing.' He grinned lecherously. 'And there'd be no risk of them telling tales to their men folk or their fathers.' He nodded towards Father Orme. 'What say you?'

Orme shrugged, apparently not offended by the man's blasphemy.

Lord Usher's fingers had already found their way between the lips of my quim, into that most intimate of places. I looked frantically at my master, praying he might rescue me from this brutal stranger, but he cruelly ignored my shame and humiliation and coolly watched the nobleman explore me.

Usher crudely plunged his fingers home, making me wince at his roughness. He smiled at my discomfort, his thumb lifting to trace the rise of my pleasure-bud. In spite of myself, my body responded to his rough caress and I shivered with shameful delight.

The man laughed triumphantly. 'See, there you have it, my lord,' he chuckled. 'Deprived of the right to answer back all women are the same. The little vixen wants nothing more than to feel my cock buried to the hilt inside her. Can you not see it in her eyes and the way she moves against me? Away with all this courtly love and poetry, give me the honest lust of a tight cunt and a fine wet mouth any day. Unless, of course, you are too old or too tired to care, don't waste conversation on harlots such as this. It is here and only here that the real pleasure lies.' As he spoke he spread the juices from my sex out onto my thighs and belly.

He addressed only my master and Orme, without a word for me or a thought for the shame and distress that I might feel at his words or his invasion of my body.

Lifting his fingers, he drew one of them into his mouth and smacked his lips as if the traces of juice it bore were the finest of delicacies. Then pulling me closer he unfastened his robe, and without prelude prodded my legs wide apart and guided his cock into me, pulling one leg up around his waist to give him better purchase. The moment of coupling was so quick, so unexpected, that I cried out in horror and surprise.

He leered as he stabbed his engorged member up into me, making me gasp with each upward thrust of his hips.

'I like it when, ah...' he grunted between clenched teeth and each shove of his groin, 'a woman calls out, ah... as you enter her, ah... 'tis an honest animal cry of desire, ah... and need... ah!'

I shivered as he forced himself deeper still, closing his eyes with the sheer pleasure of my body closing around him.

'Just as you said, dear cousin, she is good and tight,' he murmured thickly to my master when he could penetrate me no further, and then to my surprise, after no more than a dozen strokes pulled his cock out. Its livid purple crown brushed across my thighs like a wet quarterstaff.

He smiled slyly as I looked up at him, and then he forced me roughly down onto my knees. I knew then what he expected, and looking down at me with arrogant triumph etched in his eyes, he guided his shaft – that great livid horn, wet now with my own shameful juices – between my lips and into my defenceless mouth.

I gasped as the taste of my own excitement flooded my mouth. My sex fluttered like a bird's wings, and without thinking where I was or what I was doing, I slid a hand down over my belly, scrabbling up the hem of my gown to find the soft wet places that dwelt beneath. To my horror the stranger laughed loudly, even as my tongue and free hand worked furiously along his throbbing shaft.

'By all the saints, it is true what they say about country wenches, cousin!' he bellowed.

Surely it was his voice I could hear now? Although it seemed impossible that of all the places Lord Usher, the favoured and beloved friend of my master, could have come was here to the Abbey of St Joseph. Could this be the miracle I had prayed for? My heart sang. Recklessly I abandoned the linen and ran out through the kitchens, eager to follow the sound of the voices on the morning breeze.

I stood for a few seconds and looked from face to face of the fine caravan of travellers, trying to pick out Lord

Usher's distinctive features from those gathered around the tie rail, all the while wondering if I had been mistaken. But even the dust from the road could not disguise the wealth and bearing of so noble a man. There, astride a fine Arab stallion, sat Lord Usher.

Heedless of the circumstance I ran over to him. He looked once, and then twice. 'By all the saints,' he bellowed as he dismounted, 'is that you, girl?'

I nodded, and he grinned so broadly that my heart truly sang.

'By the devil's tail, fancy your being here!' he exclaimed. 'A sight for sore eyes indeed. A welcome bed mate for the weary.' And then he looked at me more closely, taking in the rags and bruises and how pale and undernourished my body was. 'What have they done to you, girl?' he asked, his expression turning to one of anger. 'Does your master know what has become of his favourite bed mate?'

It was at that moment he found out the true nature of my fall, for from the laundry Sister Judith appeared, her face thunderous. Grabbing me by the arm she dragged me back towards the door, her cold eyes for once ablaze, her temper white-hot.

'Forgive her, sir, she is but a foundling, none too bright, not versed in the ways or manners of court.' It would have been pointless to protest, but I did pull away from her. I thought she was going to hit me there and then, such was her face contorted with rage. 'Have I not told you to keep away from the main courtyard,' she hissed vehemently, 'to keep to the servants' quarters?'

Usher laughed derisively. 'Servant? I am astonished, sister. Why, this girl is a scholar, well bred, well taught. Indeed, she was charge of her master's house in his wife's absence.'

Of all the words he could have spoken there could have

been none worse than these.

'Indeed, sir, I know exactly what this creature is and what she did!' snarled Sister Judith. 'She is a liar and a whore, nothing more, and for her pains her new mistress sent her here to be taught humility and above all obedience.'

Snatching up a crop from one of Usher's men she swept it down across my shoulder. The blow was so vicious it cut the thin blouse I was wearing and drew blood. She was about to strike me again, eyes alight with fury, when Usher caught her wrist.

'Whatever her crime,' he said with remarkable restraint, 'she does not deserve so public a humiliation, sister.'

Judith looked at him with total disdain. 'And what would you know of her crimes, sir?' she sneered. 'Unhand me.'

Instinctively Usher drew back and she hit me again. This time the blow caught my face, and as I cowered blow after blow cracked across my defenceless body. I shrieked out in pure terror.

This time Usher was not so coy or so kind, and he wrestled the crop from her. 'I think you forget your position, sister,' he said, his tone full of warning.

Judith turned on him, her eyes bright and fiery. 'My position?' she shrieked. 'You mock my calling? Have you come here to feast on piety or willing flesh? Flesh I'd wager, by the look of you!'

Lord Usher's face darkened, and I realised with a sense of fear that in her fury Sister Judith had fallen into the abyss, her anger and her jealousy sparking some dark and ungodly madness. Even as I thought it two of the other sisters from the order came scurrying out from the abbey to catch hold of her and drag her back into the hall, almost having to carry her, while behind them, hurrying and looking anxious, was the abbot and his entourage.

'You have my most humble apologies, my good sir,' he

babbled obsequiously, trying to make good the damage already done. 'Know you this wench, sir?'

Usher nodded. 'Aye, indeed I am en route to the marriage feast of the man who was once her master. He and I are both kin and good friends.'

The abbot looked me up and down and then shook his head. 'When Sister Judith recovers, the girl will be in mortal danger if she stays here,' he said.

Usher nodded in agreement, having seemingly drawn the same conclusion. 'Then with your permission, I will take her with me. Though she may not be welcome in the castle where we are bound, there is always a place for a willing and comely wench such as she.'

And so it seems, in the twinkling of an eye, I am rescued from the clutches of the foul hag Judith and the equally repugnant abbot.

We left as soon as the horses were watered and tended to, I wrapped in a borrowed cloak over my rags with only a tiny basket of my most precious possessions to keep me company.

We rode all day, leaving the fortified walls of the abbey far behind. As the daylight faded Usher's men set up camp under a stand of trees, and I soon discovered the price for my salvation.

'Come wench,' said one of the serving boys, calling me from the fireside. It was dark, and the night air cold with the promise of snow on its raw biting edge. 'My master bids you come to his tent. He has need of you.'

I understood his need of old and followed the boy, my heart aflutter. I guessed at what it was that Usher might require of me. But here at least the rules of pain and passion and pleasure are mingled, not peppered with spite and cruelty for cruelty's sake.

With his valet standing by, Usher bade me stand under

the light of a lamp. 'Seems to me that you have been ill served, girl,' he said, pouring a goblet of wine and handing it to me. The table set up in one corner of the tent was heavy with food. He caught me looking, and laughed. 'Starving too?'

I did not know whether to speak.

He grunted. 'Don't worry, you will eat in good time,' he promised. 'Now, while we travel you will serve me in my bed and in all other ways I see fit. Do you understand?'

I nodded, and as he lifted his goblet in a toast I did the same, and took a swig of the heady wine, which instantly coursed through my veins like molten lead.

'Take off those rags,' he ordered. 'Let me see the stray that I have rescued from the fire.'

I did as I was commanded, and stood before him naked and still as he examined me, hands and eyes taking in every welt and mark of Judith's unfeeling brutality. His gaze was icy and made me shiver. Though he had saved me there was no hint of compassion in either his touch or his look. He slid a hand between my thighs, fingers seeking out that hidden place. Behind him, from the corner of my eye, I could see the way his young valet watched me, his eyes hungrily drinking in my body like a parched man.

Usher, meanwhile, murmured approvingly as my body opened to him. 'I see you're still warm and wet and tight, girl. Perhaps I should take you back to your master as a wedding gift. How think you the Lady Cassandra would take such a gesture?' He pushed his finger deeper and I gasped. 'Still like it rough, do you wench?' He laughed.

I cast my gaze to the floor as he pulled his fingers from me, took off his broad leather belt and folded it in two. It seems that a slave must be taught her place wherever she finds herself. Usher settled himself back on his chair and bade me come closer. I drained the wine and moved slowly to do his bidding. His expression hardened; this was his game. I lowered my gaze again respectfully; he was the master here and now it seemed my new lord. I settled across his lap, tummy on his stout thighs, legs open. He ran his hands over my body, seeking out the curves of my buttocks, and then between them, his fingers thrusting again and again into me.

I moved against his touch, feeling my body again open to him. He paused, using his fingertips to draw my juices out onto my thighs, and I sensed what would follow. I could hear my heart beating in my ears, could feel his breath on my naked flesh, and then his belt exploded across my tensed bottom. The blow made me shriek and I bent like a newly strung bow. The belt hit me again and I cried out again as the leather bit into my tender flesh, but before the pain had ebbed he hit me again and again and I cried with every blow until I knew I could cry no more.

At last it seemed Usher was done, and without a word he rolled me onto the floor like a dog, and parted his legs.

I knew what it was he wanted; the same thing he had taken in the castle gardens. His dark cruel eyes were alight with desire and need, so I crawled back to him on my hands and knees, lifted the hem of his ornate tunic, and unfastened his breeches. His thick cock was purple and ferocious, and ready for the attention of my trembling lips.

Kneeling between his sturdy thighs, bending close, I guided him into my mouth and ran my tongue around the sensitive head, working at the solitary eye, sucking and licking, my hands working up and down the shaft, grateful beyond all measure to be back in safe, even if cruel, hands – hands that I trusted.

Usher eased back in his chair, and then looking up at the young man who waited upon him, said in a throaty voice, 'Come, Sebastian, take what you will, for this sweet little creature is well versed in the arts of pleasure and will bring me as much joy as I shall have need of tonight.'

His valet, a thickset young man, settled himself behind me as I knelt between the feet and legs of Lord Usher. A moment or two later I felt him slip his hand flat between my thighs, cupping my sex, fingers working to find that place, so dishonourably wet and so desperate to be filled.

A finger pressed its way home, and it felt very good. Clearly encouraged by the evidence of my wetness, he prodded my legs wider apart without ceremony and I felt the heat of him as he crouched over me, and then I gasped as he drove his cock fully home with one thrust that nearly had me choking on the rigid flesh stretching my lips and filling my mouth.

It was all too much, and without thinking I slipped a hand down over my belly to feel the place where our bodies joined, and brushed the little nub of delight that nestles there amongst its nest of damp curls.

It seems my naughty caress was enough for Usher's serving man, and Usher groaned and gasped too, his strong fingers entangled in my hair, clamped to my head, moving it up and down at whatever pace he required to give him the maximum pleasure. I felt the tightening in his groan and then he pulled away, gasping, splashing my face and breasts with an arcing wave of his seed, while buried between my legs Sebastian snorted and bucked like a stallion, his manhood filling me to the brim with his pleasure...

In the museum vault Sarah looked up from the computer and blinked, trying to regain some sense of where she was. As always Beatrice's account of her life had carried her far away, both in time and place. Sarah already knew that she was wet, and only just resisted the temptation to follow Beatrice's lead and slide a hand down between her thighs. It was hard to disentangle her own feelings and desires from those of the slave girl.

Something made Sarah glance up, and she was stunned to find Mustafa Aziz no more than a few feet away, watching her, and it was obvious that he had been there for some time.

'W-why are you watching me?' she stammered uncomfortably, not liking the way he was looking at her, or anything about his menacing presence.

'Why?' he sneered. 'Because you are a very beautiful girl,' he said. 'But also, I think, a very rude girl to the man who arranged for you to be driven home, the man who arranged for you to have the use of this equipment and access to these manuscripts.' Although Sarah knew it was not for her to feel indebted to the man, it was true that she and Dr Casswell were only allowed access to the vaults and the diaries because of Aziz's co-operation.

'I-I'm sorry, but you startled me,' she protested, with as much contrition as she could manage. Whatever she felt about the sleazy curator on a personal level, it clearly would not be a good idea to antagonise him.

He nodded, apparently appeased – for the moment. 'I am about to have lunch, you will join me.'

His tone implied a statement rather than an invitation, and she could see no way to decline that would not have been interpreted as rude also. 'Thank you,' she blurted, her mind spinning, 'but I need to tidy away my things.'

'I can wait,' he said, and licked his fat lips, his eyes crawling down to her cleavage.

Sarah shivered, but not from the chill in the vaults.

Chapter Thirteen

In the back room of the grotty restaurant Mustafa Aziz poured more wine into Sarah's glass. She realised after the second that he wasn't drinking, and when she pointed it out he waved her protest away with a shake of his head.

'No, no, I do not drink,' he told her. 'But please, enjoy yourself.'

Sarah, sitting across the table from him, stared into his dark eyes. He may be well behaved when it came to alcohol, but she knew from experience that he behaved very differently when it came to women.

He had invited a second man to join them, a man Sarah recognised as another of the museum staff, and who drove them to lunch. Mustafa introduced him as Abdullah.

The atmosphere was tense and she felt uncomfortable, guessing that lunch was not the only thing on their mind. As Mustafa moved to top her glass up for the third time Sarah placed her hand over it.

He grinned wolfishly. 'Come on now, a little more will not hurt,' he said, and although his tone was conciliatory Sarah sensed something more threatening beneath. But she stood her ground, despite her heart pounding nervously in her chest, and refusing to be intimidated she kept her hand where it was.

The Turk's smile did not falter, but his eyes narrowed. 'Why not tell me about the diary?' he said, lowering the bottle after a few seconds of uncomfortable impasse.

Sarah shook her head. 'I don't know if I should,' she

said. 'You should talk to Dr Casswell. I only transcribe them; it's not my place. How would you feel if one of your employees betrayed your trust?'

He nodded and lifted the glass of tea he had been sipping. 'I understand, Miss Morgan. But tell me, if not the details, then how it excites you.'

The restaurant was ten minutes' drive away from the museum, and they were in a small private room that was oppressively hot and stuffy, despite a large, slowly revolving overhead fan, and with the combination of the spicy food and the wine, Sarah was beginning to feel a little tipsy and a little sick.

'You know, without me this research of yours would be nothing,' Mustafa said in little more than a whisper, leaning forward as though he had a valuable secret to impart. When she did not respond he pressed harder. 'Come on, Miss Morgan, tell me a little something about how the book makes you feel – I saw your face in the vaults. Those pretty eyes of yours were so intense... you were hardly breathing. I saw the look on your face. Tell me... tell us,' he glanced towards Abdullah, and then back to her. 'Does reading the diary make you very wet?'

Sarah blushed at the forthright, shameless crudeness of the man, but despite herself, she was a little emboldened by the wine. 'I've already told you,' she said, finding she had to concentrate a little to get the words out clearly, 'I can't talk about the diary. And I think I've paid the price already for Dr Casswell to have access to it. I've already done what you wanted...' she lowered her voice to an embarrassed whisper, '...with Anna Weissman.'

Mustafa laughed. 'Really?' he scoffed. 'Tell me, would you not like a little something more? Did you not enjoy yourself with her? Come, come, you can tell us, Miss Morgan. Confession, I believe they say, is good for the soul.'

Sarah's colour deepened, wondering if the waiter who appeared to clear some of the dishes understood what Aziz was saying. Certainly Abdullah did. His dark brown eyes were alight as they studied her discomfort with relish.

'Well?' Mustafa persisted. 'Tell us.'

Sarah was about to shake her head when the Turk leaned forward even more, and under the cover of the table he slid a hand up under her skirt, stubby fingers squeezing her thigh, inching higher. At the same time he tried to grab her nearest wrist with his free hand, but Sarah snapped out of her alcohol-induced torpor and jumped to her feet, sending her chair clattering to the tiled floor, and not knowing quite what to do, the strong wine heavy in her brain and in her legs, she backed away and pressed herself to the wall just behind her.

The fat, odious Turk threw his head back and laughed patronisingly. 'Do I make you so nervous, Miss Morgan?' He stood and lifted the chair back onto its legs, and then patted the seat. 'Come, come,' he cajoled smarmily, 'come and sit down again.'

Yes, Mustafa did make Sarah nervous, more than she could possibly say. She did not trust him any more than she trusted Uri Weissman; they were both out for themselves – for their own gain. Watching him warily, she very slowly began to back along the wall towards the door as he moved towards her, clearly being careful not to startle her again, as though tracking his prey.

'Come, Miss Morgan, this is ridiculous,' he said gently. 'Sit down and let me order you some dessert and coffee. Have another glass of wine. I do not mean to offend by touching you, and I know you like it.' Sarah shook her head, her mouth suddenly dry, but he ignored her silent denial of his insistent claim. 'Let me make you purr,' he coaxed. 'Let me make you cry with pleasure... and pain. Aren't they the two things you love the most?'

Sarah shook her head again. 'I – I want to go b-back to the Weissman's house, now,' she managed, falteringly.

Mustafa sighed heavily and held up his hands in surrender. 'All right,' he said, 'go.' And then he resumed his seat and took up a mumbled, incoherent conversation with Abdullah, the two men totally ignoring her.

So without thinking, feeling very alone and totally belittled, Sarah snatched up her bag, wrenched open the door and hurried downstairs. She was still in a confused spin; she walked quickly through the main dining area, pushed open a door, and found herself out in the kitchens. They were filled with steam and noise and a couple of grimy cooks, but not wanting to turn back and risk bumping into Mustafa, she headed for another door she could see and stumbled out into the narrow winding back streets.

The oppressive heat hit her like a sledgehammer. For a few moments she stood still and allowed her pulse and her breathing to calm, and although she had no idea of where she was, she was extremely glad to be out of the restaurant. And although this was not the way they had arrived, she glanced around to get her bearings, hopeful that it couldn't be too difficult to find her way back to Weissman's, even without Mustafa's help.

The door back into the restaurant kitchens had already swung shut behind her, not that she had any wish to go back inside and face Mustafa. So with a confidence that was little more than a veneer, Sarah set off into the maze of smelly, litter-strewn alleys. There seemed to be no one about, except a scrawny black cat curled up in the sunshine, but as she walked deeper into the labyrinth of identical lanes, she felt her panic rising. This was the native quarter, far away from the tourist beaches and stretches of modern hotels, and there was no doubt about it, she was well and truly lost.

After a while the lanes widened into narrow streets and her spirits rose a little, but it was increasingly hot and most sensible people where indoors, out of the searing sun, so there was no one to ask for directions. There were tiny shops, but they were securely shuttered. Sarah turned round and round, trying to set some sense of where the sea might be.

Should she turn left or right, try and get back to the museum, or the Weissmans' house – even though she had no idea of their address? She took a deep breath, and trying hard to control the panic, made her way quickly down another shadowy alleyway.

The houses here on either side were closed and shuttered too, their windows like unseeing eyes. Despite the suffocating heat, Sarah shivered. It was hard to keep control of the growing sense of fear. The alleyway narrowed, but Sarah carried on into deeper and deeper shadows. Maybe it would be better to find her way back to the restaurant after all, despite Mustafa probably still being there. Or perhaps she should wait until she found someone to help her out of the squalid maze.

The alley twisted back and forth ahead of her, and for a few seconds Sarah had a real sense of freedom and progress. Maybe she would be all right, after all. She was certain she could hear the rolling waves of the sea, and then, just as she turned another corner, she realised with a horrible start that the alley was a dead-end.

On either side of the end wall, which was obviously part of a building, were two tall wrought-iron gates, through which Sarah had a tantalising glimpse of terraces covered in lush plants, and places that promised the sanctuary of ordinary domestic life.

The gates where locked with lengths of chain and padlocks – there was no access through them. So she had no choice but to backtrack and try to find another way. She turned – and lifted a hand to her mouth to suppress the shriek of alarm as she saw her only way back was blocked by the bulk of Mustafa Aziz, Abdullah, and the waiter from the restaurant. The fat Turk was breathing hard, his shirt stained with sweat, dabbing at his face with his usual grimy handkerchief.

'So, there you are,' he wheezed, and before Sarah could defend herself, the waiter sprung forward and grabbed her around the waist.

'Let me go!' she shrieked, wriggling and struggling against him, but he held her tighter still and pulled her close into his body, and despite her alarm she instantly noticed a lump pressing against her hip. It seemed he was deeply excited by the thrill of the chase and the capture, and his hands crawled over her body in the struggle as he tried to restrain and quieten her, fumbling against her breasts or her thighs or her bottom. He grunted and laughed, his hold tightening, and she knew that any further movement, any spirited fight, would excite him even further.

Once she was eventually still, trapped in the man's arms, panting heavily from the exertions, Mustafa sniggered at her obvious discomfort and distress. 'Cry out all you want, Miss Morgan,' he jeered. 'It will not do you any good here. No one will come to help you.'

Sarah shrieked again, and this time the waiter clamped a hand tightly over her mouth.

Mustafa smiled with lurid satisfaction, and as he dabbed at his lips with the handkerchief, Abdullah moved closer. She had noted the way he watched her during lunch. He clearly saw this as his big chance to get some pleasure out of life for once, and with the slightest of nods from Mustafa, he reached forward, albeit a little warily, as though she might squirm free and bite him at any moment, and began to unbutton her blouse, his fingers trembling against her breasts as he did. Once it was completely undone he licked his lips, eyeing the way the material hung open and the promising shadows within. Sarah, held fast by the strong arms of the waiter, his hot breath panting in her ear, watched Abdullah anxiously, her breasts rising and falling in time with her nervous breathing, causing her blouse to open a little wider each time she inhaled, offering the obnoxious little man a tantalising glimpse of her toned tummy and her shadowy cleavage.

His hands slowly slid inside the gap to seek out the warm contours of her ribcage, cupping her soft breasts. Then, losing all reason he frantically pushed the fabric out of his way and, uttering unintelligible ramblings, clamped his hot wet mouth to her flesh, as if he wanted to eat her alive, pressing oily kisses to her shoulders, her neck, her throat, her breasts, and her nipples. He was babbling away in his native tongue and trembling with lust, and so was his companion, the waiter. Abdullah slid his hands up under her skirt, his fumbling fingers seeking entry between her thighs, and as he did he cruelly bit on her nipple, make her writhe with pain and squeal into the hand still clamped over her mouth.

Sarah renewed her fight, pulling back from Abdullah, but in doing so pressing herself even harder into the embrace of the waiter. She managed to work one hand free and lashed out at her weasel of a tormentor, but Abdullah merely laughed and, catching her wrist, licked her fingers.

'You know Herr Weissman has such plans for you,'

said Mustafa. 'And I understand why, because you are wasted on that arrogant Englishman. I will suggest that he finds a place for you in one of the local stables – there is nothing so attractive as a slave with a spirit.'

His chilling words brought an abrupt halt to Sarah's struggles.

Mustafa laughed when he saw her alarm, and the slimeball waiter took advantage of the situation to maul her breasts while Abdullah slobbered over their fresh, firm ripeness. And for that moment Sarah was too shocked by Mustafa's words to care what the two slugs were doing.

'Did you not know?' continued the Turk, with a despicable grin of mock innocence on his face. 'Weissman is going to buy you from your precious doctor – or maybe he will barter you for more manuscripts.'

Sarah felt her heart sink. Was there any possibility that what he said was true? If it came to it, she had no idea whether Casswell would choose her over the books and manuscripts he loved so dearly.

Seeing on her lovely face the distress his words had caused, Mustafa's expression returned to one of beaming triumph. He said something to the waiter, who was enjoying himself restraining and molesting her at the same time, his erection grinding against her bottom through her skirt, which made both he and Abdullah laugh.

It was all too much, the three despicable men were all too much, and Sarah began to fight again in earnest. If Casswell could not or would not save her then she had to save herself. Her newfound ferocity took the men by surprise, and the waiter had to quickly tighten his grip to keep hold of her. Sarah knew that unless she was rescued or escaped their vile clutches, all three of them planned to have her.

Abdullah grabbed her legs and, pushing a hand up between her thighs, rucking her skirt up at the same time, tried hard to prise them apart. But Sarah fought like a wildcat, her legs clamped together until Mustafa shouted something and the men, cursing and panting heavily, held off.

But then, responding to a nod from Mustafa, the waiter ushered her to one side and pressed her tight up against one of the iron gates, and with Mustafa's help they strapped her wrists together with a leather belt and then hung her from one of the ornate curls high up in the wrought iron design. Her cheek and breasts pressed uncomfortably against the vertical bars.

It was a difficult irony for Sarah to take; bound to something that just minutes earlier she had hoped would be her route of escape. Now the three men were behind her, just visible over her shoulder, and she could not resist as Abdullah slid his sweating hands up the outside of her skirt, lewdly savouring the feel of her bottom as he did, and then unfastened it and tugged it down over her hips, down her shapely legs to the dusty ground, then roughly spreading her legs apart, the tendons standing out in her thighs and calves as she strained on tiptoe.

Then, with no more ado, he crouched behind her and his tongue and fingers licked and explored and took every advantage of her vulnerability, making her cringe. Meanwhile the waiter ripped off her blouse, the fabric cutting into her delicate flesh as it tore away.

Exposed and naked, there was nothing Sarah could do to resist the three of them, and she just knew that Mustafa intended to punish her for running away and for struggling so fiercely.

'You really ought to learn to co-operate, little one,' he said, his voice thick. 'And you should also learn it is in your best interests not to upset me; I am very good friends with Uri Weissman. Very good friends indeed.'

He signalled for the two men to move back, which they did with much reluctance and grumbling, and then he felt between her legs, cupping her sex from behind, making her stiffen and gasp as he slid his thumb up into her. Sarah flinched at the crude violation, and would have spat at the arrogant oaf if she could. She knew Weissman saw Mustafa as little more than a minion, a man to be used and manipulated when it suited him, but the sweaty Turk clearly had gross delusions of grandeur.

'You have to understand who is in control here, Miss Morgan,' he growled in her ear, his breath laden with garlic. 'And trust me, I will teach you. I really will.'

He moved away, his intrusive hand leaving her, and Sarah strained to pick up some clue as to what would happen next, although she had a pretty good idea, and then she tensed as she heard an unmistakable sound, and strained to catch a glimpse from the corner of her eye of the waiter pulling his leather belt from his trouser loops and handing it to Mustafa. Her fat tormentor folded it double in his fist, and then moved out of her sight.

There was a terrible silence, a few seconds deep and dark and full of a cruel promise. Sarah swallowed hard, every sense and nerve braced for the fierce kiss of supple leather.

And it came an instant later, the first stroke wrapping around her flank like some evil embrace. There was no pain for a few seconds – no sensation at all – and then it flooded her senses and she cried out instinctively, her back arching as the second blow followed, slightly higher and harder than the first, and as she strained her head round she saw the look of lust and excitement on the faces of Abdullah and the waiter. They would get their turn with her, of that she had no doubt.

The next crack of the belt across her unprotected buttocks drove away that thought, and the next one – until every shred of her consciousness was focused in the raw kiss of the leather against her flesh. Mustafa was as good as his word; he truly meant to teach her a lesson she would not forget.

The absorbing pain of the belt was a sensation for which there was no equal, one that she both feared and yet at some strange and unexpected level delighted in. As her restrained body contorted under the kiss of it she wondered what dark magic it was that Casswell had sparked in her. Somewhere far away Sarah could hear a voice crying out in anguish, and it took a while to realise that the voice was hers. Mustafa clearly intended to punish her long and hard for her attempted escape and for her insolence. The leather bit home again and again, cracking across her back and buttocks, making her skin burn and glow until finally there was nothing left but a void, a distance from which it almost seemed she was watching herself in the alley.

At last, after what seemed an eternity, they released her. Now it was the turn of the other two to indulge themselves, and Sarah was too weary and too stunned by what had happened and by her secret reaction to it to object.

The waiter turned her around and held her under the arms, while Abdullah lifted her legs around his waist and without prelude, slid his cock deep into her. Sarah gasped; despite everything she was wet and ready for him, and instinctively her calves locked around his back as he began to rut against her. Still aglow from the belt, she writhed against his belly, unable to escape either his cock or his fingers as she impaled herself again and again on his raging shaft. It was a heady combination.

The waiter turned his attentions to her breasts, his rasping breath wafting through her hair as he watched his companion fuck her. Deep inside Sarah felt the first ragged spasms of Abdullah's approaching climax and, against all the odds, her own too. He began to writhe and groan, forcing himself deeper and deeper, and just as she thought she could take no more the first waves of orgasm crashed through her. Sarah's whole body shuddered with the sheer energy of it, arching and twisting in the waiter's arms. She cried out again and again, her cries mingling with the grunts of Abdullah as they came together in a swell of pure physical release – and then, quite suddenly, it was all over.

Breathing hard, sweating, both spent, Abdullah dropped to his knees in front of her, and for a few seconds pressed his face into the warm fragrant wetness of her sex, his tongue lapping at her clitoris, fingers still eager to explore as if he could not get enough of her. It was almost more than Sarah could bear, and she desperately tried to wriggle away, moaning her protests.

But before she had a chance to catch her breath the waiter eased her down onto the beaten earth of the alley, onto her hands and knees, and knelt behind her. Sarah sighed with shameful delight as she felt him enter her. Her juices, and those of Abdullah, eased the waiter's passage and no doubt added to his excitement. He reached for her breasts, mauling them rabidly and pinching her tight nipples, and then slid his hands back to her hips, gaining a better purchase as he drove his cock into her like a steam hammer, all the time mumbling and then crying out all manner of words that Sarah did not understand. He came in seconds.

Sarah slumped to the ground and looked up, trembling

and exhausted, her body smeared with grime. Mustafa Aziz looked down upon her, his eyes as dark as coal. She wondered if this was payment enough; had he taken enough pleasure by looking on as the two men took her in turn, watching her humiliation?

It seemed not.

Mustafa Aziz beckoned her to crawl closer, and unfastened his fly. Sarah knew exactly what it was he wanted, so on her hands and knees she made no attempt to get to her feet. At that precise moment she was not sure that her legs would support her, anyway.

She fished his shaft out with trembling hands and slipped the crown into her mouth, her trembling lips and tongue working backwards and forwards and around the glans, one hand working along him, cradling the weight of his balls, while the other eased his foreskin back and forth. He grunted and she guessed it would not be long before he ejaculated too.

He pushed his cock deep into the back of her mouth, once, twice, his fingers locked tight in her hair as he pulled her against him, almost making her gag. With her hands spread against his overhanging belly Sarah fought to hold him back; to stop him penetrating so deliberately deep, but it was impossible. Snorting like a pig and jeering gleefully, sweat running down his face, Mustafa also came quickly, his seed filling her mouth and seeping from the corners of her tightly stretched lips onto her chin. And then, before Sarah knew what the animal intended, he hauled her to her feet and kissed her aggressively, his hands tightly clutching her burning buttocks and his tongue plunging into her mouth to lap at his own seed.

Chapter Fourteen

True to his word, Mustafa arranged for Sarah to be taken back to Uri Weissman's house. Sitting in the back of the rattling, squeaking cab, wearing nothing but her shoes and the old shirt the waiter had given her, she was aware of the taxi driver's eyes crawling slowly over her as he spied her in his rear-view mirror. She shivered under his undisguised interest. Did he know, could he guess what she had been doing? What she was wearing was a bit of a giveaway, she acknowledged ruefully.

As they got closer to Weissman's house, Sarah wondered if Casswell would be there yet, even though she knew it was doubtful that he would be back from his meeting in the mountains. It seemed such a long time since she had seen him, and she longed to see his reassuring face. But conflicting with her desire to be with him was an uneasy fear of the things Mustafa had said; if it came to it, which would Casswell choose – her, or his precious diaries?

It was dark when Casswell finally got back to the harbour town, the lights of the port picked out like stars in an otherwise dark and lovely landscape.

The abbot had suggested Casswell stay overnight, but he did not like the idea of being away from either the diaries or Sarah for any longer than was completely necessary. If he was honest, he did not trust the abbot, Mustafa or Weissman any further than he could throw them. He nipped the bridge of his nose to try and short-circuit the headache that was developing. It had been a long and trying day.

It was true that the abbot had several documents that interested Casswell; tantalising fragments of accounts of a slave auction, another that referred to Beatrice de Fleur by name, and one or two interesting little erotic stories illustrated and bound in leather, but he'd had little chance to study any of the documents for more than a few minutes, watched every step of the way as he was by the hovering abbot.

He was made to feel welcome enough, and the late lunch was a simple but tasty affair; cheese, bread and olives, and a glass of the local wine, but even after returning to the vaults for another look at the abbey's erotic treasures, Casswell had an odd feeling that there was more to the trip than met the eye.

Despite his reservations it had not been an altogether fruitless journey, for the abbot, after some gentle persuasion, somewhat reluctantly agreed to loan the documents he had shown Casswell to the local museum. But only on the express understanding that Mustafa Aziz took total and personal responsibility for their safekeeping. He would arrange to have them collected the following day if the chief curator agreed to the deal.

Casswell glanced at his watch, thinking about Sarah and wondering how the transcriptions had gone, and about how long it would be before they could finally leave for home and the familiarity of Casswell Hall. It would be a relief to leave the tensions of Turkey behind.

Weissman's house was quiet and still when the car pulled up outside. Casswell wondered if the others were at dinner, or perhaps everyone had gone out for the evening. That prospect was certainly appealing.

The main salon appeared to be empty, so Casswell slipped

off his jacket, folded it over his arm and headed upstairs; what he really needed more than anything else was a drink and a shower. At the door to his room he hesitated – he had the distinct feeling that there was someone already inside.

Casswell sighed; maybe he was just tired and jumpy. It was probably Chang turning down his bed, or perhaps Sarah waiting with a pile of notes from the day's work.

Sarah.

Casswell let her name linger in his mind for a few seconds. The idea that she was waiting for him in his room was one that excited him. She was one of life's natural submissives, a creature so exquisite, so perfect, so ready to serve and obey in whatever way he commanded. She was a treasure – and one he intended to guard jealously.

The feel of her compliant and obedient body moving against his was something he relished. He sighed; if Turkey had been difficult for him, it had been considerably worse for her.

Inside the room Casswell dropped his jacket over a chair and began to unbutton his shirt, his mind still on Sarah, and turning round he was surprised to find Anna Weissman standing in the shadows by his desk. She stared at him and attempted a smile, her face a mask of contrived innocence.

Casswell was not so easily fooled, and as their eyes met he noticed that she dropped something to the floor, a single sheet of paper that fluttered and fell like an autumn leaf, down beside the desk.

'Oh, hello Rigel,' she said hastily, quite obviously trying to regain her composure by improving on her smile. 'Have you, um, have you had a good day?'

Casswell nodded, and then said with a wry grin, 'I didn't

have you down as the kind of woman who welcomed her man home after a hard day at the office.'

He watched her colour and bluster ebbing away. 'So what did you want?' he probed. 'Is there anything I can do to help you?' As he spoke he turned his back, and apparently his attention, to the drinks tray on the side table, although from the corner of his eye he could see her reflection in the dressing table mirror. The instant his back was turned she bobbed down, retrieved the paper, and added it to a pile on the desk.

'Would you care for a nightcap?' he asked, all innocence, but furtively watching her every move. 'Brandy?'

'Um, that would be lovely,' Anna gushed, overdoing it somewhat.

'Soda?' he asked, turning to her. 'Ice?'

'Uhuh.' She smiled and came over to take the glass from his fingers. 'Mustafa rang,' she said, gradually gathering her composure. 'He said you were going up to the abbey today.'

Casswell smiled; she would never make a poker player. 'And you thought I'd be away overnight?'

She was about to protest when he reached out and snatched her wrist. 'Well?' he demanded, his fingers closing hard. 'What did you really want, Anna? There is no reason on earth for you to be in here, unless of course you're checking up on, what? The linen? The housekeeping? What are you doing in here?'

She blushed and tried in vain to twist her arm free. 'I – I – please, Rigel, you're hurting me!'

Casswell bundled her over to the pile of papers on his desk. 'You were extremely interested in getting your hands on the first translation of the diary,' he stated for her. 'Was it your idea or your brother's idea to come in here and steal them?' He paused and looked down at the pages. 'Or have you already copied what's here?'

Anna's fearful expression gave the game away, and Casswell shook his head in disgust. 'I don't understand,' he said. 'You know I would have made sure all interested parties had a copy – this research is funded by a whole committee of people just like your brother. What is this all about, Anna?'

She stubbornly refused to respond, so his anger resurfacing and getting the better of him, Casswell caught hold of her hair and pulled her face close to his, and in amongst her fear he could see an intense and compelling flash of desire.

'Tell me,' he insisted, her face no more than an inch from his. He could smell the mingled scents of her subtle perfume and the soft musk of her skin. She mewled at the pain as his fingers tightened in her hair, but he was without mercy. 'Tell me,' he growled, jerking on her wrist. 'I will not be disobeyed or ignored.'

'It – it wasn't m-my idea,' she blurted through a stifled sob.

'Whose was it then?'

Anna sobbed. 'I didn't think you were coming back tonight, so I was going to take the disks and copy them and then I started to read the transcript...' she stopped, seeming to realise she'd said too much. 'He'll kill me if he finds out you've caught me.'

'Your brother?'

Anna nodded as best she could, given that Casswell still had tight hold of her. 'Yes, Uri and the museum trustees and that little shit Mustafa Aziz. They want the glory of finding and translating this book.'

'But that's ridiculous,' Casswell snorted. 'They've know about it for years.'

'Yes, but you know they couldn't translate it – and this one together with the others you've already deciphered, and your reputation, guarantees that they'll make a lot of money.' She paused as his fingers loosened their grip, and then she slowly pulled away. 'Rigel, please take me with you when you leave. I hate it here. I want to learn about those things in the diaries... about the pleasure and the pain.' Her colour intensified as she looked into his face, and her eyes filled with tears.

He stared at her. 'Don't be ridiculous. Uri would never allow you to go with me, and besides, you are of no use to me, Anna.'

She flinched as though he had hit her. 'How can you say that? Is it because I can't type?'

'No, Anna, it's because you have no integrity or sense of loyalty,' he stated bluntly. 'You are ready to run with the hare and hunt with the hounds if it suits you.'

The statuesque blonde gasped as the candid words registered, and then she launched herself towards Casswell like a banshee. Her face was contorted with fury and indignation, but before she could set foul of him he caught her wrists and held her at bay without too much difficulty.

'Anna,' he said sternly, 'if you really want to leave Uri, then do it yourself. If you come to England of your own volition then I'll help you. I'll even try to find a master to teach you all the things you so desperately desire, but I'm not taking you away from here with me. The situation is fraught enough without that.'

As she gradually began to relax he pulled her closer. 'And now,' he said, his mood quieter, 'you're going to pay for this intrusion.'

'Pay?' she said, her body instantly stiffening.

Casswell nodded. 'Oh yes. But I'll not say a word to your precious brother about your being caught stealing my work. I doubt that his punishment would be quite the same as mine.'

'Dr Casswell wants to see you.'

Sarah looked up sleepily into Chang's inscrutable face, for an instant unable to work out where she was. Since arriving back from her encounter with Mustafa, she had showered, eaten supper in her room and, having given up trying to make sense of the day's events, curled up on the bed and slept fitfully.

Her dreams were littered with intense images of twisting shadowy alleys and barred doorways as she ran back and forth trying desperately to escape an unseen pursuer. It was almost a relief to be woken up.

'He's back?' she said, with a real sense of relief.

Chang nodded.

Sarah hurried to get up from the bed; she wanted to tell Casswell about Mustafa's deceit and the awful liberties he'd taken.

Chang helped her, and then looked her up and down with the slightest hint of appreciation in his expression; she had been sleeping naked in the oppressive heat. Without another word he took a leash and collar from his pocket – familiar objects that she had not seen since leaving England – and the gesture was unmistakable. Tonight Sarah was being taken to Casswell's bedroom as his plaything. She would be a toy for his unadulterated pleasure, and it made something deep in her tummy flutter with delight.

She caught sight of her reflection in the mirror; her hair was naturally tousled from sleep, and her smooth skin had a warm glow to it, the soft curves of her body a stark contrast to the black studded leather collar. The image made Sarah's pulse race; whatever else happened to her this was where she felt closest to the indefinable hunger that drove her, the dark energy that Casswell had recognised in her when they first met. She truly was his.

Chang led her to Casswell's room. Naked and barefoot, her eyes chastely lowered, Sarah was every inch the perfect submissive, and inside her heart soared, for this was where she belonged, with Casswell, as his lover and slave.

Casswell sat relaxed on the sofa, dressed in a black silk bathrobe, barefoot too, and cradling a brandy. Sarah's heart tightened. He was as handsome as he was cruel, and she knew beneath the robe his body was lean and tanned. Excitement gripped her at the thought of his caress.

She shivered. Nothing she experienced at the hands of any other man came close to the passion and the desire experienced when in Casswell's company… or his bed.

He indicated that she should turn around for him, and she did so without an instant's hesitation. Sarah knew from experience how much he enjoyed looking at her body, touching and stroking and admiring his prize possession. He beckoned her closer, so she backed up close, and following his unspoken instructions, knelt on the floor on her hands and knees, so he could pet her like some favoured animal.

He smiled and ran his fingers through her hair and then something – a movement or a noise, it was hard to decide exactly which – caught her attention. Sarah looked over her shoulder, and saw to her surprise that Anna Weissman was in the corner of the room. She gasped as she took in the details.

Naked, tied, her legs spread wide, the elegant blonde hung from a hook in the ceiling. She was trembling, her large eyes wide with fear and anticipation. It was a state of mind and body that Sarah recognised only too well.

The trussed woman refused to meet the kneeling girl's stare.

Sarah would have known Chang's handiwork anywhere. He had shaved Anna's sex mound, and smooth and naked, it looked vulnerable and exposed and at the same time like some erotic, ripe fruit. He had oiled the blonde's sleek skin too, until it seemed that she glowed from within. Her wrists were tied above her head, exposing her breasts to perfection, and her feet were parted wide and held by a metal retaining bar and ankle straps. She looked quite magnificent, hanging there in the soft lamplight like a living trophy.

For a terrible, insecure instant Sarah's heart sank – could it be that she had lost everything? Had Anna taken her place?

And then Casswell's dulcet tones seeped into her fears, soothing and reassuring. 'Miss Weissman needs to be punished,' he said gently. 'I caught her this evening, trying to steal our work. It seems we've been set up.' As he spoke he handed Sarah an ornate riding crop.

She looked up at him with uncertainty in her eyes, feeling the braided handle cradled in her palm, catching the subtle fragrance of the well-worked leather. Sarah was not sure how she felt about what he was proposing. It had been one thing to whip the unknown girl in the nightclub – but to do the same to Anna Weissman? To her surprise, she felt tears welling up in her eyes. This was against her nature, but his gaze did not falter.

'If you do not do it,' he said with calm assurance, 'I will hand her over to Chang.'

Sarah glanced across the room again. Casswell's manservant was watching and waiting by the door, his expression totally impassive, although Sarah could guess the direction his thoughts were turning. She knew very well that whatever punishment she administered, it would be nothing compared to what the duplicitous blonde might expect at the hands of Chang, although she also knew, without a shred of doubt, that even though she had no desire to hand Anna over to the oriental, this was not what she was made of. She searched Casswell's face again, hoping he would offer her some clue, some glimmer of what he was thinking, but his eyes were dark and unreadable.

'Well?' he pressed.

Sarah knew exactly what she had to do, although with Casswell she always had the choice. It was implicit to their unspoken arrangement; it was the reason she trusted him with her body and her soul. His cruelty, his love of dominance, his love of her, was a magical bond that she both loved and dreaded; the mixture of light and dark, the passion and pain were as compelling an enchantment as she could ever imagine. But she also knew where her passions lay, and it was not in beating Anna Weissman.

Each to their own – let Chang do what he had a natural gift for. So without a word she handed him the whip back.

Casswell smiled, and on silent feet Chang came over and took the crop from his master. On the other side of the room Anna whimpered in fear. Casswell beckoned Sarah to move beside him so he could touch her as he sat and watched the entertainment unfold.

She stood as he ordered, and watched as across the room Chang drew the whip up and back and brought it down across Anna's buttocks with a terrible and deadly accuracy.

The blonde screamed and spun slightly. Her voice was heavy with a mixture of indignation and pain. A great blush of red rose on her skin, marking the kiss of the whip like a photographic image.

'You bastard, Rigel,' she moaned as the crop bit again. 'I hate you. I hate you!' She writhed and tugged at the leather straps as she babbled.

In Casswell's company Sarah had seen many scenes like this before, but this was perhaps the first in which she truly had a vested interest. The elegant ice-cold blonde contorted and twisted against the leather and the leg irons, and Sarah could not help but wonder how much of Anna's behaviour and intervention had been at her brother's behest.

The blonde's body glowed like spun silk under the lamplight, glistening with a subtle mixture of sweat and oil as Chang continued relentlessly with her punishment.

The whip cracked repeatedly, the sound filling the room. Anna shrieked, she mewled, and she swore like an alley cat until gradually she became lost in the maze of pain, the sounds slowly changing to something more instinctive and less coherent.

Chang was relentless, each stroke as accurate and cruel as the one before.

And all the while Casswell stroked Sarah, almost as if he was settling her, comforting her, consoling her. She moved under his touch to let him have greater freedom with her. His fingers idly made their way over her breasts, and then down the smooth plain of her ribs and belly until he could cradle and explore the gentle mound of her sex and those soft, wet, fragrant lips between her thighs.

His touch was driving Sarah wild with desire, and eventually he looked up at her and she knew exactly what he wanted. She sank gracefully to her knees, curled up between her legs, and unfastening the waist-tie of his robe, took his throbbing cock into her mouth. How different from doing the same to Mustafa; this was an act of worship at a revered and adored altar.

She sighed with pleasure as her senses filled with the smell and touch and taste of him. He was already wet, his erection warm and salty on her eager tongue. Sarah wriggled closer, cradling his heavy balls with one hand. She loved this so much, the act of obedience and submission making her heady with desire. First she licked the crown, teasing around the rim with the tip of her tongue, sliding his foreskin back, tracing spirals around the sensitive head before drawing it deep into her mouth, while her other hand worked up and down the swollen, rigid shaft. The first strokes were long and slow, not too tight nor too intense, but a breathtaking counterpoint to the light brushing and nibbling and sucking of her mouth around his glans.

Casswell groaned softly and lifted his hips towards her face, and all the while she was honouring him with her lips and tongue she could hear the cut and hiss of the whip and the muted cries of Anna Weissman, although as the seconds passed she became so involved in pleasing her master that the sounds faded to a distant corner of her mind, and so she was shocked when a few minutes later she felt a hand slide apprehensively between her thighs. She shivered and, with her mouth still full looked up at Casswell with wide, enquiring eyes, as a finger slipped into the wetness it found there. Although she was in no position to turn, she guessed from the gentleness of the exploration and the knowing touch, that it was Anna Weissman.

It seemed the blonde's penance was not yet over. She eased Sarah's thighs apart, and the kneeling girl felt a warm tongue flick over the tight puckering of her anus, and then down over the delicate bridge of skin that lay between it and her throbbing quim. Anna's tongue slid in and out, sucking her juices much as Sarah was sucking Casswell's cock.

He smiled. Sarah's eager tongue and lips were taking him closer and closer to the point of no return – and it was the sweetest of tortures. Anna Weissman had taken the place he had ordained for her – serving his beautiful slave.

He nodded, and Chang dropped to the floor between the blonde's legs and, lifting her hips slightly, positioning her just as he wanted her, used some of the oil he had previously used to coat her body, to lubricate that spot he loved so dearly. There was a tremor that echoed through each of them, a chain reaction, as Chang fed his cock very slowly deep into the tight dark confines of Anna's bottom.

The blonde cried out – her pain, her shock, her trepidation, and the sense of humiliation muted by the soft warm press of Sarah's shapely thighs and buttocks to her face. Casswell pressed deeper into Sarah's willing mouth, and she responded instantly by increasing the pressure of her fist around his shaft, her lips closing tight, working him harder and harder. They both knew it would not be long before she took him to the point of release, and Casswell briefly wondered if he could hold out long enough so that each player could reach the goal they most desired simultaneously.

Despite the humiliation at the hands of Chang, Anna was writhing and moaning as the artful oriental applied his fingers to the engorged ridge of her clitoris. Sarah groaned around the column of flesh in her mouth and ground her sex back onto the face of the Austrian woman, and Casswell knew from the way she was moving, the tightness in her shoulders and the dreamy expression on her face, that she was as close as he was.

Suddenly Sarah jerked forward, a little moan of pure pleasure echoing and vibrating through his cock. It was enough to take him over the edge, and the effect on the others was explosive as if that one little shudder, that one little gasping sob, was the touch paper that lit a stunning and volatile fuse.

Waves of ecstasy rolled through him driving away everything, every thought, except the suction and heat of Sarah's mouth tight around his cock and the pulsating rise of his orgasm. Sarah suckled and hummed with avid delight, and her mouth filled with his seed.

Anna Weissman shrieked, her hips lifting to meet Chang stroke for stroke as she impaled herself on his shaft, and for an instant all four of them were linked by an intense communal pleasure, which only very gradually subsided and left them replete and drained, the silence of contentment punctuated only by the sounds of their breathing.

'Well, well, well... what have we here? And why wasn't I invited?'

Casswell opened his eyes. Uri Weissman, cradling a glistening glass of brandy, was standing by the door, his eyes alight with interest. Was his expression one of envy, or was he hoping his sister's mission had not been thwarted?

'I thought you were spending the night in the mountains,' he went on.

Casswell smiled, making no effort to move. 'And miss the comforts of your hospitality? I don't think so.'

Weissman laughed. 'You are a cool customer, Rigel,' he said, and lifted his glass in salute.

Chapter Fifteen

While Chang poured their host another glass of brandy Sarah remained curled up on the floor beside Casswell, watching Weissman's every move.

'We will be leaving at the end of the week,' Casswell informed the Austrian, his hand lingering on her shoulder.

While Weissman had settled himself in an armchair, his sister slipped away to retrieve her clothes and what little remained of her dignity.

Weissman looked at Casswell inquisitively. 'Are you serious?' he asked. 'Are you that close to finishing the translation?' Casswell knew Weissman had a good idea how much more he had to do, but he was a far better liar than his sister. His questioning expression did not falter for an instant. Casswell nodded.

'And what about the extra manuscripts from the abbey?' Weissman continued, probing.

Casswell smiled. 'They're just a simple matter of translation; anyone could do it. What makes the diaries so much more complex is that not only are they in a little known dialect, but much of the more sensitive material is encrypted. Beatrice was a clever young lady. She knew how potentially explosive and dangerous these accounts of her life could be if they fell into the wrong hands.'

Weissman nodded. 'We will be sad to see you go,' he said. 'It has been a pleasure to have your company. And of course, we will miss the company of your lovely assistant. Such a talented little creature.'

He smiled at Sarah, who shivered under his stare. His

eyes moved over her, exploring her nakedness, as intrusive as tangible fingers, his attention lingering for a few seconds on the leather collar she wore.

'A nice touch,' he said, rolling the ice around in the bottom of his glass. 'Perhaps I ought to get my sister one. What do you think?'

Sarah looked away, she would be glad to put their stay in Turkey behind them.

The sound of Anna returning broke Weissman's concentration. As the blonde crossed the room, now dressed, with her hair and make-up immaculately restored, he abruptly got to his feet. 'If you will excuse me, Rigel, my sister and I have a family matter to sort out. I will see you both tomorrow.'

Anna looked taken aback; it was extremely late and quite obvious that the 'family matter' was a complete surprise to her, but she did not question her brother or offer a word of protest.

Once the two of them had left Casswell dismissed Chang, rose from the comfort of the chair, and taking Sarah's hand, led her to his bed. It seemed that at least for tonight the status quo had been restored, and with a warm glow enveloping her, Sarah slipped between the sheets beside him. As he turned to her in the darkness and held her in his arms, she sighed with contentment and a sense of coming home.

When Casswell and Sarah arrived at the museum the following morning, Mustafa Aziz was gleeful. Rubbing his hands together with delight he showed Casswell the box of books and manuscripts that had arrived at first light from the abbey. Even Casswell was surprised how quickly it had all been delivered, assuming that Mustafa's agreement to keep everything safe would have to be confirmed in writing. But apparently not. It seemed Casswell's genuine interest and Mustafa's word over the phone had been enough. Although he did not say so much, Casswell thought the abbot a fool, or perhaps, it occurred to him as he looked at the crate, the old man was just happy at last to rid the abbey of the salacious material. Whichever, the chest was made from the finest tooled red leather, faded now with age, and bound with two stout straps. It took a couple of men to carry it down to the vault.

Casswell very carefully opened it and examined the contents without removing anything.

'You made a very fine impression on the abbot,' Mustafa told him. 'He rang me last night to say how impressed he was by you. He considered you a true gentleman.' Casswell glanced at the Turk, wondering why all the flattery. 'This material is only here because of your excellent and honourable reputation,' gushed Mustafa.

'And held in your safekeeping?' Casswell asked.

The Turk nodded. 'Indeed. The deal is we keep it all safe, translate it and return it without the contents ever becoming public knowledge.'

'And those are your true intentions?'

Mustafa snorted, as though insulted by the suggestion otherwise, but then a smile slowly broadened his loose lips. 'What can I say?' he chuckled. 'If the material is commercial, what man would not be tempted to turn a coin or two. We both know there are interested parties out there who would relish something new.'

'Sell them, you mean?'

Mustafa very nearly blurted something, but paused and then stopped himself, as if remembering who he was talking to. 'No, no, the originals, of course not,' he snorted, as if the very idea that he was suggesting such a thing was a slur on the integrity of his family name. 'But, a good copy of the translated version, perhaps?' he opened his arms expansively, as if the proposal was only natural and totally acceptable. 'The abbot need never know, need he?'

Sarah knew from Casswell's expression that he was offended by Mustafa's dishonesty, and his dismissal of the abbot's trust.

With a withering look that expressed Casswell's opinion on the matter perfectly, he turned away from the sweating oaf and focussed his attention on the handwritten script on the desk before him. But thick-skinned as ever, Mustafa merely grinned at the rejection and dabbed his forehead with his usual grubby hanky.

'I wondered if you might look at them, Dr Casswell, and then perhaps recommend a trustworthy translator, given the potentially delicate nature of the contents,' he said, undaunted.

'Well, there are several good scholars I would be happy to recommend,' Casswell replied. He glanced again at the chest. 'And yes, I would certainly like a greater opportunity to look through the collection. I'd appreciate it if you would leave it here for the time being.'

Mustafa nodded curtly. 'Of course, no problem.' With a wave of his hand the two porters were dismissed.

Pulling on a pair of light cotton gloves, Casswell returned his attentions to the job in hand. Lifting his magnifying lens closer he began to work, and getting the message that he had been summarily dismissed, Mustafa backed away.

Sarah glanced at Casswell. It was so unlike him to be rude that she suspected he was deeply annoyed with not just Mustafa, but the whole distrustful set up they had found in Turkey.

Finally alone, it was not long before a comfortable silence settled between the two of them. Then Casswell read the words from the page in front of him, taking Sarah by surprise, for normally he wrote the translations down, but today it seemed important for him to hear Beatrice's words aloud.

Sarah picked up a pencil and started to take notes, locked into the story not just by the events unfolding, but also by the sensual hypnotic timbre of Casswell's beautifully modulated voice.

...The days riding back to the castle are long and arduous, the nights longer still, but I am learning that with Usher as my new master at the very least I am safe. The pain and the kiss of his belt is tempered by the knowledge that he will protect me from whatever the journey brings, and his cruelty is fired by an animal passion, not by revenge or spite.

I ride alongside him, wrapped in a cloak from his war chest, dressed in clothes he has bought for me along the way, my mind returning again and again to what will become of me when at last I ride under the gates of my master's castle.

To mark my servitude and obedience, Usher found me a collar from his chest that once graced the neck of his most favoured hound. Set with studs and precious stones it is a pretty trinket, and all the while I wear his mark, in my imagination Lord Usher takes me, stripped naked and bound hand and foot, and passes me over to my lord – a wedding gift for the man who, as the miles and the abbey are left behind us, fills my every waking thought.

In my dreams my master smiles, and without looking back at those knights and ladies and fine noble folk who are gathered for his wedding breakfast, carries me up to his chamber and makes me his once more. He must take me back for himself, reclaim me from the life I have suffered away from the castle, and in my wild dreaming I feel the bite of leather as the whip wraps around me, I feel his body pressing on mine, his cock buried deep, deep inside me, inside my mind, I smell him, I hear the soft whisper of his breath in the dead of night when he sleeps and the heady groans of his excitement as he fills my body with his pleasure.

At present it is Lord Usher who reaps the sweet harvest of these imaginings, for by the time I climb down from the horse each day my body is yearning with the most desperate hunger, my sex wet and ready, longing for satisfaction.

Usher knows women well, and sees and understands only too well the raw lust in my eyes as I turn to him – for I dare not look at any of the other men who ride with him. Often he dismisses his body servants and will take me then and there, against a tree, or if we have stopped at an inn, up against the wall, caring not who witnesses the coupling, pushing up my skirts, driving his cock deep into me, or order me to the floor and take me like a beast on all fours amidst the dust and dirt.

Worse by far he will make me wait, but not in a way that lets my blood settle. Instead, as the day darkens, he will summon me for all manner of trivial reasons, or brush against me or cup my breasts as he passes. As I wait on him he will press a kiss to my neck and slide his hands up between my thighs, so by the time night falls I am like a bitch on heat, or sweated up like a mare, with a hunger that will not abate.

Usher knows too my worth as cold hard currency, and likes the games and power my body offers him. At the house of a merchant he will trade my services to an older son, or a father, or both for a little silver, and though he has no need of the coin he loves the sport of it. A second calling, he tells me as he impales me after they have had their fill – a pimp to willing whore. What better trade for a landed man?

Last night at a farm on the outskirts of a town, he took me out to the barn once supper was done on the pretext of looking at a filly he had bought, and on which he would value the farmer's opinion. Waiting in one of the stalls were the farmer's sons, three big boys, and a father who they favoured.

'Come,' Usher said, and held a hand towards me. I stepped out from the shadows in a lamp lit circle.

'What nonsense is this, sir?' the farmer snorted. 'I came to see a horse.'

Usher laughed. 'I told you, sir, I had a fine mount with me, a ride that would put any other to shame, did I not?'

For an instant the farmer looked puzzled, and then his face split into a wide grin. 'Aye, indeed you did, but I'm wary of so fine a beast as this. I need a workish creature that will bear a heavy load.' As he spoke he rudely cupped the front of his breeches.

Usher's expression did not falter. 'Do not be deceived by these fine bones,' he said. 'This creature comes from working stock. Let me show you it unrugged.'

There was a pause, and Usher looked at the farmer's sons, whose mouths were hanging open at the very prospect of what might follow, clearly already erect at the very notion of seeing a girl uncovered.

'I presume they would like a little ride too,' said Usher, watching their eager, oafish faces. 'To get the feel of a good mount.'

The old man wiped his mouth with the back of his hand. 'Aye, but after me, not afore. Tis the right of age before youth to try a new ride out.'

'Indeed,' Usher nodded, every ounce the horse dealer. He stood behind me, and gripped the cloak that covered me. He waited until he had their full attention and then slowly, with a sleight of hand that would have served a magician proud, he unveiled me. There was a mumbled murmur of approval.

'Yours?' said the farmer, indicating the collar.

Usher laughed. 'Indeed, have you never had a bitch that strays?'

The farmer laughed and looked me over again. I could see the lust in his dark eyes. 'She's still a little too fine for my tastes,' he declared. 'Little bones, easy broken, easily bruised. No staying power.'

Usher pulled a face and made as if to cover me up with the robe. 'Ah well, if she's not to your tastes then we'll away to our beds,' he said. 'Come, Beatrice.'

But before he could wrap me up again the farmer caught hold of his wrist. 'Not so fast,' he said hastily. 'Perhaps we could manage her.'

There was a lusty murmur of agreement from the farmer's sons.

The farmer looked me up and down again, and circled me like I was prize stock, and as he did Usher backed away into the shadows.

'Will she bite or bolt?' the farmer asked, reaching out to touch my face. 'Will she run away if I ride her a little rough?'

'Who knows,' Usher shrugged. 'Would you like her better bound? You can tie her if you prefer it.'

The farmer's eyes narrowed with intent, and from one of the stalls he pulled a length of rope. This man was better suited to tying sheep or cattle than women, but even so he bound my wrists and hung me from a rafter, all the while his desires mounting as he worked, his labours watched wide-eyed by his boys.

The air around us was alive like a storm in that barn. When I was well and truly bound the farmer took a rag from his pocket and gagged me, for fear I do believe that I might cry out and rouse his wife. Strange though, I was not afraid with Usher there to protect me.

Ready now, the farmer took in the details of his handiwork. I could feel the boys eager to take their turn, eager to touch and have me. But what was it the old man wanted from me? As he circled me once more he fell to his knees at my feet, and with his great hands cupping the orbs of my backside, he pulled me forward onto his tongue, and moaned in delight as he sniffed and lapped and sucked eagerly at all those most secret and scented places.

I moaned in pleasure as his leathery tongue found my pleasure-bud and drew it like a little teat between his thick lips, sucking at it, nibbling and caressing it with the very tip of his tongue, making me shiver with pure animal pleasure.

Lifting me in those large hands of his he pressed my little body to his lips, like a poultice, parted my legs wider still, and taking my weight, let his tongue move back, sliding deep in and out of my sex, and then back further over that little area of flesh between one ripe pleasure and one even darker. I held my breath, as now his tongue brushed even that secret entrance, back and force, sucking and lapping at that most forbidden and unnatural of places. The sensation lit a strange ache in my belly and I moaned and writhed with the most terrible mixture of deepest shame and wildest pleasure.

The man was truly wise to have gagged me, for I cried as his tongue teased and tickled and he sought entry there.

As I looked across into the stall I could see the look of desire on the faces of the boys, and wondered what would happen to me once their father was done, for the excitement rumbled and roared like a gathering storm, but such thoughts did not last, for the farmer's tongue was working a dark and compelling magic so mesmerising I could scarcely believe it.

With one great paw he pulled me closer still, a thickset thumb brushed my pleasure-bud, and a rough and unwieldy finger slipped deep into my sex. All this while his tongue worked back and forth until I knew my quim was as wet and as hungry as those boys who watched us. I trembled with sheer need, and he knew it too, this old man who made his living from the land, who understood animals and knew me to be one. As I began to ride his face, pushing my wet quim eagerly onto him, he looked up at my rapt expression and knew he had me. I was as eager as any filly for the coming of the stallion.

Slowly the man got to his feet and unfastened his breeches, and my eyes barely believed what stood proud of the nest of thick curly hair in his groin. The man was a giant, his cock no less.

I gasped behind my gag. Without his tongue and fingers exciting me beyond measure and getting me so very wet, he would have split me wide, but as it was my body opened as tame and willing as a newly broken filly under the relentless press of his manhood.

As I sighed through the gag at the feel of him finding his way home, he lifted me up onto to him with those large hands and moved deeper still. He lifted my breasts to his mouth, and his lips closed first on one nipple and then the other, sucking hard and biting at my teats. And now despite the glow in my belly and the wetness that seeped between my legs I was afraid, for it was the biggest cock I had ever seen, and even with his ministrations I couldn't help but be fearful as he began to move deeper into me.

The old man looked me in the eye, and spitting into his palm, began to rub around that place where our bodies where joined, at the same time his thumb finding my nub. The sensations were almost more than I could bear. Holding me to him he began to move in and out, slowly at first as if allowing my body to settle, to lose its apprehension, and indeed it did, and as I felt my pleasure rekindle he began to move faster, all the while his eyes locked on mine as if he were looking into my very soul.

And now he began to ease me along the length of his shaft, holding me so that with each stroke his great cock grazed and brushed the seat of my pleasure.

T'was more than I could bear, my body began to close around him, and he began to thrust in earnest, his whole frame seemed locked into the thrust, pushing me and pulling me as if I weighed no more than a feather. And feather I felt, for my mind was reeling and floating with the pleasure that this great brute of a man was gifting me with. And then I knew that I could bear no more; I was within a whisper of that madness, that instant when all reason is lost and all we are left with is pleasure, and I knew he was there too.

Deep inside I felt the roaring pulse of his cock as his seed exploded inside me. It was like a tidal bore making me gasp, making me writhe, and then he was spent and sliding from me.

In those moments when I had expected him to leave me to the mercy of his boys, who bayed like hounds at the leash, he fell to his knees and buried his face in the wet pit of my sex and lapped at me again, his tongue exploring the dregs of his own passion.

His touch made me gasp, for I was so close to that moment of release that every part of my body shivered and quivered, and what an instant before had been pleasure was now pain, and was now again a roaring fire that made me cry out despite the gag. He looked up at me, his face wet with his pleasure and my own, and began to slowly circle the seat of my desire.

So calculating was his touch. I could not fight the sensation; only submit to the flow of it. In the stall the boys bayed for more. My cries were muffled, my body crying out for a moment's respite, but all to no avail. Waves of ecstasy began to roll through me again; hot and angry like water boiling. Against all odds I began to writhe and shudder and tremble, my whole body alive and glowing.

At some signal unseen by me in my reverie, he moved away, and like a hunting pack the farmer's sons fell on me to take their fill. Strong hands held me while others cut me down. As I opened my eyes the first, a thickset boy who so favoured his father that they could almost be twin, was unfastening his breeches. It seemed he was as blessed as the one that sired him. Setting me down on the dusty floor like a dog, he slid into my cunt, so wet and yet still so accommodatingly tight, and drove home. He had not his father's touch, though, yet despite the gag I screamed and cried as he filled me to the very brim.

One of the younger brothers, who could bear it no more, pulled away my gag and knelt before me cradling his manhood in his hands, and I took him into my mouth, the scent and salty taste of him flooding my already overwhelmed senses. The third knelt down alongside me and began to touch and stroke me, fingers straying to the pit of my sex, brushing the place were cock and quim met, cupping my breasts, sniffing at my hair, touching and kissing me, while his hand worked back and forth along his own shaft, although I thought this was only to sustain the pleasure until his own chance came. And then the one impaling me began to gasp and my sex flooded with his seed, and within a heartbeat his brother filled my mouth equally. The third splashed his seed onto my throat and breasts, his hands working it into my skin like the most precious unguent.

Awash with their pleasure, I cried. Slumped there on the floor between them, I was reduced to the very essence of my sex, not a person, not even a girl, but just an available creature meant purely as a vessel for their pleasure.

As I looked up through weary eyes, Usher was still there, watching me from the shadows, his face as hungry as any of the others, and I knew, without any doubt, that when the boys were done he too would want his fill…

At the desk in the vault Casswell looked across at Sarah, the air electric between them.

Sarah set the pencil she had been using down on top of the desk, and moved closer to him.

In an instant Casswell was on his feet and locked his fingers in her hair, dragging her too him. She sobbed with delight and misgivings, and at the very edges of pain he kissed her feverishly, and then turned her facedown amongst the books and notepads and glass cases. Spreading her legs he pressed his hand between her thighs and opened her. She gasped as his thumb prodded into her sex, knowing fingers teasing her clitoris. She was already wet, and a moment later she felt his cock battering at her. It took her breath away as he sank deep, deep inside. With one hand he continued to caress her, and his other was still locked in her hair, pulling her up and back, pulling her closer. Sarah cried out, helpless as he aggressively fucked her. She felt he was reclaiming her, from Mustafa Aziz, from Uri Weissman, and from Turkey. As his stabbing hips found some sort of a rhythm, she slid her fingers down between her thighs, joining with his to bring them both to a shattering climax.

Chapter Sixteen

Sarah turned on the computer to type up the final entry in Beatrice's diary.

As she settled down Casswell looked at her. 'You know, as soon as this is finished we can go,' he said. He sounded tired, his eyes heavy from hours of concentration.

They had both worked for the remainder of the day, eating lunch in situ, ignoring the call of siesta, both united in their desire to get the work done and put the events of the trip far behind them.

Sarah nodded, expecting him to collect his things together and go back to the house. After all, all she had to do was put the day's work onto a disk. Casswell got to his feet and looked at the chest sent down to the museum by the abbot and, crouching over it, opened the lid. For an instant he paused.

'Weissman has already got copies of the translation we've done so far,' he said. 'I caught Anna in my room last night. She's copied the disks, and Mustafa may well be taking a copy of this machine when we leave, to ensure that between them they're getting everything. If it weren't for the fact that I caught her reading my notes, I'd never have known. And he certainly had no plans of handing them over to the committee that's paid for the trip. Oh no, our dear friend Uri Weissman has his own distributors in mind.'

'But we've got a copy too,' Sarah pointed out.

Casswell nodded. 'We have, that's true, except that Weissman has probably already got the work we've done so far to the printer. Add in today's work and his job is done. Print it off, bind it up, it could be in the hands of his readers within hours.'

He turned his attention back to the chest of documents, while Sarah looked down at the notebook she had been working in all day.

'And if we don't transcribe it?' she said. 'If I don't put it on the computer?'

Casswell stared at her. 'What?'

Sarah picked up her briefcase and dropped her shorthand pad inside. 'I could do it when we get home. Usher and the farmer's boys, and what happens when Beatrice gets back to the castle.'

A slow smile crept onto Casswell's face. 'My dear girl, why didn't I think of that before? It's so simple, and they won't know how it all ends.'

Sarah smiled, feeling pleased with herself, as Casswell reached out and gently touched her cheek. 'Now, before we leave I want to take a quick look at the abbot's treasures, and then we'll go. This time tomorrow we could be back at Casswell Hall.'

Sarah stretched, feeling better already, and looked across at the crate that contained the section of pillar Mustafa had presented Casswell with, as a 'gift'. 'Are they going to have that shipped back for you?' she asked.

'Don't worry,' Casswell said, seeing what she was looking at. 'I've already arranged to have it taken to the airport. Chang will sort it.'

She glanced towards the chest. 'Interesting?' she asked.

He nodded. 'Oh yes, there are some amazing things in here, and most of it is far too good for that heathen Mustafa, and his tin pot museum.'

Sarah looked at him affectionately; she knew how passionate Casswell was about his precious research. 'You said you could help him get it translated,' she reminded him.

'Indeed I did, Sarah,' Casswell agreed. 'Come on, it's time we went back to the Weissmans.'

'But I thought,' she indicated the trunk, 'I thought you were going to look at the papers.'

Casswell smiled. 'Don't worry, there is all the time in the world,' he told her.

Was this some spiritual reflection on the nature of time, Sarah wondered, or did it mean they would have to come back to Turkey in the future? She hoped with all her heart that he had not meant the latter.

The following afternoon, Sarah relaxed in the sumptuous surroundings of first class with a glass of chilled champagne and the final pages of Beatrice de Fleur's diary, and it seemed that Sarah was not the only one going home.

...We are close now to the castle. Usher's groom says perhaps a day, two at the most before we reach the borders of my master's land. But all is not well and I am afraid that we may be forced to turn back. There is a sickness in the air, a fever that has laid low half the population, it seems. Lord Usher is determined to go on with our journey, as it appears that the worst of it has passed, but his serving men are less certain and are more eager to turn for home.

I am torn, but for different reasons. I want nothing more than to see the man who was my love and my lord, but as the miles unfold I fear more and more what my fate will be once we arrive. Even the prospect of sickness does nothing to shake those fears and doubts and wonderings. If the Lady Cassandra sees me, what will become of me? This time I fear her fury, this time there will be no return to the convent – and if my master sees me first will he be strong enough to save me from her wraith? Will he even remember me? The miles only compound my fears.

At last, as night fell, we came upon an inn that I recognised. It can surely be no more than half a day from the castle walls.

And it is here that my worst fears fill me. As we are shown to the stables Usher talks to the lad who works there. Mentioning that we are come for the wedding feast at the castle, the boy grows pale. It seems that even those folk up at the castle have not been spared the rigours of the fever.

He beckons Usher closer, and I push my way through the horses and his entourage, too anxious, too fearful to worry about whatever punishment Usher might see fit to mete out for impudence.

The marriage of the lord of the manor, which should have been a time of joy, is a time of gloom and tragedy, and glancing nervously over one shoulder to make sure that none were listening save Usher and I, he says in a whisper, 'There is those as feels it is a terrible omen for the match. His betrothed, she is not well liked, folk say she is in league with dark forces.'

'What of the lord of the manor?' I asked. 'What of his lordship?' Usher casts me such a glance, I know only too well that I am overstepping the mark and yet can do nothing but beg for news of my beloved.

The boy shrugged. 'I cannot tell you, people have stayed close to home over the last few weeks and had to deal with their own tragedy. They have no news of events up at the castle.'

As night falls Usher summons me to his chamber. He was sitting before the fire in a tub of hot water. His face is pale and drawn, both I believe with anger at my forwardness in the inn yard, but surely too for fear of the fate of his old friend.

He had his manservant pour me a glass of wine and indicated the fine four-poster bed that graced one corner of the room. But there was something more; laid out upon it was a fine red dress, and a corset of the finest black silk, boned and laced, beside high boots and a long black hooded brocade cloak.

I looked across at him, uncertain.

'I had thought to give you this as a gift, pretty trinkets to wear when we ride into the castle tomorrow, something to make that bitch Cassandra sit up and take notice and make your master realise what a fool he was, but now I have no idea what awaits us.' He looked up at me, and for an instant our eyes met and we both knew the words that went unspoken.

I slipped out of my robe and knelt beside the wooden tub, soaping my hands and working them over his muscular frame. For all my nights and days in his company I had never seen Usher totally naked before, his body is much scarred with the mark of the blade – a warrior and a soldier – as was my lord. I felt sobs press up into my throat and then remembered my place there; a willing slave to a strong and superior master. I lowered my gaze and set about the task of bathing him.

As my hands slipped down over his broad shoulders he pulled me to him, a wave of water splashing out onto the wooden floor.

His face was an unreadable mask. 'And if tomorrow, girl, there is no home for you, for whatever reason, then you will come back with me. Do you understand?'

I nodded, there were no words to describe the feelings his promise evoked in me. But before I had time to order my thoughts he caught hold of my hair and kissed me hard, making me cry out, more water splashing over me.

Wet now, my hair dripping, Usher nodded to his serving man, who picked me up bodily and set me in the tub alongside him. It was the most pleasant of sensations. The water was warm and soft with soap and between them they began to wash me, hands exploring my sex, my breasts, and the curve of my hips and bottom.

The feel of the water between us added something more to their dark game. T'was no time at all before the manservant slipped off his clothes and stepped in the tub alongside me. I turned to soap his muscular thighs, my mouth and lips seeking his pendulous cock and heavy balls, fingers closed tight around his manhood as Usher pressed his hand between my thighs. I groaned and felt him kneeling, seeking entry, and with a hand between my legs I helped to guide his throbbing shaft home into my wet and eager quim.

It seems that in that moment, held between them, caught up in their desire, I forgot what lay ahead of us. There was a certain wildness in the air, and when they were spent, wet and dripping suds the two men carried me to the great bed and continued to take me between them with tongue and fingers and cocks and I, lost in the place of lust and hunger, satisfied the two of them as best I could with quim and mouth and hand. It was almost day afore we finally slept, a tangle of limbs slick with sweat and the heady perfume of mating...

'Not finished your champagne yet?' Casswell looked at Sarah, and she realised she had barely touched the glass she was cradling.

Casswell pulled the jacket she had been wearing over her lap, and slid his fingers up over her thigh. Sarah knew better than to resist; she was aroused and she could not help but gasp as his hands slipped under her skirt and a thumb brushed her clitoris. She saw the man in the seat over the aisle was watching them keenly. Casswell, it seemed, knew too, and pushing her jacket and skirt up a little higher, prised her thighs apart so the stranger could just glimpse the soft pinkness of her sex.

Sarah moaned; Casswell's touch set her alight, and knowing they were being watched added another dimension to it. His caress began to find a rhythm, and he resisted her efforts to slide a hand onto his crotch.

But just as she began to relax and lift her hips in time to his fingers, he smiled and cruelly moved away. 'I'm just going back to check on Chang,' he informed her.

Sarah stared at him, bemused and frustrated. Casswell got to his feet, and whispered in his most convivial tone to their eager observer, 'Would you like to keep my seat warm for a while?'

The man's eyes widened, but he needed no second invitation. As he stepped across the aisle he brought with him a travelling rug, and settling into the seat next to Sarah, draped it over both his lap and hers.

Then, wasting not a second, he feverishly tugged her skirt even higher so that she was totally exposed to his touch, and began to stroke the rise of her mound, gently toying with her sex lips. With his other hand he guided her fingers beneath the blanket to his tented groin, used them to unzip his fly, and wrapped them around his throbbing cock.

He began to explore her, tentatively at first, stroking the delicately moist flesh between her thighs, dipping in and out of her, seeking the hardening ridge of her clitoris. He was eager and totally focused on exploring her, and despite her chagrin, she gasped softly as her excitement began to mount. His hand guided hers, working with her up and down his pulsing shaft, as if there was some chance she might forget that he wanted to enjoy a little pleasure too.

Sarah worked diligently on the stranger's cock, knowing Casswell would expect nothing less from her, one hand pumping his foreskin up and down, holding it tight in her fist, while with her other she burrowed into his open trousers and underwear for his heavy balls. He hissed, fighting to suppress any outward display of the pleasure he was experiencing so as not to alert anyone, but clearly delighted by her skilled touch and not quite able to believe his incredible luck.

Sarah saw Casswell return, take the stranger's seat and, selecting the in-flight magazine, begin to read, his apparent indifference somehow intensifying her shame. Beneath her fingertips she felt the man's scrotum tighten, felt the surge and spasm of his orgasm, felt his sticky seed seep down over her hands, and at the same instant was astonished to find herself coming with him, grinding her hips against his fingers, gasping and breathless.

The two of them sat quietly for a few minutes, then the man took a white linen handkerchief from his jacket pocket, slipped it under the blanket and wiped both her and himself. Sarah then straightened her blouse and smoothed her skirt down over her thighs, and without a word being spoken between them, he got to his feet, exchanged seats with Casswell for the second time, and Sarah, still trembling, turned to the next page of Beatrice's diary.

Casswell pressed the button for a stewardess and ordered more champagne. He looked pleased. 'Chang's fine, and so is my gift from the museum,' he said, with a broad grin.

Sarah looked at him, knowing full well that he had hated

the reproduction pillar.

The grin widened. 'Which is currently in residence somewhere in the depths of Mustafa's precious vault.'

Sarah's eyes widened. 'But I saw the crate being loaded at the airport.'

Casswell tapped the side of his nose conspiratorially. 'Indeed you did,' he acknowledged. 'The crate was loaded, together with the documents lent by the obliging abbot.'

'The manuscripts from the chest?'

Casswell nodded. 'Chang filled the abbot's precious red leather box with some of the things lying around the vault,' he disclosed. 'That little creep Aziz said he hadn't had a chance to have half of them dated, catalogued or translated anyway. So now he will.' His expression was almost as unreadable as Chang's always was. It was just a mischievous glint in his eyes that revealed his delight. It seemed that justice had been served, after all.

And now there was only Beatrice. Sarah took a sip of her champagne and turned to the next page.

...I dozed fitfully all through the dark of the night, woken by Usher or his manservant as they stirred and found me there ready for their every want. It seemed as if we were all three of us clutching at life, our desire and our hunger seeing off the darkness that hung over the end of our journey. It was both a relief and a worry when the sun finally rose.

There was no putting off the last miles of our journey. I washed in the cold water left in the bath on the hearth, and dressed in the finery Usher had given me. He watched me and for once acted as the maid who helped me fasten the laces of the corset that cinched in my waist, and then helped me slip the final scarlet dress over it. T'was not a modest churchwoman's robe, but the gown of a favoured mistress, a courtesan, a harlot.

When my hair was dressed and decked Usher looked me up and down. 'You look truly magnificent, Beatrice, and whatever becomes of us today nothing can take away this moment.'

My eyes filled with tears. It was the first time he had called me by name. He unfastened the leather collar I had worn since he saved me from the clutches of Sister Judith, and from a twist of velvet set upon a side table brought out a fine metalled choker set with precious stones.

'A gift,' he murmured, pressing his lips to my neck as he fastened it tight shut.

A while later we walked back to the courtyard where the horses were saddled and ready. Without another word we mounted up and headed towards the castle. I cannot tell you how anxious I was nor how close to tears, but as the miles passed I began to feel easier; at least whatever the outcome, by the time the sun set I would know my fate and that of my master.

As we rode through the fields it was impossible not to feel the air of neglect and sadness in the landscape. All along the roadside the fields and cottage gardens were untended, the crops not harvested, and we saw many cottages where no smoke rose from the chimney.

I sensed the unease of Usher's men. We could be leading them into a plague, and yet I knew Usher would not turn back, and neither would I.

And then at last we saw the outline of the castle against the skyline, and my heart rose into my mouth. It was all I could do not to kick my mount on and gallop up to the gates. Usher looked across at me.

'Stay here,' he said. 'My man and I will see if we may enter, find out what news we can.' And so he rode on with just his man at his side and I waited with the rest of Usher's entourage, who looked anxiously over their shoulders as if there was some chance that they might spot the fever creeping up on them.

We waited and waited just beyond the walls, and then I saw at last the gates open and Usher's manservant riding towards us. 'We are bidden to go inside,' he said.

I searched his face to see what else he might know. He looked me boldly in the eye.

'What other news is there of the castle?' I asked.

He shook his head. 'None, my lady, only that I am to take you to Lord Usher.'

Take me to Lord Usher? So that he may comfort me, console me?

I mounted up and rode with him to the castle.

The great courtyards look unkempt; where there should be wedding banners and bows there was nothing but a sense of death and illness. I looked from face to face, trying to find one I recognised; some I knew were Cassandra's servants, but what unnerved me more was that each and every one wore a black band on their arm. Who was it that had passed on? My eyes filled with tears again.

Looking up to the main steps I saw Lord Usher staring down at me, and beside him a face that made my heart stand still in my chest.

He was alive!

My master stood alongside him, eyes heavy, his whole demeanour pale and weak. I dismounted and ran up the steps, not caring whether the Lady Cassandra saw me or not, my relief was such that I would have lost my life for that instant. He opened his arms to me and I rushed into them without an instant's hesitation. The smell of him, the touch of him, the feeling of his arms around me; I had truly come home. He held me at arm's length and looked deep into my eyes.

'Oh sweet Beatrice,' he murmured, pulling me close, his lips pressed into my hair. 'I never thought I would ever see you again. The Lady Cassandra is dead,' he said in little more than a whisper, and without any emotion. 'She was amongst the first to succumb to the fever, but I was too ill to seek you out. I thought you were lost forever.'

I shook my head. It did not matter. I was home now.

'But I will see to it that you will never leave me again,' he vowed, and taking my hand, led me inside.

I thought I knew what devil drove him, but I was wrong. To my amazement Father Orme was standing in the main hall. 'Marry us,' my master said.

Orme looked from face to face.

'You heard me,' my master said. 'My cousin Usher and his men have come to celebrate a wedding, and by God there will be a wedding for them to dance at.'

After a few awkward moments Orme lifted his hands and smiled. 'Indeed,' he said ingratiatingly.

And so it was done. I was married in the gown Usher had given me, my master dressed as I had seen him at the top of the steps.

And afterwards, while Usher danced, my lord took me to his chamber.

'Take off your clothes, wench,' he said, settling down upon a couch. I did as I was bidden, revealing the fine lines of the black silk corset beneath that nipped my waist and lifted my breasts like a feast for his hands and eyes.

My master beckoned me closer, and I dropped to the floor and crawled to him. He ran his hands over my face and throat and shoulders. 'Bring me my riding crop,' he ordered.

I looked up into his eyes as I handed him the ornate leather handle.

'Now, on your hands and knees, I will teach you never to leave me again,' he said, drew back the whip, and brought it down across my warm and eager flesh so hard that I screamed in a wild and hungry mixture of delight and pain. He brought the whip back again and once more it explode across my full buttocks. Again and again, and with each new blow I cried out, writhing and gasping from the hurting.

Finally, when my punishment was done, he dropped to his knees behind me and with no prelude drove his cock deep inside me, hands on my hips to pull me back onto him. As he began to move I slid my fingers down between my thighs to rub the little bud that glowed deep within. One hand of his joined with mine and the brush of his fingertips was enough to take me to the place of no return. Driving his hips hard, he pressed his fingers and cock home. I cried out, this time in pure pleasure.

'Welcome home, sweet wife,' my master murmured, as he drove me out to the very shores of madness...

Sarah lay the last few pages down on her lap and looked at Casswell, who smiled. 'Time for us to go home, too,' he said.

More exciting titles available from Chimera

1-901388-23-9	Latin Submission	*Barton*
1-901388-19-0	Destroying Angel	*Hastings*
1-901388-26-3	Selina's Submission	*Lewis*
1-901388-29-8	Betty Serves the Master	*Tanner*
1-901388-31-X	A Kept Woman	*Grayson*
1-901388-32-8	Milady's Quest	*Beaufort*
1-901388-33-6	Slave Hunt	*Shannon*
1-901388-34-4*	Shadows of Torment	*McLachlan*
1-901388-35-2*	Star Slave	*Dere*
1-901388-37-9*	Punishment Exercise	*Benedict*
1-901388-38-7*	The CP Sex Files	*Asquith*
1-901388-39-5*	Susie Learns the Hard Way	*Quine*
1-901388-40-9*	Domination Inc.	*Leather*
1-901388-42-5*	Sophie & the Circle of Slavery	*Culber*
1-901388-11-5*	Space Captive	*Hughes*
1-901388-41-7*	Bride of the Revolution	*Amber*
1-901388-44-1*	Vesta – Painworld	*Pope*
1-901388-45-X*	The Slaves of New York	*Hughes*
1-901388-46-8*	Rough Justice	*Hastings*
1-901388-47-6*	Perfect Slave Abroad	*Bell*
1-901388-48-4*	Whip Hands	*Hazel*
1-901388-50-6*	Slave of Darkness	*Lewis*
1-901388-49-2*	Rectory of Correction	*Virosa*
1-901388-51-4*	Savage Bonds	*Beaufort*
1-901388-52-2*	Darkest Fantasies	*Raines*
1-901388-53-0*	Wages of Sin	*Benedict*
1-901388-54-9*	Love Slave	*Wakelin*
1-901388-56-5*	Susie Follows Orders	*Quine*
1-901388-55-7*	Slave to Cabal	*McLachlan*
1-901388-57-3*	Forbidden Fantasies	*Gerrard*
1-901388-58-1*	Chain Reaction	*Pope*
1-901388-60-3*	Sister Murdock's House of Correction	*Angelo*
1-901388-61-1*	Moonspawn	*McLachlan*
1-901388-59-X*	The Bridle Path	*Eden*
1-901388-62-X*	Ruled by the Rod	*Rawlings*
1-901388-63-8*	Of Pain and Delight	*Stone*

1-901388-65-4*	The Collector	*Steel*
1-901388-66-2*	Prisoners of Passion	*Dere*
1-901388-67-0*	Sweet Submission	*Anderssen*
1-901388-69-7*	Rachael's Training	*Ward*
1-901388-71-9*	Learning to Crawl	*Argus*
1-901388-36-0*	Out of Her Depth	*Challis*
1-901388-68-9*	Moonslave	*McLachlan*
1-901388-72-7*	Nordic Bound	*Morgan*
1-901388-27-1*	A Strict Seduction	*del Rey*
1-901388-80-8*	Cauldron of Fear	*Pope*
1-901388-74-3*	In Too Deep	*Beaufort*
1-901388-73-5*	Managing Mrs Burton	*Aspen*
1-901388-75-1*	Lucy	*Culber*
1-901388-77-8*	The Piano Teacher	*Elliot*
1-901388-25-5*	Afghan Bound	*Morgan*
1-901388-76-X*	Sinful Seduction	*Benedict*
1-901388-70-0*	Babala's Correction	*Amber*
1-901388-06-9*	Schooling Sylvia	*Beaufort*
1-901388-78-6*	Thorns	*Scott*
1-901388-79-4*	Indecent Intent	*Amber*
1-903931-00-2*	Thorsday Night	*Pita*
1-903931-01-0*	Teena Thyme	*Pope*
1-903931-02-9*	Servants of the Cane	*Ashton*
1-903931-04-5*	Captured by Charybdis	*McLachlan*
1-903931-03-7*	Forever Chained	*Beaufort*
1-903931-05-3*	In Service	*Challis*
1-903931-06-1*	Bridled Lust	*Pope*
1-903931-07-X*	Stolen Servant	*Grayson*
1-903931-09-6*	The Carrot and the Stick	*Vanner*

* * *

All **Chimera** titles are available from your local bookshop or newsagent, or direct from our mail order department. Please send your order with your credit card details, a cheque or postal order (made payable to ***Chimera Publishing Ltd***) to: **Chimera Publishing Ltd., Readers' Services, PO Box 152, Waterlooville, Hants, PO8 9FS**. Or call our **24 hour telephone/fax credit card hotline: +44 (0)23 92 783037** (Visa, Mastercard, Switch, JCB and Solo only).

To order, send: Title, author, ISBN number and price for each book ordered, your full name and address, cheque or postal order for the total amount, and include the following for postage and packing:
UK and BFPO: £1.00 for the first book, and 50p for each additional book to a maximum of £3.50.
Overseas and Eire: £2.00 for the first book, £1.00 for the second and 50p for each additional book.

*Titles £5.99. All others £4.99

For a copy of our free catalogue please write to:

Chimera Publishing Ltd
Readers' Services
PO Box 152
Waterlooville
Hants
PO8 9FS

or email us at:
sales@chimerabooks.co.uk

or purchase from our range of superb titles at:
www.chimerabooks.co.uk

Sales and Distribution in the USA and Canada

LPC Group
Client Distribution Services
193 Edwards Drive
Jackson
TN 38301
USA

Sales and Distribution in Australia

Dennis Jones & Associates Pty Ltd
19a Michellan Ct
Bayswater
Victoria
Australia 3153

* * *